Sam told himself to stay as far away from Lisa as he could get.

This was no time to get involved with a woman. Especially one he didn't trust.

But, damn, she was something else. He couldn't remember when he'd been so affected by a woman. Something about her made him want to grab her, kiss her, hold her and touch her until they both went a little crazy.

He'd gone a little crazy last night. Wanted her so badly, he'd thought if he couldn't have her, he'd bust a gut. Or something even more vital.

Lisa was like satin and lace and perfumed softness, delectable from her blond curls down to her toes.

All of which made Sam grumpy as a 'gator with a toothache.

But he was damn well going to leave Lisa alone.

Wasn't he?

Dear Reader,

This month marks the advent of something very special in Intimate Moments. We call it "Intimate Moments Extra," and books bearing this flash will be coming your way on an occasional basis in the future. These are books we think are a bit different from our usual, a bit longer or grittier perhaps. And our lead-off "extra" title is one terrific read. It's called *Into Thin Air*, and it's written by Karen Leabo, making her debut in the line. It's a tough look at a tough subject, but it's also a top-notch romance. Read it and you'll see what I mean.

The rest of the month's books are also terrific. We're bringing you Doreen Owens Malek's newest, *Marriage in Name Only*, as well as Laurey Bright's *A Perfect Marriage*, a very realistic look at how a marriage can go wrong before finally going very, very right. Then there's Kylie Brant's *An Irresistible Man*, a sequel to her first-ever book, *McLain's Law*, as well as Barbara Faith's sensuous and suspenseful *Moonlight Lady*. Finally, welcome Kay David to the line with *Desperate*. Some of you may have seen her earlier titles, written elsewhere as Cay David.

Six wonderful authors and six wonderful books. I hope you enjoy them all.

Yours,

Leslie Wainger
Senior Editor and Editorial Coordinator

Please address questions and book requests to:
Silhouette Reader Service
U.S.: 3010 Walden Ave., P.O. Box 1325, Buffalo, NY 14269
Canadian: P.O. Box 609, Fort Erie, Ont. L2A 5X3

MOONLIGHT LADY

BARBARA FAITH

Silhouette
INTIMATE™MOMENTS®
Published by Silhouette Books
America's Publisher of Contemporary Romance

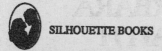

SILHOUETTE BOOKS

ISBN 0-373-07623-1

MOONLIGHT LADY

This edition published by arrangement with Harlequin Enterprises B.V.

® and TM are trademarks of Harlequin Enterprises B.V., used under
license. Trademarks indicated with ® are registered in the United States
Patent and Trademark Office, the Canadian Trade Marks Office and in
other countries.

Printed in U.S.A.

Books by Barbara Faith

BARBARA FAITH

is a true romantic who believes that love is a rare and precious gift. She has an endless fascination with the attraction a man and a woman from different cultures and backgrounds have for each other. She considers herself a good example of such an attraction, because she has been happily married for over twenty years to an ex-matador she met when she lived in Mexico.

Chapter 1

It was hotter than the hinges of hell. The only things moving were the miragelike waves of heat floating up from the black asphalt. There was nothing in sight, only this long, lonely stretch of road with tall green mountains on both sides.

Lisa Collier, who until a week ago had been Lisa Collier Matthews, took off the jacket of her pink suit and fanned herself with the brochure that extolled the beauty of Jamaica and told of the trade winds that almost always cooled the island. But today wasn't one of those days. There were no trade winds, only the bright, blazing sun.

Noël Coward, who had lived here, had written a song about only mad dogs and Englishmen going out in the noonday sun. She wasn't English, so apparently that made her just the least bit mad.

The driver of the taxi she'd hired at the Kingston airport had assured her that he, Moses Begrande, was the most reliable driver in all of Jamaica and that he could get her to Ocho Rios in less than two hours, since it wasn't high season and traffic would be light. With a cheerful smile he'd loaded her luggage into the trunk and held the door open for her. Gears grinding, they'd set off, driving as the English did, on what Lisa considered the wrong side of the road.

An hour out of Kingston, on a winding twist of a mountain curve, the taxi had coughed, sputtered and wheezed its last wheeze.

"Be not worried, madam," Moses said as he hurried to lift the hood. "I be A-number-one mechanic."

The number-one mechanic stood with his hands on his hips and frowned at the intricacies of the motor as if seeing it for the first time. He jiggled a wire, patted the carburetor as though he were patting the head of his favorite dog and studied the battery. Then he got back into the taxi and tried once more to start the motor. When nothing happened, he said, "I believe there is a small problem. It is best that I go for help."

They were in the middle of nowhere. There were no houses, nothing to indicate help of any sort might be nearby. In the last half hour they'd seen only one car. Since then there had been nothing, not even a horse cart.

"Are we near a town?" Lisa asked.

"Alas, no." He smiled as though to reassure her. "But perhaps there be a village, madam, and if there is I will telephone for help and soon we will be rescued. However, since I do not know when that will be, should a car or another taxi pass by while I am gone perhaps it be best you ask for a ride. When my taxi is fixed I will take your luggage to the hotel. It be the Poinciana, yes?"

"Yes," Lisa said.

With a nod and a smile that showed every one of his even white teeth, Moses had started up a small mountain path. That had been a little over an hour ago. Nothing had come by since then, not a taxi or a car or a bus, not even a bicycle. Lisa flicked the sweat off the end of her nose. She was hot, thirsty and cranky enough to wish she'd never left Miami.

But she had left, both Miami and Philip. Soft-spoken, well-mannered, impeccably dressed Philip, who even in a circumstance like this would not have sweat. He'd have adjusted his tie, straightened his tailor-made jacket, studied his manicured nails and, lighting one of his French cigarettes, would simply have waited to be rescued.

Of course Philip would never have come to Jamaica in the first place. He much preferred the south of France or Spain's Costa del Sol. "But only in the off season," he said. "Otherwise you run into all sorts of people, tourists who've barely managed to scrape enough money together for a two-week trip so that when they return to Ohio or some other ungodly place they can say they've been to Europe."

Lisa was from Ohio.

She'd been twenty-two when she'd met Philip. Fresh out of the University of Miami with a degree in fine arts, she had been impressed by the fact that he was the famous art critic everyone talked about. And she'd thought him attractive in a slender, aesthetic way.

He'd courted her for a year, and finally, because she refused to go to bed with him, he'd married her.

Philip was a snob, but it had taken some growing up on her part to realize that. Artists from Maine to California lived in fear of his often witty, but almost always scathingly sarcastic reviews. He made fun of everyone. Usually he saved his sharp-edged verbal criticisms for the occasions when, at an art opening or a large party, people gathered around him. Then, with a martini—very dry with a twist—in hand, he would tear to shreds whatever artist happened to be in the public eye at the moment.

Lisa mopped her forehead, angry and upset because she hadn't come to Jamaica to think about Philip. All she wanted to do was lie on the beach with a tall, cool tropical drink in her hand, and maybe stir her bones once or twice a day for a swim. A swim. Lord, wouldn't she love that right now.

With a sigh, she walked around the taxi and stood in the middle of the road as though to will a bus or a taxi or a vehicle of any sort to come around the curve of the mountain. She paced up and down, fanning herself with the hotel's brochure, but stopped when she finally heard what sounded like the roar of a motor. Shading her eyes, she peered toward the noise. Let it be a car, she prayed. Let it be...

Like a big, black beast, the motorcycle zoomed into sight. The man astride the machine slowed for the curve, leaned into it and gunned the motor for a straight run. But when he spotted Lisa, he slowed and pulled to within a yard or so of her.

"Trouble?" He shoved the dark glasses up onto his forehead and regarded her with eyes as blue as the Jamaican sky.

"Uh-huh." She gestured to the taxi. "I was on my way from the Kingston airport."

"Where's the driver?"

"Somewhere up that path."

"How long has he been gone?"

She glanced at her watch. "An hour."

"Where you headed?"

"To Ocho Rios. The Poinciana Hotel there."

"That's where I'm staying." He swung a leg over the motorcycle and stood beside her. Over her. He was big, about six-four, and brawny as a bear. "Maybe you'd better come along with me," he said.

I don't think so, Lisa thought, but didn't say it. She wasn't into motorcycles or the type of man who rode one. This was a rough-looking, he-man type, exactly the kind she shied away from. His jeans were faded and tight around his thighs. There was a spot of grease on the denim shirt with the rolled-up sleeves. His biceps were muscled. His black hair looked shaggy and longer than she approved of.

"Name's O'Shaughnessy." He offered a hand the size of a five-pound slab of beef. "Sam O'Shaughnessy."

"Lisa Matthe—Lisa Collier." She hesitated. "Maybe I'd better wait for the driver to come back."

O'Shaughnessy shook his head. "You don't know when that'll be. Hell, he's probably sitting in some shack up in the mountains drinking a cold Red Stripe and wondering where he can find somebody who knows more about cars than he does. Could be dark by the time he comes back."

Lisa looked at the motorcycle. "I've never ridden one of those before."

"It's simple. All you have to do is hold on and lean into the curves when we take 'em." He glanced toward the taxi. "What about your bags?"

"The driver said he'd bring them to the hotel as soon as he got the car fixed."

"Then what're we waiting for? Let's go."

She didn't want to go anywhere with this hulk of a man, but she didn't have much choice. She couldn't wait here by the side of the road forever.

"I'll get my purse out of the taxi." She looked up at him. "I don't suppose you have any water," she said.

"Nope. Sorry. If we hit a village farther down we'll stop for a beer."

She put her jacket back on, took her purse out of the taxi and slung it over her shoulder.

He swung his leg back over the motorcycle. "Hop on," he said.

She looked at him, then at the cycle. Her pink skirt came to a more-or-less discreet five inches above her knees. She hiked it up and frowned when O'Shaughnessy, instead of having the decency to look away, gazed with open admiration at her legs.

There wasn't anything she could do. She couldn't very well ride sidesaddle; she had no choice except to swing her leg over the seat behind him.

"What do I hang on to?" she asked.

"Me." He turned around and grinned at her. "Hang on to *me,* Miss ... Collier?"

"Yes," she said, tight-lipped.

"Put your arms around my waist."

She fastened both hands on the sides of his shirt.

"That won't do it. The first bump or curve and you'll go flying off. Hang on to me, not my shirt."

Tentatively, she encircled his waist with her arms.

"Here we go," he said, and gunned the motor.

The wind whipped at her short, ash blond hair. She tightened her arms around his waist and hung on. They started around a curve. When he yelled, "Lean in," she followed the movement of his body and leaned.

This wasn't at all like Philip's silver Mercedes. She felt open, exposed, wanting the assurance of a closed-in car with sturdy metal surrounding her. This was scary, as though any minute she'd go flying off, spattering all over the asphalt or hurtling against the side of the mountain.

She shouldn't have come with him. He was a stranger. How did she know he would take her to Ocho Rios? Maybe he was headed up into the mountains to...what? Rape and ravish? God, she hoped not! It was too hot for raping and ravishing.

With an ironic smile, she closed her eyes and pressed her face into Mr. O'Shaughnessy's back. He smelled like woodsy fresh air, nothing at all like the scent of Philip's hundred-dollar-an-ounce French cologne, which he bought in three-ounce bottles.

Don't think about him, she told herself. That's over, kaput, *fini,* final. I don't need him or any other man. I'm self-sufficient.... They whipped around a curve she hadn't seen coming because her eyes were closed. She cried out in alarm and dug her fingernails into O'Shaughnessy's midsection. His muscles tightened. He didn't say anything, but reduced the speed, and when he did she took her nails out of his skin and opened her eyes.

Everything looked pretty and green, she noted as she began to relax. The air smelled of the sea and of whatever the flowers were that grew alongside the road. She leaned back a couple of inches and relaxed her grip around his waist. Actually it was rather pleasant, skimming along this stretch of open road that was such a far cry from the busy Miami traffic, the superhighways she was used to driving on.

They passed a man with a horse-drawn cart, two women with clay water jugs on their heads and a gaggle of small boys who waved as they went by.

"Must be getting to a village," Sam said, and when they rounded a curve, Lisa saw a cluster of small, thatch-roofed houses nestled at the foot of the mountain.

He slowed the motorcycle when they hit the narrow, dusty road, and came to a stop in front of a store with a tin sign hanging over the door that read Red Stripe Beer.

"It's not the Poinciana," O'Shaughnessy said, "but it'll do. You want a beer?"

"I'd rather have a cola."

"Okay." He swung his leg over the motorcycle just as a boy of ten or eleven came out of the store. He was barefoot and dressed in ragged cutoffs and a torn shirt.

"You in charge?" Sam asked.

"I be the boss today, mon." Hands on skinny hips, legs sprawled, the boy looked past Sam to the motorcycle. "That a Harley?"

"Yup."

"Big damn bastard, mon."

"That it is. You ever ride one?"

The boy shook his head. "Go like hell?"

"Damn straight." Sam held out a hand to help Lisa off. "Red Stripe cold?" he asked the kid.

"It be cold." He tore his gaze away from the Harley and looked at Lisa. "You want a beer, too?"

Lisa shook her head. "A cola, please."

"The beer be cold, the cola be warm."

"Beer then."

He went into the small, dark store. By the time he came back with the two beers, other people had strolled over to see what was going on. They looked curiously at Sam and Lisa, but it was the Harley that drew their attention.

The boy frowned at the crowd. "Don't be puttin' your hands on it," he said to a man who ran his fingers over the leather seat. With the part of his shirt hanging out of the cutoffs, he rubbed the place the man had touched.

An old woman with no teeth grinned up at Sam. Hooking a thumb in Lisa's direction, she asked, "This be your woman?"

He took a long swallow of his beer. "Yep." He wiped his mouth with the back of his hand. "Been married eight years," he said.

"You have many children?"

"Seven. Four boys and three girls."

Lisa choked on her beer, coughed, then sputtered an indignant, "Wait a *minute!*"

"She be fine looking." A scrawny, toothless old man with a fringe of white curly hair around his otherwise bald head pointed a finger at his bony chest. "I have twenty-eight, with four wives all gone to glory. How do you call your children?"

"Hortense, Tallulah and Matilda, Ismael, Zachariah, Siegfried and Waldemar," Sam said without hesitation. He drained the beer and handed the empty bottle to the boy. "What's your name, kid?"

"I be Joshua."

"Well then, Joshua, how'd you like to take a ride on the Harley?"

The boy's eyes widened pearl white in his dark-skinned face. "For true, mon?"

"For true." Sam swung his leg over the machine and reached out a hand to pull the boy up in behind him. "Back in ten minutes," he told Lisa, and, gunning the motor, he took off.

Lisa stared at the retreating Harley, then smiled a hesitant smile at the village people who'd gathered around.

"That be some fella," a woman said.

"Bet he be strong like a bull." Another woman laughed and poked the woman standing next to her.

"Be makin' strong babies," someone else said.

Hot color rushed to Lisa's cheeks. If she had any idea how far it was to Ocho Rios, she'd start walking. As it was, all she could do was force a smile and drink her beer.

Fifteen minutes later the motorcycle zoomed up the dusty street of the village. When it stopped, Joshua, his mouth split in a grin, hopped off the back. "That be a fine machine," he declared. "I thank you, sir."

"You're welcome. How much for the beer?"

"For you there is no charge."

Sam shook his head. "I'll be back this way in a few days. Wouldn't feel right stopping if I didn't pay." He took a five out of his jeans and stuck it in the pocket of Joshua's shirt. Turning to Lisa, he said, "Hop on, Mrs. O'Shaughnessy."

She shot him an if-looks-could-kill glance, and hiked up her skirt.

The old man gasped and stared at her legs. "You one lucky son o' bitch," he said to Sam.

"Yeah." Sam grinned before he swung his leg over the motorcycle and climbed on. Then he held out his hand to Lisa. "Ready, dear?" he asked.

Grim-faced, she ignored his hand and climbed onto the Harley.

She didn't say anything until they rounded the curve out of sight of the village. Then she said, "How dare you tell those people I was your wife?" and smacked his shoulder. When he threw his head back and laughed, she smacked him again.

He liked her, maybe because she wasn't like most of the women he knew. And he knew a lot of them.

Being a New York cop, he met all kinds—hookers and show girls, librarians and Park Avenue society dames. They were streetwise and hip, sophisticated and worldly. He liked 'em tall and lanky, big-breasted and wide of hip, with shoulder-length hair, preferably dark, that swung in the breeze when they walked—his wife had been like that.

Lisa Collier wasn't his type. For one thing her blond hair was too damn short. Curled around her face like a kid's. Didn't swing, didn't bounce. She was short, maybe five-two, with small breasts, a little waist and hardly hip enough for a man to get his hands on. But swell legs. Back at the village the old man's eyes had almost dropped out of his head when she'd hiked her skirt up.

She was pretty enough in an elfin kind of way, but still, definitely not his type. Even if she were, he hadn't come to Jamaica looking for romance. He was here to find Juan Montoya. That was serious as well as dangerous business.

Two days ago the DEA had gotten a tip that Montoya had been seen in the vicinity of Ocho Rios, and Sam, an NYPD lieutenant who had been working with the DEA on the Montoya case for the last year, hopped a plane for Kingston. When he arrived, he'd gone directly to the Kingston Police Department, where he'd met with a captain of police, Filoberto Hargreaves.

Hargreaves, a slim, well-dressed man in his middle forties, with cocoa brown skin and surprisingly blue eyes, had welcomed Sam with a smile and a tot of good Jamaica rum.

But his expression had been all-cop when he said, "How could your police in the United States let a man like Montoya get away from you once you had him?"

"Wasn't easy." Sam took a slug of the rum. "He'd been indicted for murder—"

"Which one?" Hargreaves asked, raising a quizzical eyebrow. "He's murdered . . . how many?"

"Fourteen that we know of."

"What happened?"

"They were taking him out of the courtroom after the indictment. Somebody jostled him and slipped him a gun. He walked out with the guard, then shot him, and at the same time his accomplice took the other guards down. I wasn't there, but apparently it was one hell of a mess. Four guards dead and three bystanders injured."

"And Juan Montoya got away." Hargreaves poured another splash of rum into both of their glasses. "We'll work with the DEA and with you," he said, "but we want to be informed about what's going on. You have a problem and you need backup, you call me."

He opened a manila folder and studied the papers inside for a moment. "There's a drug deal going down somewhere on the island," he told Sam. "Montoya's probably masterminding it. They dealing in something a lot heavier than ganja, Jamaican marijuana. It's something new, more expensive, more dangerous, maybe even deadly because we think they're mixing it with a powder that may very well be contaminated. Believe me, Mr. O'Shaughnessy, we want the men behind this. Most of all we want Montoya."

"The DEA's got first dibs. I'm taking him back to New York."

Hargreaves lit a cigarette. Through the pale gray smoke he looked at Sam. "Just be sure you get him and he doesn't get you, my friend."

They had lunch, and afterward Sam asked where he could rent a car.

"You know how to handle a Harley?" Hargreaves asked.

"Sure. I had my own until a couple of years ago."

"Then take mine. It's faster than a car and better on the mountain roads. Of course, if you'd rather have a car, I'll arrange it."

Sam shook his head. "The Harley's fine."

Now here he was, racing around the mountains with a dame who wasn't a lanky brunette hanging on behind him.

He slowed for a curve, and when he did, she tightened her arms around his waist and leaned into him. He felt the brush of her cheek against his shoulder, the press of her breasts against his back. He took a gulp of the clean sea air. To hell with lanky brunettes, he thought, and with a wolflike grin sped on toward Ocho Rios.

Chapter 2

Lisa was windblown and frazzled. There was a smudge of grease on her skirt, the heels of her new pumps were scuffed and she was afraid, when O'Shaughnessy turned the motorcycle into the curved driveway of the Poinciana Hotel, that she would forever walk bowlegged.

"Well, we made it." He shot her a grin and offered a hand to help her off. "You okay?"

"More or less," she said once she was on solid ground again. "Thank you very much for the lift, Mr. O'Shaughnessy."

"Sam."

"Yes, well..."

A bellman, smiling a greeting, hurried out of the hotel. But the smile faded when he saw the Harley. "You be checking in?" he said doubtfully.

Sam nodded. "Where's the registration desk?"

"Inside, sir. But—but you have no luggage?"

Sam reached behind where Lisa had been perched, grabbed a duffel bag and tossed it to the bellman. "Only this," he said as he took Lisa's arm to lead her up the red-carpeted stairs of the hotel.

The lobby, though small, looked clean and cool. Through the floor-to-ceiling windows that faced the sea, Lisa could see the wide outside patio with the striped chaises, umbrellaed tables and swimming pool. Beyond lay the beach, palm trees and the turquoise sea.

"May I help you?" The man behind the desk looked first Lisa, then Sam up and down.

She ran both hands over her hair to try to smooth it. Before she could say anything, Sam said, "We'd like to check in."

The man wrinkled his nose in a sniff, raised his eyebrows and said, "I'm afraid we're all booked up."

"But I have a reservation," Lisa protested.

"I think not."

"But I do." Lisa stepped closer to the desk. "It was made by a travel agent in Miami."

"Under what name? Mr. and Mrs.... ?"

"I'm O'Shaughnessy," Sam said. "This is Miss Collier."

The thin lips pursed. "I'm afraid we can't accommodate you."

"But my reservation," Lisa started to say. "I..."

The desk clerk, as though he had other, more important things to attend to, turned his back on her. Before he could step away, Sam reached across the desk, swung the man around and, grabbing his tie with one meaty hand, pulled him smack up against the registration desk.

"My name is Sam O'Shaughnessy," he said in a pleasant voice. "My reservation was made by Captain Filoberto Hargreaves. This lady is Miss Lisa Collier from

Miami. We are not together, but even if we were, that would be none of your business. Miss Collier, who had taken a taxi from the Kingston airport, was stranded on the highway when the taxi broke down. I offered her a ride on the motorcycle Captain Hargreaves was kind enough to loan me."

The clerk began to struggle. When he did, Sam tightened his grip and raised the man up onto his toes. "Her luggage will be along later," he went on in the same pleasant voice. "Your bellman already has mine."

"Please..." The man's face had started to turn an interesting shade of red.

"I'm sure you didn't understand the situation," Sam continued, sounding like somebody's kindly, if somewhat strange, uncle. "But you were rude to Miss Collier and I think you owe her an apology."

The clerk bobbed his head and Sam let him go. "I—I...Miss Collier, is it? Well, yes, I believe we do have your reservation. And I..." He glanced at Sam. "I most certainly apologize for any misunderstanding."

She'd been appalled, actually she'd been scared out of her wits when Sam had grabbed the man and all but hauled him across the front desk. But appalled or not, she was finding it hard to keep a straight face. She managed, however, and said in what she hoped was a haughty voice, "I'd like to be shown to my room now."

"Yes, yes, of course."

"Oceanfront," Sam said. "With a balcony."

"I'm not sure we..." The clerk took a deep breath. "Yes, of course, sir."

"I'd like oceanfront, too."

"I'll see to it." He put two registration slips in front of them, and when both Lisa and Sam had filled them out, he banged the bell on his desk. The young man who'd taken Sam's duffel bag ran forward. The clerk said, "Show Miss Collier and Mr. O'Shaughnessy to their rooms."

Sam said, "Thank you so much, Mr. . . . ?"

"Abercrombie."

"You'll send Miss Collier's bags to her room when they arrive." It was a statement, not a question.

"Yes, sir. Of course, sir."

They followed the young man, who seemed barely able to keep a straight face, up the flight of carpeted stairs to the third floor.

"This be your room, ma'am," he said, when he stopped in front of a tall white door. "Mister's room be right next door. Best rooms in whole damn hotel." He chuckled and with a wink said, "That be because big mister here be scaring de livin' sheet out of old Abercrombie."

"Mr. Abercrombie needed the livin' sheet scared out of him." Sam dug in his pocket, and before Lisa could open her purse to tip the young man, said, "This is for both of us." And to Lisa, "You go ahead in. It's been a long day. I imagine you're pretty tired."

"All the way down to my bones," she admitted.

"See you later then."

"Very likely." She started into the room, then hesitated. "Thank you again for helping me, Mr. O'Shaughnessy."

"Sam. Remember?"

"Of course. Sam." And with a smile at the boy, she started into the room.

"How about dinner?"

"Dinner? Well, I. . ." She hesitated. He wasn't the kind of a man she would ever be interested in. He was too big and brash. Too everything she disliked in a man. Still, if

it hadn't been for him, she might very well still have been
sitting on the side of the highway waiting for Moses Begrande to reappear. She'd have dinner with him, and
starting tomorrow she'd do her best to avoid him.

"I'm not sure my luggage will have arrived by then,"
she said, stalling.

"Then wear what you've got on. Eight o'clock?"

"All right."

"I'll meet you out on the patio."

The bellman opened the door to Sam's room. She
turned away, not at all happy to have him right next door.
And when she heard the young man laugh and say to
Sam, "Convenient, yes, Boss?" she went in and closed
the door, none too gently, behind her.

He was standing at the bar drinking a beer when she
stepped out onto the patio. He saw her hesitate and look
around, but he didn't move or make an attempt to go to
her because he liked looking at her. She was wearing blue.
The dress was short, coming to an inch or two above her
knees, but unlike the pink skirt, it flared out around her
drop-dead-gorgeous legs, enticingly splendid in three-
inch heels.

She spotted him and he hurried toward her. "I see your
luggage arrived," he said.

Her blond hair curled softly around her face and she
smelled like peach blossoms. In her high heels she came
just to his shoulder, a nicely wrapped package of a
woman, delicate and altogether delectable. *Almost small
enough to put in my pocket,* he thought suddenly. *Could
take her out whenever I wanted to, put her back in when
I didn't.* That made him grin, and she looked up at him,
puzzled.

A white-jacketed waiter approached. Sam said, "Table for two," and took Lisa's arm. The table was on the edge of the patio on a small rise of land overlooking the Caribbean. Red hibiscus surrounded the glass-enclosed candle in the center of the white linen tablecloth.

"Would you like a drink?" Sam asked.

"A martini, dry, with a twist."

He raised an eyebrow.

"And for you, sir?" the waiter asked.

"Planter's punch."

Most of the other men were in lightweight suits or white dinner jackets. A few wore white *guayaberas*. Not O'Shaughnessy. He wore a blue denim shirt exactly like the one he'd worn today, only cleaner, white Dockers and sneakers without socks.

Their drinks arrived. Sam touched his glass to hers and, in a rough imitation of Bogart, said, "Here's looking at you, kid." He took a sip of his drink. "What do you do in Miami?" he asked.

"I'm a commercial artist."

"Here on business or vacation?"

"Vacation."

"Married?"

"You ask a lot of questions."

He grinned. "I'm a cop. It gets to be a habit." He took another sip of his beer. "Well, are you?"

"What?"

"Married."

"I was until last week." She looked out toward the sea. "I'm divorced," she said.

"How do you feel about it?"

She turned back to him, wanting to say, "This isn't any of your business," but found herself saying, "I'm not sure. I think I stopped loving Philip, that's my husband—ex-husband—a couple of years ago. I married him when I was twenty-two. We were together for almost seven years.''

She took a sip of her martini and put it down, wondering why she'd ordered it. It was Philip's drink, not hers. And though he'd always ordered martinis for both of them without asking her what she wanted, she'd never really liked the drink. Yet out of force of habit she'd ordered it tonight.

''Something wrong with your drink?''

''No.'' A reluctant smile softened her lips. ''This was his drink, not mine. I don't know why I ordered it.''

''How about a planter's punch?''

''I've never had one.''

''Then it's time you did.''

''What's in it?''

''One of sour, two of sweet, three of strong, four of weak.'' He grinned. ''All you need to remember is that it's made of a couple of kinds of rum.'' He motionned for the waiter, ordered the drink and asked for menus.

He wondered what her husband had been like, and because he was curious, asked, ''What does he do?''

''Philip? He's an art critic.''

''And art critics do what? Criticize other people's work?''

Lisa looked at him, a little startled, then she laughed and said, ''That's about it.''

The rum drink came. She tried it, smiled and began to feel better about the evening. O'Shaughnessy was all right in a rough-hewn sort of way. He was different from anyone she'd ever known. With the exception of her father. Sam was like him—big, brawny....

A sudden wave of nausea started in the pit of her stomach, and the palms of her hands went damp. She tightened them around the planter's punch and downed half of it. She didn't notice Sam's questioning look, and said yes when he asked her if she'd like another. He ordered her drink and gave their food orders to the waiter.

"The pepper-pot soup is good," he told Lisa. "Want to try it?"

"You've been to Jamaica before?"

"Couple of times." Because she seemed tense, he talked about some of the other Caribbean islands he'd been to—Trinidad, Barbados, Haiti. "But I like Jamaica," he said. "I like the people and the pace of life here."

The waiter brought the pepper-pot soup. Made from Indian kale and kalalu, okra and chopped meat, it was spicy and good. That was followed by a green salad and steak, bloodred for Sam, barely pink for Lisa.

The second drink had relaxed her, and for the first time since she'd arrived, she began to enjoy the surroundings. A full moon shone over the sea. The trade winds the brochure had promised rustled through the palm fronds. The air was scented with frangipani blossoms, gardenia and ginger. At one end of the patio a five-piece orchestra began to play, and a few couples got up to dance.

Sam ordered coffee and soursop ice cream. Just about the time they finished, the band started a slow, sensuous bolero. He pushed his chair back and said, "How about a dance?" And before Lisa had a chance to refuse, he pulled out her chair and, taking her hand, led her to the dance floor.

"I don't do fast," he told her. "Watching a woman waving her arms and jerking around like she's got Saint Vitus' dance doesn't do a damn thing for me. I like to hold a woman in my arms." He put his arms around her. "Like this," he said.

He was a surprisingly good dancer. She felt enfolded by him, which wasn't, as she had thought it would be, half-bad. He tucked one of her hands up against his chest and held her that way. She felt the least little bit dreamy and wondered if she should blame it on that second planter's punch.

"What kind of a cop are you?" she asked, looking up at him.

"Just a cop."

"Like in a squad car?"

He shook his head. "Like in plainclothes."

"You hunt down the bad guys in tennies and jeans?"

"And the bad girls." He smiled down at her. She really was pretty and feminine, all nicely done up in her blue dress, with soft skin, sweet scents and fragrant hair. The moonlight cast pale shadows across her face. When a breeze ruffled a loose tendril, he reached up to brush it back from her face.

She flinched. He looked at her, surprised. "What is it?" he asked.

"What?" Pretending not to understand, Lisa forced a smile. "Beautiful night, isn't it?" she said.

"Yeah." He wondered what had spooked her, but decided not to ask because he had a hunch she wouldn't answer. So he held her, contenting himself with the feel of her in his arms. She felt snug against him like this, her small fingers curled in his hand. He wondered what it would be like to kiss her.

Whoa, he told himself. You're not here for romance, pal. You're here to track Montoya down and haul his Cuban hide back to New York. No matter how cute a dame this is, you haven't got time for any kind of female distraction. You catch Montoya and maybe someday you look her up in Miami. But for now...

He felt her breath against his throat as they began to move to the rhythm of yet another bolero, the slight, soft pressure of her breasts against his shirt, the slim and lovely legs pressed close to his. Legs a man could die for if they were wrapped around him.

He stepped away from her. "How about a walk on the beach?" he asked.

"I don't think so."

"Not a walk then. We'll just take a look, okay?" And when she hesitated, he said, "You have to see the beach at night. There's a full Jamaican moon. It'd be a crime not to. C'mon."

"Five minutes."

"Sure. Just a look." They crossed the patio and went down the few steps to the sand. "Better take your shoes off," he said, and she stepped out of the pumps. Her legs were bare, sleek and smooth. He reached for her hand.

The sea looked phosphorescent in the moonlight, like sparkles of stardust were riding atop the incoming waves. "Oh," she said, and pulling away from him, she ran down to the shore. Warm water lapped over her bare feet and she bent down to scoop some of it up. He kicked his sneakers off and went toward her. "What're you doing?" he asked.

On one knee, she turned and laughed up at him. "Catching moonbeams," she said.

Nuttier'n a fruitcake, he thought. A pocket-size blonde trying to catch moonbeams in her hands. Loony tunes.

He grasped her shoulders and brought her up beside him. She looked at him, surprised, her lips still parted in a smile. "Damn," he whispered, and kissed her.

For a moment she was too startled to move away. When she did, he tightened his grip and held her there. Her mouth trembled under his; her lips tasted of salt spray. He had a sudden urge to scoop her up in his arms and carry her down the beach to some dark, secluded cove where he could kiss the stuffing out of her. Instead, he let her go.

She stared up at him. "You—you shouldn't have done that," she said.

"Didn't mean to. Sorry." He tried for a grin. "Blame it on the moonbeans."

The ghost of a smile touched her lips. "I want to go back now."

"Sure." He picked up his sneakers, and when he took her hand, she didn't pull away. When they reached the steps, he held her arm while she slipped into her pumps. At the top of the stairs, he said, "How about a night-cap?"

"No, thanks."

"I'll walk you to your room, then."

"That's really not necessary."

"Sure it is." The band was playing a soft rumba. He thought about asking her to dance again and decided not to because he was afraid if he held her in his arms he wouldn't be able to let her go.

They crossed the lobby and went up the three flights of stairs. At the door of her room, he hesitated, because he wanted to kiss her again. While he was thinking about it, Lisa said, "Thank you for dinner."

"Any time."

She smiled uncertainly. "Well…" She reached into her purse for her key. When she found it, Sam took it out of her hand and opened her door.

"Get some rest." He handed her the key. "You've had a long day. You must be tired."

"Yes, I am."

"Well..." But still he hesitated, not wanting to say good-night. "Probably see you at the beach tomorrow."

"Probably." She offered her hand. "Good night, Sam. Thank you for dinner and thank you again for rescuing me."

He managed to resist the urge to pull her into his arms, and said, "Good night, Lisa."

With a nod, she went in and closed the door. He stood there for a minute or two, then with a sigh went next door to his own room.

But it was a long time before Sam went to sleep. And when he did it was to dream of a small, fairylike young woman with moonbeams in her hair.

Chapter 3

Breath coming in painful gasps, heart thump, thump, thumping. She ran through darkness and swirling foggy mists of Spanish moss that hung like gray and wispy ghosts from gnarled and bony branches of twisted trees. Had to get away! The roar of a motorcycle came from behind her. Gaining on her. Oh, no! Please, God, no...!

Straining with the effort to breathe, drowning in waves of fear. Feet mired in sand. Everything in slow motion. He was gaining on her. His heavy hand was on her shoulder. "Got you," he cried. "Now you'll pay..."

The whistling slash of the strap. Strangled cry. Piercing scream...

She awoke, shivering and frightened in the stillness of the night, with her heart beating so hard against her ribs she could scarcely breathe.

She tried to take deep breaths, to still the frantic pounding of her heart, to will herself back to sleep. But every time she closed her eyes, the dream came again.

The palms of her hands grew damp, her throat went dry and she was afraid to go to sleep.

She got out of bed and went into the bathroom, poured water into a glass and held it in both hands so she could drink. But she didn't put on the light because she didn't want to look at herself in the mirror.

When she came out of the bathroom, she shivered in the coldness of the air-conditioned room. Sliding back the balcony door, she stepped outside and went to stand at the railing to look out at the sea.

It had been almost five years since she'd last had the dream, but it still had the power to terrify her. Just as the thought of her father, though she hadn't seen him in almost eleven years, still terrified her.

In her mind's eye she saw the farm—row after row of potatoes she had to dig, row after row of beans she had to pick. The field of corn where she tried to hide. The gray clapboard house.

Whenever she thought of the house, the room irrevocably burned into her memory was the kitchen. Table and four chairs. The refrigerator and the stove with the broken oven door. And the kitchen door, with the strap that hung from the hook there.

And her father, big Matt Collier, who ran his Ohio farm, his animals and his family with cruel and heavy hands. His wife, Margaret, whom he never called by name, and Jimmy, his son, four years older than Lisa. She had grown up always afraid, almost always silent, trying to shrink into herself so that her father wouldn't notice her.

Jimmy wasn't like that. Unlike Lisa, who had learned early on never to talk back to their father, Jimmy kept trying to stand up to him.

"It wasn't the horse's fault he couldn't pull that heavy load," he'd say. "You shouldn't have hit him with the hoe. You didn't have no right to do that. You made him bleed."

Very carefully, with slow, precise movements, their father would put his knife and fork across his plate and push his chair back from the table. She would sit there frozen, looking from her father to Jimmy, too paralyzed with fear to move.

"Now, Matt..." Her mother's voice would quiver. "The boy didn't mean no harm."

He'd take the strap off the back of the kitchen door and reach for Jimmy. And the beating would begin. Jimmy wouldn't cry, at least not at first, but finally the sobs would come. And when they did, she would feel the tears streaking down her own cheeks.

When he saw them, her father would turn his gaze on her. "What's the matter with you?" Holding Jimmy by the back of his shirt, he'd tower over her, big, threatening. "You want something to cry about? You want a lick or two?"

"No, Daddy." Snuffling back her tears, biting hard on her lips, she'd stare down at her plate, her fear like a living thing growing inside of her.

She'd had her share of whippings, but she hadn't suffered nearly as much as Jimmy had. He'd run away a few days before his seventeeth birthday. She didn't blame him, but she'd never forgiven him for not taking her with him.

Her mother—her poor, ineffectual mother—had died a week after Lisa's high-school graduation.

"It's your place to stay home and take care of things now," her father had said to Lisa after the funeral. "I'll be wanting my lunch on the table at noon like always and my supper at six. You give me my meals on time and keep the house clean and we'll get along. If you don't, I reckon you know what'll happen to you."

Two days later, when he went into Dayton to buy a new set of tires for his truck, Lisa took a bus to Miami. She had seventy-eight dollars her mother had somehow managed to save and keep hidden, and a check for twenty-five dollars her mother's sister in Cleveland had sent for her graduation.

She got a job waiting tables at a restaurant on the beach, and by scrimping and saving, she managed to put enough aside to pay for a term at the University of Miami. She worked for the four years she went to the university, and all the while, like an escaped criminal, she'd lived in fear that her father would find her. And dreamed the recurring dream that he did.

But always in her dream he'd been in his pickup, chasing her through fields of corn or among Florida oak trees hung with Spanish moss. Never before had he chased her on a motorcycle. She tried to analzye this new version of the old dream, and though she told herself it was nonsense, she knew that it had something to do with Sam O'Shaughnessy. O'Shaughnessy, who was big and brawny like her father. Tough like her father. The kind of man she would always be afraid of.

She had known a few years after her marriage that she had been drawn to Philip because he was so unlike her father. Philip, for all his faults, was a slender, quiet man. He never raised his voice, and though he may have belittled her verbally, he had never physically harmed her. For all his faults, he was in his own way a gentleman. Perhaps, though she had fallen out of love with him a long time ago, she would have stayed with Philip had it not been for his affair with a Fort Lauderdale artist who had managed to win his praise. The affair had ended the seven-year marriage.

Without warning, Lisa's chin began to tremble and she started to cry. She hadn't wept during or after the divorce, but she did now. She cried for the broken marriage, and for Philip, because she no longer loved him. She cried for her dead mother, for her lost brother and for the child she had been, the little girl who had lived in fear.

Sam liked to hear the sound of the waves at night. That's why he'd shut off the air-conditioning and opened the sliding door to the balcony. He slept stretched out naked on top of the sheet. No dreams disturbed his sleep, but suddenly he came awake, cop instincts alert, listening.

It took a moment to identify the sound of a woman crying. He sat up and reached for his shorts, and when he put them on, he went to the open door and looked out. Lisa Collier stood by the railing, head bent, shoulders shaking, one hand over her mouth to try to smother the sobs that would not be smothered.

He said, "Lisa?" very softly, but she didn't hear. He started to climb over the three-foot wall that separated their two balconies. But he stopped. He knew about that kind of grief. It went gut-deep, too terrible, too personal to infringe upon.

He drew back into the shadows, feeling the pain that was her pain, yet reluctant to interfere.

He went back into his room and lay upon his bed. In a little while she stopped crying. He pictured her standing by the rail, a small, sad woman clad in a thin nightdress, looking out at the vast and endless sea.

A while later she went in and he heard the sliding door close. He hoped that the crying had exhausted her. He hoped she would sleep.

But he did not. The sound of her weeping stayed in his ears, the picture of her in his mind.

No matter how badly he slept the night before, Sam always awoke a little before six, ready for the first cup of coffee of the day. Even in Jamaica.

He lay for a few minutes wondering about the woman in the next room. She'd told him that she had only recently divorced. Was that what she'd been crying about? Did she still care for her husband?

He wondered what kind of a man she'd been married to, what kind of a wife she had been.

He got up and dressed in a pair of khaki shorts and a T-shirt, shoved his feet into a pair of sneakers and went looking for coffee.

The dining room hadn't opened yet, but that didn't stop him. He followed the blare of reggae music coming from the radio in the kitchen, pushed open the swinging doors, and when the two men working at the stove turned, said, "How about a cup of coffee?"

One of them poured him a cup. He hefted one haunch on a counter and drank two cups while he shot the breeze with the two men. When he finished, he said he'd see them later and headed down to the beach.

The skies were gray and heavy with clouds that threatened rain. The waves crashed against the shore and the air was misty. It was the kind of day Sam liked. No sunshine and roses for him; this was weather that stirred a man's blood and made him want to beat his chest. He took a few deep breaths, swung his arms around a cou-

ple of times, did a few knee bends and started running up
the beach.

Jamaica was a far cry from New York. It was good to
be away from traffic noise, the squeal of brakes, the
shouted insults of cabbies, the panhandlers and drugged-
out weirdos. From the smell of the precinct, peeling green
walls, phones ringing, uniformed buddies, guys in handcuffs, the clack of typewriters.

Five years ago he'd made lieutenant. He'd worked
homicide first, then drug enforcement. He'd been in a
few shootouts and gotten a couple of medals for bravery
in the line of duty. He could sniff out a drug house ten
blocks away and he'd gotten a reputation as a blood-
hound, a cop who never gave up, who wouldn't stop until every drug lord in New York was behind bars.

A year ago the DEA had summoned him to work for
them. He didn't want to leave the NYPD, so they'd
worked out an arrangement where he was on loan to the
DEA for special jobs.

He liked the men he worked with and he felt a sense of
satisfaction in bringing down the dealers and the push-
ers. But there were times when he felt as though he'd seen
too much, done too much. In the last few months he'd
felt so soul weary, so disillusioned that he'd wanted to
throw in the towel. But he hadn't. He never would because he had his own demons to deal with. And because
drug lords like Juan Montoya were responsible for deaths
he didn't want to think about. He wanted the bastard so
badly he could taste it.

The DEA hadn't wanted to send him on this job because something big was going down in Kansas City. It
had taken a lot of persuading on his part to convince
them, when Montoya escaped, that he was the man for
the task.

"I know every inch of Jamaica," he'd said. "I know the people, I've got connections on the island. If anybody can ferret Montoya out it'll be me."

Still thinking about Montoya, Sam rounded a curve in the beach, stopped for a moment and looked out at the sea. He narrowed his eyes and tried to see through the mist. "What the hell?" he said aloud. Five-foot waves were sweeping in, and some damn idiot was swimming out beyond the breakers.

He ran down to the shore and waved his arms. Whoever it was spotted him, and now he could see that the swimmer was trying to make it back to shore. He'd advance a few strokes, then a wave would hit and he'd be right back where he'd started, arms flailing the air when he went under, fighting the surge of water every time he bobbed to the surface.

The way he was going, he'd never make it.

With a muttered curse, Sam kicked his sneakers off and, yanking the T-shirt over his head, plunged into the surf and started swimming. The fellow spotted him again, then again went under.

Sam swam as hard as he could. The swimmer came to the surface, and all of a sudden Sam realized it wasn't a guy, it was Lisa Collier. What in the hell was she doing swimming in weather like this? Then he remembered last night on her balcony, the way her body had hunched in pain, the sound of her sobs. Had she swum out this far deliberately, knowing she couldn't make it back?

Grunting with effort, Sam plowed through the waves. He was close enough now to see her face, to see the terror there, to know that she was trying with every bit of her strength to reach him.

Two yards away, one. He grabbed for her hand, snagged her wrist just as a six-foot roller hit. They went down together. He tightened his hold, hung on and fought with his free arm and with his legs for the surface. They broke through. He swung his head to get his wet hair out of his eyes. "Hang on to my shoulders," he cried.

She nodded her understanding and he started for shore. But the current was against him, and halfway there he had to stop and catch his breath. He turned, treading water. He saw the fear in her eyes and the determination, and he knew she hadn't been trying to do herself in. She put her arms on his shoulders and treaded water with him.

"You all right?" he managed to ask.

"Yes."

But her face was chalk white and she sounded exhausted.

He got his breath. "Okay, let's go," he said.

She kept one hand on his shoulder and tried to swim along with him. Thunder cracked, lighting split the sky and it started to rain. The undertow sucked at his legs, trying to drag him down. His arms were tired; the breath rasped in his throat. He kept his eyes on the shoreline. Come on, you bastard, he said to himself. You can do it. Couple of more strokes. God, I'm tired. Yeah, so what? Swim, damm you, swim!

His feet touched bottom. She let go of his shoulders and he put his arm around her waist. It was still hard going, but they were almost there. Another couple of yards. Water to his thighs, his calves, ankles. They struggled up onto the beach. She slumped down onto the sand; he sagged beside her on his knees.

"You okay?" he asked when he got his breath.

She lay on the wet sand, breathing hard, her face still chalky. A shudder ran through her. She brushed a strand of wet hair out of her eyes and rolled over onto her back. "Yes," she managed to say. "I'm—I'm all right." She took a deep breath and looked up at him. "Thanks. If it hadn't been for you..."

The words trailed off. She closed her eyes, spent, breathing hard. Finally she pushed herself up to a sitting position. "I'm a good swimmer. I thought I could handle it. I didn't mean to go out so far. I didn't realize the tide was so strong."

He started getting angry, knew it was a reaction to the fear that they weren't going to make it, but couldn't stop himself. "It was a stupid thing to do," he said.

"I—I know."

He stood and, reaching down a hand, pulled her up beside him before they headed back for their things. "If I hadn't come along..." The thought scared him so much that for a minute he couldn't go on. His anger was all mixed up with fear because he knew that if he hadn't come along when he had, she'd probably be fish bait by now.

"What in the hell were you thinking of, swimming this far from the hotel on a day like today? You almost drowned!" His anger got the best of him. He grabbed her arms and shook her. "Dammit!" he shouted. "You—"

"Don't!" Her face was frozen in fear, her eyes wide with terror.

He let her go. He said, "Lisa?" and stared at her, shocked, stricken. He raised a hand to wipe the wet hair back off her face, and when he did, she jerked her head away as though from an expected blow.

When he'd first started with the NYPD and he'd been on patrol-car duty, he'd seen battered women. He knew how they reacted to the slightest touch, how they flinched away. Had Lisa been battered?

He felt her tremble. "I—I'm sorry," she said. "I guess I overreacted." She tried to smile, but her lips quivered and she still looked afraid.

He wanted to put his arms around her, but he feared if he did she'd be scared again. "You've got to get into some dry clothes," he said in a matter-of-fact voice. "You're shaking."

He picked his T-shirt and sneakers up off the sand and she reached for her beach bag. He started to take her hand, but stopped himself.

When they got to the hotel, he walked her up to her room. She took the key out of her beach bag and, when she had opened the door, turned back to him. "There really aren't any words to thank you," she said. "But I do thank you. If you hadn't come along . . ."

"But I did." He summoned a grin. "Let me know next time you decide to take an early morning swim. Okay?"

"Okay." She held her hand out and he took it in his. It was very cold and very small. He thought again of the way she had reacted to his anger and felt a stab that was like a physical sickness in the pit of his stomach because someone—he didn't know who but suspected it might have been her husband—had hurt her. He wanted, as he had on the beach, to put his arms around her and tell her that she was safe and that nobody would ever hurt her again. But he didn't. Instead he said, "You'd better get right into a hot shower."

"Yes, I will. You, too."

"Yeah." It was hard keeping his hands off her, so he turned away and put the key in his door. "See you later?" he said.

"Yes, probably." She went in and closed the door. Without taking her bathing suit off she went into the bathroom and turned on the hot water in the shower. She stripped out of her suit, then leaned against the shower wall and let the steaming water wash over her.

"Fool," she said aloud, not because she'd done a stupid thing by swimming alone on a day like this, but because she'd let Sam O'Shaughnessy see her fear. Because she'd thought that, like her father, he had meant to strike her. Would the fear always be there? Whenever a man made a sudden gesture toward her would she always recoil?

When she felt the beginning of tears, she said, "No! I'm not going to cry. I won't feel sorry for myself because my father was rattlesnake-mean or because my mother was too afraid or too weak to try to help me. He'll never find me, but if he does—if he or anybody else ever tries to lay a hand on me again—I'll chop it off."

That made her feel better. She got out of the shower, and when she had toweled her hair dry, she put on a terry-cloth robe and went into the other room. Five minutes later somebody knocked on her door and called, "Room service."

She opened it a crack. "I didn't order anything," she said to the waiter who stood there.

"Mr. O'Shaughnessy did. This be your breakfast."

"Mr. O'Shaughnessy?" Lisa opened the door wider so the waiter could come in. He put the tray he carried on the table in front of the sliding glass door that led to the balcony and began to set the dishes out.

"There be orange juice, papaya and mango and banana, ham and eggs and fried plantains." He poured coffee into a cup, took a snifter of brandy from the tray and poured a small splash into it and handed the cup to her. "Mister say you need this."

Mister taking a lot on himself, she thought, but didn't say it. And because the man was looking at her, waiting, she took a sip of the brandy-flavored coffee. It slid like a not-unpleasant fire down her throat, and she felt some of the cold seep out of her bones.

"Yes?" the waiter said.

"It's very good." She went to the dresser and took some money out of her purse, but he held his hands up as though to ward her off. "Bossman O'Shaughnessy take care of it," he said. And with another wide smile, he hurried out of the room.

Bossman O'Shaughnessy? A small smile curved her lips. She took another warming sip of the coffee, then sat down and picked up a piece of papaya. It was sweet and tasty. She took another bite and washed it down with the rest of the coffee in her cup.

The rain came harder. Thunder rolled and the rain pelted down. But it didn't matter. She was warm and safe in her room where nothing could touch her. Ohio was another lifetime away.

She curled her feet up under her, took another sip of the brandy and tried not to think how deep and dark the sea had been. Or of what would have happened if Sam O'Shaughnessy hadn't pulled her to safety.

Chapter 4

The phone call came at five that afternoon. "Hargreaves here," Filoberto said in his clipped British accent when Sam answered. "I have a bit of news you might find interesting."

"What is it?" Sam hooked his leg around a chair, dragged it closer to the phone and straddled it.

"We've gotten a lead on a dealer who we have reason to believe has a connection to Juan Montoya. They've worked together before and they were in prison in Cuba's Isle of Pines at the same time a couple of years ago. The information our man has gathered confirms your suspicion that Montoya is in Jamaica working with a group that used to deal in ganja. They're into stronger stuff now, something called splat. From the information we've been able to gather, it's a cheaper, easier-to-produce form of heroin. It's exactly the kind of thing our friend Montoya would be in on."

"How'd you get the info? How do you know it's straight?"

"One of our men has been working undercover with the group for over a year. A few days ago he found out that a connection in Miami is coming to Jamaica to expedite a shipment."

"From Miami?"

"That's right. The man from Miami, or possibly a woman, may have already arrived. We'd thought before that Kingston was the center of their operations, but now we believe it's on the north coast, somewhere around Ocho Rios. The Poinciana is a popular hotel, so there's a possibility that whoever it is we're looking for will stay there. Keep an eye on any new arrivals and let me know. We'll check them out with Miami PD from here."

"You have any idea where Montoya is holed up?"

"Possibly in the area around Port Antonio, but of course he could be anywhere, even in Ocho Rios."

"Montoya might be here?" Sam stood and shoved the chair back. "If he is I'll . . ." He stopped, swung around and saw Lisa standing at the open balcony door of his room.

Without taking his gaze from hers, he said into the phone, "I'll call you back," and hung up.

"I'm sorry," she said. "I didn't know you were on the phone. I didn't mean to disturb you."

How long had she been standing there? How much had she heard? He took a shot at looking casual and said, "It's okay."

She was holding a tray with two planter's punches and a bowl of fried banana chips.

"I thought you might like a drink. The sun, if there had been any sun today, would have been over the yardarm by now."

It seemed like a nice gesture and maybe that's what it was. Maybe.

He took the tray from her and put it on the table by the open door. "Nice idea," he said.

"I wanted to say thank you for what you did this morning."

Like hell, he thought. "No need, but thanks." He pulled out the other chair.

"You're sure I'm not intruding?"

"Of course not." He took a long swallow of the drink and reached for a handful of chips. Hargreaves had said someone was going to arrive, or had already arrived, from Miami. A man, possibly a woman. But Lisa Collier?

She looked out toward the sea and he gave her the once-over. In white shorts and a red knit shirt, barefoot with no makeup and her hair soft around her face, she looked like the girl next door. Fresh as a daisy, innocent as a lamb. But was she as innocent as she looked or was that part of her cover?

He tightened his hand around the glass and took another swallow. If Lisa Collier was involved, if she had any connection to Montoya, he'd bring her down along with the drug king.

He leaned back in his chair. "You said you're a commercial artist. Tell me more about yourself," he said. "What do you do in Miami, I mean besides being married to... what's his name?"

"Philip Matthews."

Matthews. He'd check it out. See if there really was a Philip Matthews or if she was making it up. He sat forward, pretending to look interested.

"I free-lance for a few Miami ad agencies," she said.

"Where'd you go to school? Miami?"

She bit into a banana chip and nodded.

"You from there originally?"

"No, I'm from Ohio."

"Oh, where?"

"Tipp City. It's a small town near Dayton. What about you?"

"Chicago, Detroit, then New York."

She took a sip of her drink. "I've never been to any of those places. I wanted to travel—before I married Philip, I mean. He went to New York several times a year, but he never took me with him. Maybe now that I'm free I'll do some traveling."

"When you get to New York, look me up," he said. "I'll show you the sights." And if you're working with Montoya, it might be a lot sooner than you think, dollface. He studied her with different eyes now, trying to see behind the innocent goody-two-shoes mien, trying to figure out who and what she really was.

Sensing the intensity of his gaze, she moved a little in her chair. He caught a glimpse of smooth, tanned thigh, and an unexpected heat zinged through his belly and sizzled downward. He looked away and gulped the last of his drink. "Want another?" he asked her.

"None for me, but you go ahead."

"Maybe later." He was still trying to figure her out, trying to see behind what she looked like to who she really was. He had to get closer to her, had to find out.

She finished her drink and stood. "I've intruded enough," she said.

"How about dinner?" And before she could refuse, he said, "There's a place a few miles out of town I think you'd like. I haven't been there for a couple of years, but I remember that the food was pretty good."

"Well, I—"

"Seven okay?"

She nodded.

"Great. Come over when you're ready."

She reached for the tray, but he said, "Leave it. I'll have somebody pick it up later." He walked her out onto the balcony, took her hand to help her over the wall and stood on his side until she went into her room and slid her door shut. Then he went back inside and closed his own door.

He called Hargreaves.

"What happened?" the Jamaican asked. "You hung up quite abruptly."

"Somebody at my door." He knew he had to find out about her, but still he hesitated. This was a woman he'd danced with, a woman whose life he'd probably saved. A woman he had kissed. Checking her out was distasteful, but if she wasn't who she seemed, he'd be a fool not to.

"I want you to check on somebody," he said into the phone. "A woman. Her name is Lisa Collier. Until a week ago she was Lisa Collier Matthews. Ex-husband is a Miami art critic named Philip Matthews. She's from Ohio, a small town near Dayton. That's *D-A-Y-T-O-N*. The town is Tipp City. Got it?"

"Yes, but—"

"Find out if she's got any kind of a record, either in Ohio or Florida. See if she's ever been to Cuba."

Hargreaves whistled. "The lady a friend of yours?"

"Maybe," Sam said. "Maybe not."

"If she is—a friend of yours, I mean—what happens if you find out she's connected to Montoya?"

Sam's expression hardened. "She goes down right along with him."

He'd said it; he meant it. If Lisa Collier had any connection to Montoya or anyone like him, he'd bring her
down. But first he had to make sure who she really was.

She found herself humming along with the radio while
she showered and dressed. She'd been a little shy about
accepting Sam's dinner invitation, but now she was glad
she had. It was time she got over her irrational fear of a
man just because he was as big as her father.

At the university, when she'd been asked out on dates
by football-type jocks, she'd always turned them down.
The two friends she'd shared an apartment with, Marian
Jones and Betty Kendall, had thought she was crazy.
"Half the women here would give their teeth for a date
with any one of the guys you turn down," they'd said.
"What's *wrong* with you?"

"They're not my type," Lisa always answered.

Because that type of man reminded her of her father.
Because she was terrified of big, brawny men.

She'd never told anybody how she felt, not even Philip during the years she was married to him. God knows
Philip had his faults, but at least she hadn't been afraid
of him.

She didn't think, after this morning, that she was
afraid of Sam. He'd saved her life. He'd taken her from
the frightening power of the waves and brought her to the
safety of the shore. He had been brave and decent and
gentle. He wasn't like her father.

She took extra care with her makeup and her hair and
decided to wear the new, pale green, summery dress she'd
bought at an expensive boutique in Bal Harbour the day
after the divorce. It wasn't the kind of thing she usually
wore—it plunged too low in front and the skirt was
shorter than she was used to. But because she needed

cheering and because she felt adventurous, she'd bought it.

But now she looked at herself in the mirror. Was the dress too daring? Would it be all right or should she change? No, she decided, this is my vacation. It's time I was a little daring.

She put a dab of perfume behind her ears, at her wrists and between her breasts, and pearl earrings, an anniversary present from Philip, in her ears.

It was five after seven when she took a last look at herself in the mirror and wondered why she felt excited at the prospect of having dinner with Sam when she'd seen him only a little while before. Then, with a smile, she went out and closed her door.

When Sam answered her knock he took one look at her and decided they'd better not take the motorcycle. She looked like a wood nymph in a green dress the same color as her eyes. She wore high heels and her hair was fluffed out in a golden halo around her face. He had a sudden almost irresistible urge to cup her face between his hands and say, "Tell me you're not a part of this drug thing. Tell me you're as innocent as you look, that you'd never be mixed up in anything as dirty as the drug trade."

The thought that she might be roughened his voice when he said, "Since you're all dressed up, I guess we'd better take a taxi."

The restaurant was up in the mountains, away from the beach. A low, white building set back among a stand of West Indian cedar, it looked homey and inviting.

At the door they were greeted by a tall, handsome man who sported a wild Afro, one gold earring and a devilish smile.

"A romantic table for two," he said in a wonderfully musical Jamaican dialect, and he led them past other diners to a secluded table set in an alcove bower of ferns and orchids.

"You be having drinks? A love potion made with good Jamaican rum to warm the blood and stir the passions? A wildly exotic drink for the beautiful lady, something hot like love for the mon?"

"How about a couple of planter's punches?" Sam raised an eyebrow. "Or would you prefer something wildly exotic, Lisa?"

"I'll stick with a planter's punch." Lisa grinned up at the Jamaican. "With a bit of wildly exotic on the side."

He grinned back at her. "My name be Deuteronomy. It is my extrafine pleasure to serve you. I will return with your drinks with the speed of a number-five hurricane."

"Nice man," Lisa said when he walked away.

"He's flirting with you."

She looked surprised and, with a shake of her head, said, "He was only being friendly."

Sam gave an ungentlemanly snort. "Friendly, hell." And once again he wondered if the innocence she projected was real or a put-on for his benefit. He decided then that before the evening ended he'd make a stab at finding out.

Deuteronomy brought their drinks along with a bowl of banana chips and a gardenia for Lisa. With a flourish he placed the flower next to her drink.

Lisa picked it up and brushed the cool white petals against her cheek. "Thank you, Deuteronomy. It's lovely."

"As you are, my lady."

Sam growled, an actual low-in-the-throat growl of a wolf about to spring. Deuteronomy's eyes rolled. He backed up a step, said a hasty, "I be going now," and hurried away as though the winds of an actual hurricane were nipping at his coattails.

Lisa grinned, and when Sam said, "I don't think it's funny," she laughed out loud. It was a good sound.

They chatted while they sipped their drinks. When they'd finished, Sam signaled to a different waiter, and without asking Lisa, ordered two more.

The planter's punches were good—smooth, not too sweet, not too sour. They went down easily.

Sam drew her out, asking questions about her work, about where she'd lived with Philip and where she planned to live now that she was divorced.

"We had a house in Miami Shores," she said. "Philip paid me what my share was worth and he kept the house. I found an apartment on the beach before I left."

She seemed open about her life in Miami, but when he asked her about Ohio, she clammed up.

"What's it like growing up in a small town?" be asked.

"I don't know—well, not really. My father..." He saw her hands tighten around her glass. "We had a farm," she said.

"Near town?"

She shook her head. "Twenty miles away."

"Different from big-city life, I guess."

"Yes."

"What was it like? Growing up there, I mean."

"It—it was all right." She looked down at her drink. A thin film of perspiration made a sheen on her forehead. She picked the drink up and drained it.

Why was she suddenly so nervous? he wondered. Because she was lying? Because she wasn't from Ohio and she'd never even seen a farm? He'd find out. Maybe her name wasn't really Collier; maybe there had never been a Philip Matthews. He wouldn't be snookered by green eyes deep enough for a man to drown in, or a fine little body he had a yen to cradle in his arms. Her looks wouldn't matter if she was tied up in any way with Juan Montoya. If she was, he'd personally see that she got everything coming to her.

They had shrimp-and-crab gumbo, a spinach salad, then scampi for Lisa, a blood-rare steak for Sam.

The food was good and the drinks were delicious. Maybe too delicious. Sam had ordered a third when their entrées came. She hadn't meant to drink it, hadn't realized she had until she looked and saw that her glass was empty.

Sam was talking about his early days with the New York police, and she'd gotten so interested she'd sipped the drink but barely touched her shrimp. It was all right, though—she wasn't in the least tipsy. She felt a little warm, maybe, but nice, more relaxed than she'd been in years.

When a small band began to play at one end of the room, Sam asked her to dance. She tucked the gardenia Deuteronomy had given her behind her right ear and let Sam lead her onto the dance floor.

He enfolded her hand up against his chest the way he had the night before. She leaned her head on his shoulder and sighed.

A woman with a soft Jamaican voice began to sing.

Sam was a good dancer. He didn't look like he would be, but he was. He had nice shoulders. Philip's shoulders were bony. He thought himself a good dancer, but he wasn't. He'd taken lessons, he knew all the right steps, but he was too stylized. Too precise. Sam wasn't. He held her close, her body snugged to his, and moved to the music with a natural rhythm.

The band played a French song done calypso style. Lisa hummed along, eyes closed, happy as a kitten who'd just finished a saucer of milk.

The hand on the small of her back urged her closer. Sam felt the press of her breasts against his chest and wanted to touch them, see how they felt in his hands.

Steady, he told himself. You brought her here to feel her out, not *up*.

"Nice place," he said in a too-hearty voice.

She looked up at him. "Umm," she said. And captured him with her eyes.

He looked away. "Good band."

She nodded, tickling his chin with her hair. He caught the scent of the gardenia and of her. She was as light and as soft as a cloud in his arms. He wanted to keep on holding her, dance all night with her. Wanted to take her down to some lonely stretch of beach and do all manner of things to her. With her.

He had to get a grip on himself. Think about other dames.... What other dames? His mind was a blank. Okay, he told himself, so you're attracted to this little pint of cider. So what? He'd been attracted to women before. It didn't mean anything.

She smiled up at him, a sleepy, lopsided smile, and his insides turned over.

He stepped away from her. "Getting late," he said.

Her lower lip came out in a pout. He wanted to bite it. Instead he took her hand, led her back to their table and signaled to a waiter for their check. Five minutes later Deuteronomy appeared with the check and two snifters of cognac.

"Compliments of the house," he said. And gazing down at Lisa he added, "It has been my pleasure to serve you."

She beamed a smile at him. He took her hand and kissed it, then glanced at Sam and backed away.

"What a nice man," Lisa said. "I love this restaurant, Sam. Thank you for bringing me here."

"You're welcome." He frowned at the glass in her hand. "You going to drink that?"

"It'd be rude not to." She took a sip, said, "Good. Really good," and ran her tongue over the rim of the snifter.

Sam shoved his chair back. "Time to go," he said.

She took a deep, sighing breath. Her breasts pressed against the fine material of her dress and he felt his own breath clog somewhere between his chest and his throat. You do that again, he almost said, and I'll take you out behind one of those trees and kiss you till you're dizzy.

He pulled her chair out and helped her up. She put her hand in his. It wasn't until they were outside that he remembered he had to call for a taxi. "Wait here," he said, and hurried back into the restaurant.

She wasn't where he'd left her when he came back out. He called, "Lisa?" and heard her answer, "Over here, Sam."

She stood under one of the trees, away from the reflected light of the restaurant. "Look at these wonderful old cedars," she said when he reached her. "They must be hundreds of years old." She rested a hand on one of the thick, gnarled branches. "I'm glad I came to Jamaica, Sam. I'm really happy for the first time in a long time and it feels . . ." She lifted her shoulders, trying to find the words to tell him how good she felt, how free. "Wonderful," she said with a smile. "It feels wonderful and so do I."

"You've had too much to drink."

"Have I?" She tilted her head to one side and looked up at him. "Are you mad at me?"

"Of course I'm not mad." But he sounded mad, ferocious as a bear with his foot in a trap. "Dammit, Lisa," he growled, "don't look at me like that."

"Like what?" She rested a hand on his shoulder, honestly puzzled. "Like what, Sam?"

With a groan, he put his arms around her. "I don't want this," he muttered under his breath. Then he kissed her.

For a moment Lisa was too startled to resist. He tightened his arms around her. Her mouth softened and she sighed.

She was as fragile as a butterfly, as delicate as a rose. He kissed her more gently, kissed her eyelids, her nose, her mouth. He said, "Part your lips for me," and when she did he ran his tongue across them. He took the pouty lower lip between his teeth and, as he had wanted to do in the restaurant, bit it just enough so that he could feel it between his teeth, then ran his tongue over it.

He heard the gasp of her breath, but she didn't pull away.

He wanted to drown in her mouth, wanted to crawl inside her, to hold her and caress her until they both went a little crazy. He was crazy now, crazy to touch her, have her.

He ran his hands down over her bare shoulders. He cupped her breasts.

Soft, so soft, so small in his hands. He kissed her again and ran one hand across the rise of her breasts. Her skin was smooth as satin. He slipped his hand down inside the décolletage. She wasn't wearing a bra. He cupped her bare breast and a groan escaped his lips.

She whispered, "You shouldn't." But she leaned toward him, filling his hand, murmuring with pleasure when he rubbed his fingers over the pebbled tip.

"We…" She was struggling for breath now. "We have to stop."

"I know."

But the kiss deepened. He squeezed her nipple between his fingers, and when she moaned into his mouth, the soft sound of her pleasure burned through his body. He felt himself grow, grow to bursting. He had to have her. Had to take her back into the stillness of the trees.…

A beam of light cut through the darkness; the sound of a motor cut through the stillness. He let her go. "The taxi," he said hoarsely. "It's here."

He took her hand. They left the protection of the trees and crossed the grass.

The driver hopped out and opened the back door. Lisa's legs were trembling and it was difficult to keep up with Sam. He helped her into the back seat and got in beside her. They didn't speak or touch.

When they reached the hotel, he walked her into the lobby. Abercrombie was behind the desk.

Sam cleared his throat. "You're probably tired," he said to Lisa. "You'd better go on up. I'm going to have a nightcap."

"All—all right. I—I guess I'll see you in he morning. Tomorrow. At the beach, I mean."

"Yeah, probably." He wanted to kiss her again and knew he didn't dare. He only looked at her mouth, and let his gaze drift down over her breasts.

A flush rose in her cheeks. She said, "Good night, Sam. Thank you for—for dinner. It was wonderful. I really enjoyed…" Her voice drifted off. She held her hand out. He took it, but only for a moment.

When he let it go, he mumbled another good-night, then turned and walked away from her. At the door leading to the patio he stopped and looked back. She was at the top of the stairs. She turned and saw him watching her, and stood for a moment, her hand on the banister.

He almost went to her. Wanted to. Wanted to go bounding up the staircase after her, pick her up and carry her into her room or his. Wanted to kiss her again, touch her again.

But he didn't move. He only stood there watching her until she turned and disappeared around the corner of the stairway.

Chapter 5

He told himself he'd stay as far away from her as he could get. This wasn't the time to become emotionally involved with a woman, especially one he wasn't sure he trusted. But damn, she was something else. He couldn't remember when he'd been so affected by a woman, wasn't sure he ever had been. There was something about her that knocked the pins right out from under him, made him want to grab her, kiss her, hold her and touch her.

Last night he had wanted her so badly he'd thought for a minute that if he couldn't have her he'd bust a gut. Or something even more vital. She was like satin and lace and perfumed softness. She had skin like the petals of a gardenia, breasts to get lost in, pebble-hard nipples he wanted to take between his teeth to lap and tease until she cried for mercy.

Lisa Collier was delectable from the top of her curly

blond head right down to the tips of her toes. And he was damn well going to leave her alone.

That's what he told himself when he awoke the next morning, grumpy as a gator with a toothache because he'd spent most of the night dreaming about her. Lisa wearing nothing but gardenias, smiling a teasing smile as, one after another, she began plucking the flowers from somewhere on her body and tossing them to him. He could smell the heavy fragrance as he started toward her. But when he reached out to her, she backed away, whispering, "Catch me if you can. Catch me...."

"Wait," he'd called out. "Wait for me...." And he came awake sitting straight up in bed.

At six he got up and, pulling on his swim trunks, went down to the beach. He plunged into the surf and swam as hard as he could, swam until the breath rasped in his throat and he'd almost stopped thinking about her.

Back on shore he toweled himself, combed his fingers through his hair and headed for the kitchen. The same two cooks were there. Without asking, they poured him a mug of coffee. They called him "mon" and "boss-mon," and with a wink, one of them pulled a bottle of Tia Maria out of a bottom cupboard and poured a splash into his coffee. Two cups later, Sam felt ready to face the day.

But not Lisa.

He headed back to his room, showered, then pulled on a pair of jeans and a T-shirt and went down to see Abercrombie to ask about new arrivals. At first the clerk pursed his thin lips and said, "I cannot possibly give out that information." But when Sam leaned forward as if he might grab the man's tie the way he had that first day, Abercrombie said there'd been two parties check in late yesterday afternoon—a Mr. and Mrs. Perret from Idaho and a single man, a Mr. Howard Reitman, from Florida.

"Where in Florida?" Sam asked.

"Miami," Abercrombie said.

Could Reitman be the contact Montoya was waiting for? Sam wondered about that while he ate a breakfast of fruit, three eggs and a couple of slices of ham. Then he went outside to have a look around.

Most of the guests were down at the beach. Only Lisa lay stretched out on a chaise beside the pool—wearing, God help him, a red bikini and a big straw hat with a red ribbon around it. The top of the bikini was about as wide as the ribbon.

She sat up when she saw him, and when she smiled, his heart did a flip-flop and his mouth went dry.

"Good morning." And probably remembering last night, she blushed. "You're—you're not going to swim?"

"Had my swim earlier."

"Oh." She looked at the beach chair next to her like she was waiting for him to sit down.

But he didn't. He stood over her and he wasn't smiling, "Better be careful of the sun," he said. "If you get a burn you'll ruin your vacation."

"I'm used to the sun."

"That's what all the tourists say."

"I put sunscreen on."

"Your back's red."

She sat up and, turning a little away from him, asked, "Would you mind rubbing some lotion on me?"

Mind? Hell yes, he'd mind. Her back was bare except for about half an inch of material, and smooth as silk all the way down to the bikini bottom that stretched low across her hips.

She handed him the bottle of sunscreen, then lay down on her stomach and scooted over a little so that he could sit beside her.

He drizzled some of the lotion onto her shoulders and carefully, with only the tips of his fingers, rubbed it in. Her skin was warm from the sun. He stopped.

"The rest of my back," she said. "Not just my shoulders."

He gulped like a fourteen-year-old looking at a nudie magazine, poured the cream down the length of her spine and with the flat of his hands began to rub. God, she was beautifully made. Small bones, narrow waist, slight flare of hips, saucy bottom.

He was tempted to undo the top. Afraid she'd object; afraid she wouldn't.

"I'm going to unhook the top." His voice sounded rough. "You'll get a better tan, no white line."

"Well..."

He unsnapped it and she brought her arms up, hugging her body with her elbows, hiding her breasts.

The lotion was smooth and warm on his hands when he rubbed. She groaned with pleasure and his body tightened. It was heaven and it was hell to touch her like this—up and down the length of her back, trying not to slide his hands around to touch her breasts. But tempted, oh damn, he was tempted. Nobody was here; nobody could see. Just slide his hands under, pretend he hadn't meant to, pretend it was a mistake, but keep on touching.

He remembered the way she'd reacted when he'd touched her breasts last night. Now, lulled by the sun and the warmth of the lotion, of his hands, maybe she wouldn't stop him. Maybe he could just slide around and touch her. Maybe . . . He stopped, hands poised over her back, took a deep breath and said, "That ought to do it."

"Legs," she mumbled.

How much could a man take? He picked up the bottle and drizzled some of it on her legs. Legs? Hell, these were works of art. Smooth, shapely, warm. He clasped his hand around her narrow ankle and wondered if there'd ever been a more beautiful ankle. Up and down both legs, clasping, rubbing, soothing. She sighed, stretched as sensuously as a cat and murmured her appreciation.

What would it be like to entwine his legs around hers? What would it be like to have them wrapped around his back, holding him close while he . . . ?

He snatched his hand off her leg as though he'd been burned. "Got to go," he said. "Got things to do. Can't waste my time like this."

Still trying to cover her breasts, Lisa looked up at him, eyes slumberous, lower lip pouty. "Will I see you later? At lunch maybe?"

"I'll be busy."

She clutched her bikini top and rolled over so that she could see him. "You took me to dinner last night. I'd like to take you tonight."

"Sorry. I've already made plans."

"Tomorrow night then?"

"Don't think so." He saw the sudden embarrassment that brought a flush to her cheeks, but he couldn't help it. This, whatever the hell it was between them, had to stop right now. He was in Jamaica on a job that demanded every bit of his attention. He couldn't let himself get distracted by a dame, especially one who might be connected with Juan Montoya. Maybe Lisa wasn't as innocent as she looked. Maybe she'd been sent from Miami with the express purpose of keeping him off balance while the drug deal went down. It was too big a chance to take. He'd keep an eye on her, but at a distance.

He handed her the bottle, said, "See you around," and strode off before he could change his mind.

Lisa fastened her top back into place and put her face down on the back of her hands, ashamed and embarrassed and mad because she'd made a fool of herself over a man she'd known for only a few days.

"Lunch?" she'd asked. "Dinner tonight? Tomorrow night? Would you mind putting some lotion on my back?"

Her face burned, but it wasn't from the sun. It was because she'd made a fool of herself. Thrown herself at Sam, asked *him* for a date!

She wanted to crawl under the chaise. To go bury herself in the sand. Instead she got up, walked to the edge of the pool and, holding her nose, jumped feetfirst into the deep end.

Sam made the call to Filoberto from his room. "I want you to check on a Howard Reitman who's just come in from Miami." he said. "Check with both NYPD and Miami PD."

"Right away. Anything else?"

"That'll do it for now."

"By the way," Hargreaves said before Sam could hang up, "I checked on the woman you mentioned. Lisa Collier Matthews."

Sam held his breath.

"She appears to be clean as a whistle as far as Miami is concerned. A fairly successful commercial artist. No record of any kind."

Sam let out the breath he hadn't known he'd been holding.

"Married for seven years to Philip Matthews, Miami art critic. He, too, seems straight-arrow."

"Okay, thanks."

"One thing, however. I called that place in Ohio you said the Collier woman was from. Tipp City. Seems the police there have an outstanding warrant for her arrest."

Sam tightened his hand around the phone. "What for?"

"Strangely enough, they didn't seem quite clear on that. Whatever it was happened quite a long while ago…ten or eleven years. At the time they'd had an APB out on her."

All-points bulletin. Why? What had she done?

"You haven't any idea where she was before she went to Miami?" Hargreaves asked.

"No." Sam swallowed hard. "Thanks a lot," he said. "I'll wait here for your callback on Reitman."

When he put the phone down he went to stand out on his balcony. There wasn't any evidence that she was mixed up with Montoya, that she'd ever been mixed up in any kind of drug business in Miami. But she had been in some kind of trouble back in her hometown. He wished he knew what kind. But did it matter? The fact that she was listed with the Ohio police meant she wasn't as lily-white as she seemed.

A lot of the bastards who dealt in drugs operated undercover. Both men and women from all levels of society were attracted because of the big money to be had in the sale of drugs—respected professionals, city officials, housewives, dirty cops, shop girls, secretaries. Lisa Collier could be one of the smart ones who'd never been caught, who had no record. Except back in Tipp City, Ohio.

When the phone rang, Sam hurried back into the room.

"I have something on Reitman," Hargreaves said. "He's a big name with the operators in the south Florida area. Been arrested half a dozen times, but has always gotten off, through lack of evidence and a smart lawyer. One arrest for suspicion of murder, one for assault, one for rape. No convictions. I'd venture to guess he'll be up to no good in Jamaica. He's probably the man you're looking for."

"Thanks," Sam said. "I'll keep an eye on him."

"There's one other thing. On a hunch I checked with Miami to see if there was any possible connection between Reitman and Philip Matthews, the ex-husband of the Collier woman."

"And?"

"They know each other."

Sam swore under his breath.

"Seems that Reitman is into art. He goes to art openings and from time to time buys something expensive, I imagine as a way to launder the syndicate's drug money. At any rate, he and Phillip Matthews are acquainted. When Matthews knows of a piece of art that will very likely increase in value in a few years, he lets Reitman know. They have dinner together several times a month."

"You're sure about this?"

"Oh, absolutely." Hargreaves cleared his throat. "Seems a bit strange, doesn't it, that both he and the former Mrs. Matthews are staying at the same hotel?"

"Yeah," Sam said. "Strange."

When he hung up the phone, he sat on the edge of his bed. He felt as though he'd just lost his best friend.

* * *

"Lisa? Lisa Matthews? My God, is that you?"

She looked up from the luncheon salad. "Mr. Reitman?"

"Yes. Small world. What're you doing here?"

"Vacationing."

"Are you alone? May I join you?"

"Of course." She indicated the chair opposite her. "Please, sit down."

"Thanks." He took a cigarette out of a silver case and lit it. "You're about the last person I expected to see here."

Lisa offered a tentative smile. She'd never particularly liked Howard Reitman, though she couldn't really say why. The few times he'd had dinner with her and Philip he'd been quite pleasant. Still, there was something about him that bothered her.

He was attractive enough, short—five-eight or -nine, she guessed—and in his early forties. The first time she'd seen him she'd been a little surprised, because he wasn't the type of man Philip usually associated with. For though he dressed well, there was a rough edge to him. Sam had a rough edge, too, but he wasn't like Reitman. There was a blunt honesty about Sam that made her trust him.

Still, after his rebuff this morning it was nice having a man pay attention to her, and when he asked her to have dinner with him that night, she accepted.

She wore the dress she'd worn the first night at the hotel, and when she met Reitman in the lobby, he gave her an appreciative once-over and whistled.

"You're a knockout," he said, linking her arm through his. "Philip was crazy to let you go."

Lisa didn't answer.

"I know it's none of my business," he went on as he led her through the lobby to the patio, "but what happened with the two of you? I thought you were the perfect couple. Whenever I saw you together it looked to me like everything was fine."

"Things happen," Lisa said with a shrug.

"Like what?" he persisted.

"Another woman."

"You're kidding!"

"A Fort Lauderdale artist."

He swung around and shot her a look. "Claire Montgomery? Hey, she's good."

"I'm sure she is," Lisa said, tight-lipped.

"I saw her with Philip once, thought it was strictly business. Nice looking, but skinny as a board. Can't hold a candle to you."

A waiter led them to a poolside table. When they were seated and he asked if they would like something to drink, Reitman said, "Planter's punch, Lisa?"

Remembering last night, she shook her head. "White wine, please."

"Aw, come on. You're on vacation, right?"

"Well . . ."

"Nothing like Jamaica run." He turned to the waiter. "Two tall ones." And when they were alone, he said, "How long are you staying?"

"Another week. What about you, Mr. Reitman?"

"Two or three days. Then I'm going to Kingston to attend to a little business." He reached across the table and took her hand. "My name's Howard. Call me Howard."

She started to pull her hand away, but just as she did, she glanced up and saw Sam watching her from the bar. He was leaning back against it, drinking a Red Stripe beer. Even from here she could see the angry, speculative look in his eyes.

She smiled at Reitman. "Howard," she said.

The waiter returned with their drinks. Reitman touched his glass to hers and they drank. It was good, potent with rum. She needed it.

The band began to play a Bob Marley song, fast reggae with a jungle beat. "How about a dance?" Reitman asked.

"Love to," Lisa said.

He took her hand and led her to the dance floor. They faced each other, a couple of feet apart, and she remembered that when she'd first danced with Sam, he'd said, "I don't do fast. I like to hold a woman in my arms when I dance."

Well, she wasn't dancing with Sam now and could dance any way she wanted to. Listen to the music, she told herself. Forget about him. Forget that he lied when he said he had plans tonight. He didn't. He just didn't want to be with you.

She smiled at Howard Reitman and gave herself up to the music. It was primitive, wild. She let herself go, moving with the flow of the beat—arms swaying above her head, head thrown back, doing intricate steps when the music grew faster, caught up in the junglelike rhythm of the drums. A whirling turn made her skirt swirl up over her thighs. She wasn't aware that other couples on the floor had stopped dancing to watch.

Sam had said watching a woman waving her arms and jerking around didn't do anything for him. Well, it was doing something for her. She was having a wonderful time.

The beat quickened and the drums reached a climactic frenzy of sound. Howard grabbed Lisa's hand and whirled her, fast. She twisted away, full skirt floating outward. The music stopped and the band and the couples on the dance floor cheered. Howard pulled her up against him and kissed her full on the mouth.

And Sam, standing at the bar, muttered, "Son of a bitch!"

It was after midnight when Howard walked Lisa to her room. "Well . . ." He smiled and started toward her.

She backed away and, offering her hand, said, "Good night, Howard. It's been fun."

"Can I come in for a minute?"

"No, I'm sorry. I'm a little tired."

"See you in the morning for breakfast."

"I don't know. I—"

"Eight-thirty too early?"

"No but—"

"I'm going to run in to Ocho Rios right after breakfast, so I won't be able to see you for lunch. But how about dinner?"

Lisa hesitated. She didn't dislike Howard, neither did she especially like him. The one thing in his favor was that he wasn't a stranger. If she accepted his invitation, at least she wouldn't have to have dinner alone. He'd said he was only going to be here for two or three days. So she'd see him for dinner tomorrow night and then he'd be gone.

"All right," she said. "I'd love to."

"Eight o'clock?"

"Fine, Howard. Thank you."

Before she could step back, he put his arm around her neck and, pulling her toward him, kissed her.

She did step back then, said a quick, "Good night," and went into her room.

It was just about then that Sam started along the corridor. He passed Howard, saw the satisfied smirk on his face and had a sudden urge to wipe it off.

Eight minutes had gone by since he'd seen them going up toward Lisa's room. A hell of a lot could happen in eight minutes.

He stopped in front of her room, went to his own, put the key in the lock, then took it out. Grim-faced, he knocked on Lisa's door. When she opened it, he said, "I want to talk to you," and without waiting for an invitation, walked into her room.

She'd stepped out of her high heels. Now she looked like *half* a pint of cider. He glared down at her.

Hands on her hips, she glared right back at him. "I didn't invite you in," she said, and started toward the door to open it and usher him out.

He blocked her way.

"Please leave," she said.

"When I've had my say."

"I'm tired."

"You should be, the way you were behaving tonight."

"What's that supposed to mean?"

"Flaunting yourself out there on the dance floor. Showing yourself off that way."

Hot color rushed to her face.

"Bare legs. Skirt halfway up around your neck."

"What I do isn't any business of yours," she said, getting angry.

"Yeah? Oh, yeah?" Brilliant repartee, Sam, he told himself, knowing he sounded like a six-year-old. What are you going to do now? Jump up and down and swat her?

"Listen," he said, trying to sound reasonable. "You shouldn't be running around with some stranger you don't know anything about." And testing her, he asked, "Who is that bird, anyway?"

"His name is Howard Reitman. He isn't a stranger. I knew him in Miami." She clenched small fists against her hips. "But whether I know him or not isn't any concern of yours."

"Isn't it?" He advanced a step, and before she could get away, he grabbed her shoulders. "Isn't it, Lisa?" he asked. And he kissed her.

She struggled, but he clasped her in his arms and held her there. He ground his mouth hard on hers, angry again, more at himself than at her because he didn't want to give in to this, didn't want to hold her like this, kiss her like this.

He loosened his grasp, and when he did, she broke away from him and ran out through the open doors of her balcony. He followed her.

"I want to talk to you," he said.

"Go," she whispered. "Just go."

"No." He turned her around to face him and held her there, searching her eyes as though trying to see what lay behind the mystery in their green depths. Who was she? Only a tourist from Miami here in Jamaica recovering from a broken marriage? Or somebody in the drug underworld, somebody connected with dirtbags like Juan Montoya and Howard Reitman?

That thought made him mad again, but sure as hell didn't cool him off. With a muttered curse he pulled her back into his arms and kissed her with all the force of his anger and desire. He took her pouty lower lip between his teeth to taste, clamping hard while he ran his tongue back and forth across the fullness. He nibbled the corners of her mouth, and when she protested, he said, "Kiss me back. Kiss me the way I'm kissing you." And when she parted her lips to say no, he slipped his tongue past her lips.

Her mouth was sweet and moist. He touched his tongue to hers and heard the intake of her breath. She tried to move away, but he took her face between his hands and held her until her lips parted and with a cry her hands crept up to encircle his neck.

"Lisa." He breathed her name and his mouth softened against hers. He held her close, letting her know she was safe here in his arms.

A breeze stirred, bringing with it the soft strains of Caribbean music from below and the crash of waves against the shore. The night was scented with jasmine, and with her. She drugged his senses and made him long for things he hadn't even known he wanted.

He felt her warmth through the silky material of her dress and thought of how she'd looked out on the dance floor when the dress had swirled up around her pale thighs. He wanted her more than he'd ever wanted a woman before.

He pressed his hand against the small of her back and moved against her. He took her gasp of shock into his mouth, moaned when she snuggled closer and ever so slowly answered his movements with her own.

Like a drowning man gasping for air, he took her breath, as she took his. He knew he had to stop. If he didn't right now, he wouldn't be able to. If she was mixed up in the drug thing... The thought stunned him enough to let some sense back into his brain. He held her away from him.

All slumberous and warm, she looked up at him. Her lips were bruised by his kisses. Moonlight touched her hair.

He looked past her to the bed and knew that if he picked her up and carried her there, she wouldn't fight him. He could lay her down and strip the dress off. He could cover her with his body, hold her, make love to her. He could . . .

He touched her hair. "Moonlight lady," he said. And let her go.

"Sam?" She reached out to him.

"No," he said, his voice rough with all that he was feeling. "This isn't any good."

"I—I don't understand."

"Maybe you do, maybe you don't." He backed away. "I shouldn't have come in, Lisa. I'm sorry. I won't do this again."

Her green eyes were wide. "What is it?" she whispered. "Why are you . . ." She shook her head. "I don't understand," she said again.

"Don't you?" He took a deep breath to steady himself and reached for the doorknob, hanging on to it as though to a lifesaving ring. "Good night," he said. "I won't bother you again."

Then, as though all the demons of hell were after him, he went out and closed the door.

Leaving her alone, there in the center of the room. Alone while her body thrummed with desire.

Chapter 6

Filoberto Hargreaves showed up in Ocho Rios at seven-thirty the next morning, dapper in a white linen suit, blue shirt and a conservative tie. He took a room on the second floor of the Poinciana overlooking the patio, a room he would use for only a few hours.

Sam joined him for breakfast.

"Which one is Reitman?" Filoberto took a sip of his coffee and indicated the tables around the pool. "Is he down there?"

"Guy with the yellow sport shirt," Sam said. "Rusty-colored hair."

"Sitting with the blonde?"

"Yes." Lisa. In a white bikini with a short, white, terry-cloth coverup.

"Is that the Collier woman?"

Sam nodded.

Hargreaves raised an eyebrow. "Quite nice looking, isn't she?"

"She's all right."

"All right?" Hargreaves studied her. "From here she looks quite spectacular. I rather hope she isn't involved is this nasty business. It would be a shame to put a woman like that behind bars."

Sam tightened his hands around the balcony railing, but he didn't say anything.

"You're not involved with her, are you?"

"Involved? Me? Of course not."

The Jamaican gave him a piercing look. "One must not let one's hormones get in the way of duty."

"Not a damn thing wrong with my hormones," Sam snapped.

"That's what I'm afraid of." Hargreaves turned away from the balcony and went back into the room. Sam followed him. "I have something to tell you," the Jamaican officer said.

Sam leaned against the dresser and waited.

"I told you we've had a man working undercover with the local group for over a year. Last night we found his body on the beach near Runaway Bay." Hargreaves reached for a cigarette and when he had lit it, said, "His throat had been cut."

"Damn!"

"He was a good man. We will miss him. So will his wife and their three children in Kingston."

For a minute Sam didn't say anything. Then he said, "Can I have one of those?" and indicated the cigarette.

Filoberto offered him the pack. Sam shook one out, lit it and took a deep drag. "I quit a couple of months ago," he said.

Filoberto waited.

"How'd they catch on to him?"

"We don't know. But his murder suggests that whatever it is that's going down will take place soon."

"And it has something to do with Reitman's arrival here in Ocho Rios."

"I would suspect so. He arrived yesterday?"

Sam nodded.

"And made almost-instant contact with the Collier woman?"

"They had dinner together last night."

"And now breakfast." Hargreaves ground out the cigarette. "They knew each other in Miami, of course. But still, one wonders if he was simply a business acquaintance of her husband's or if the three of them were involved with this from the beginning."

Sam didn't say anything. The thought of Lisa being involved with the bastards who had murdered Hargreaves's man sickened him.

Hargreaves went back out onto the balcony. "Reitman's getting ready to leave," he said. "I'm going to follow him."

"Be careful."

"Always, my friend." Hargreaves started toward the door, then turned back and said, "I leave you with the not-unpleasant task of keeping an eye on the young lady."

"I'll keep an eye on her," Sam said.

His voice was so hard, so cold that it stopped Hargreaves. "Do not do anything foolish. Remember, we want Reitman, Montoya and all the rest of them in one piece. So do you when you take them back to New York." He paused. "The Collier woman is attractive, Mr. O'Shaughnessy. It wouldn't be wise to let yourself become emotionally involved with her."

"I don't intend to," Sam said, tight-lipped.

When Hargreaves left, Sam went back out on the balcony and looked down at the people having breakfast on the patio below. Lisa was alone now. As he watched, she left the table and walked toward the pool. She took the terry-cloth robe off and tossed it onto a chaise. Her body was slim and tanned and beautiful. He tightened his hands around the rail. Then he swore under his breath and went back into his room.

She wished she hadn't told Howard Reitman she'd have dinner with him. She didn't want to see him or anybody else. Not even Sam, at this point.

She didn't understand him, or the way she acted when she was with him. She'd never responded to Philip that way. Their marital relations had been more or less okay, if a little bland. Never once in the seven years she'd been with him had she felt the sexual excitement she felt with Sam O'Shaughnessy.

She was not a promiscuous woman. Philip had been the first and only man she had ever made love with, and only after they were married. Yet last night, if Sam hadn't stepped away, she would have oh-so-willingly been his.

But he had stepped away.

She didn't understand him. Sometimes he acted as though he couldn't keep his hands off her. But there were other times, like last night, when it was as if it made him mad that he'd kissed her.

Was there something wrong with him? Some physical ailment, or, God forbid, a disease that made him draw back? Whatever it was, from now on she'd keep her distance. She had another week here in Jamaica and she intended to enjoy it. By herself. She'd have dinner with Howard tonight because she'd said she would, but that was it. When he left tomorrow she'd be glad to see the last of him.

She'd sun and swim, maybe do some sketching, take long walks on the beach, and do everything she could to avoid Sam, even if it meant having dinner alone in her room. That wasn't an especially pleasant prospect, but anything was better than being rejected again.

She tried to tell herself it didn't matter that Sam had rebuffed her. She told herself that, after all, he was just someone she'd met on vacation, a man she'd kissed a couple of times because she'd been a little vulnerable after her divorce. Though not movie-star handsome, he was attractive in a rough, virile sort of way. She knew he was attracted to her, but it was pretty obvious that he didn't want to get involved. So that was it. From now on she'd stay out of his way.

She didn't hear from Howard all day, but a little before eight that night he called to remind her of their dinner date.

"I've rented a car," he said. "Slappy... oops, I mean *snappy* red convertible."

"That's nice," she said, and frowned because his speech was slurred.

"We're going to drive up to a restaurant in the mountains," he went on. "Great place. You'll like it."

Lisa didn't think so, especially if he'd been drinking. She was about to tell him she had a headache, but before she could speak, Howard said, "See you in the lobby in a few minutes," and hung up.

She'd assumed they'd be having dinner here at the hotel; that way she could have escaped to her room whenever she'd had enough of Howard. She didn't like the idea of driving up into the mountains with him, but she wasn't sure how to get out of it.

She frowned at herself in the mirror, and once again firmed her resolution that after tonight she'd be on her own. No more dates, not with anyone.

She checked herself over—new, white silk pantsuit, green silk shirt and white sandals. She picked up her white bag, put a small makeup case and her key into it. With a sigh, because she really didn't want to go out tonight, she turned off the bedside light and started toward the door. She hesitated when she heard a sound.

"Excuse me." Sam stood in the shadows of her still-open balcony door. "I didn't mean to startle you," he said. "Are you going out?"

"Yes."

"With Reitman?"

She nodded.

"Where?"

"Is that any of your business?"

"I'm making it my business." He took a step into the room, then, because he knew he was going about this all wrong, he said, "Sorry. I don't mean to interfere, I just want to make sure you're going to be okay."

"I can assure you I'm going to be quite okay." And relenting, she said, "He's taking me to a place somewhere up in the mountains."

"Don't go."

"I beg your pardon?"

"You don't really know the guy."

"Of course I know him. I told you last night, he's a friend of Philip's."

"And that makes him okay in your book?"

"For heaven's sake, I'm only going to have dinner with him. He's leaving tomorrow and I doubt I'll ever see him again."

"Tomorrow? Where's he going?"

"I think he said to Kingston." She switched the light back on. "Why are you asking me all these questions?"

Why indeed? If she was mixed up with Reitman, and through him with Montoya, he ought to let her have free rein. Let her go with Reitman, follow them, see what they were up to. Dammit, why did he have this overwhelming urge to protect her?

He thought then that what he'd like to do would be turn her over to Hargreaves and tell him to stash her somewhere until all of this was over, so that when it all came down, she wouldn't get too badly hurt.

But he couldn't do that, because if she was involved, she'd take the rap just like the rest of them.

She stood there, waiting for an answer. And because he couldn't tell her, he said, "Don't go out tonight, Lisa."

She looked up at him and there was an expression of determination on her face he'd never seen before. "Good night, Sam," she said.

He chewed the inside of his cheek, feeling tempted to keep her here, slap a pair of handcuffs on her, tie a handkerchief over her mouth and fasten her to the bathroom sink. But even as the thought came, he knew he couldn't do that. Not to Lisa.

Without another word he walked out of her bedroom and vaulted over the wall to his own balcony.

She stood for a moment, then quickly crossed the room to close and lock the balcony doors. Sam wasn't any different from the other men she'd known. He, too, wanted to tell her what to do—just like her father, just like Philip. For while Philip hadn't been physically cruel, he'd been verbally cruel. He'd ordered her about, as her father had. Now Sam was doing the same thing.

She'd decided when her divorce was final that nobody was ever going to do that to her again. If she made mistakes they'd be her own. But she would not be told what she could or could not do. Not ever again.

With a determined look, Lisa picked up the white purse and left her room.

Reitman drove erratically. He sped up on the curves, slowed down on the staightaways and veered to the right or left on the narrow mountain road every time he turned to say something to Lisa.

She'd been right about his having been drinking, and she knew now that she should have refused to go with him. She would have if Sam hadn't told her not to go out tonight.

They came to another, sharper curve. There were no guardrails on this mountain road, only football-size rocks to mark the drop-off. Suddenly Reitman veered to the left, hit one of the rocks, then swung back onto the road and came within a foot of hitting the side of the mountain. When Lisa gasped, he patted her knee.

"Not to worry," he said with a laugh, and inching over, gave her leg a squeeze. "I know the road like the back of my hand."

She moved away from him. "I wish you'd slow down."

"Sure. All you have to do is ask." He slowed to thirty. "I'm used to driving fast. Sorry." He eased his right arm over the back of the seat and rested it on her shoulder. "I've always liked you, Lisa. Right from the first time we met. I'm going to be busy for the rest of my stay here in Jamaica, but I'm thinking that maybe we could see each other when we're back in Miami. I never would have said anything while you were married to Philip, but you're free now, so I can. There's no reason why we shouldn't get together."

She murmured, "Well, perhaps," and thought, not on your life, fella. Once tonight was over she never wanted to see Howard Reitman again.

She had absolutely no idea where they were. With every turn of the road they seemed to be getting farther and farther from civilization. If he let her out of the car now, and she almost wished he would, she'd have no idea how to get back to the main road or to the hotel. She didn't like being this vulnerable. It frightened her.

"Are we almost there?" she finally asked.

"Almost." He squeezed her shoulder. "Another couple of miles. I know it's a little far from the hotel, Lisa, farther than I remembered. Place isn't too ritzy, but the food is good and I know everybody. It used to be a popular hangout for people from both Ocho Rios and Kingston and some of the resorts in between, but not too many people come here now." He slowed the car. "See the lights up there? That's it. Mountain drops down to the sea on the other side."

They wound up another corkscrew curve, came to a driveway and stopped at last in front of the restaurant. There was only one other car, a black sedan.

Reitman parked, then hurried around to open her door. "Great steaks," he said. "I know you're going to like the place."

She nodded and forced a smile. All she wanted to do was eat dinner as quickly as possible and get back to the safety of the Poinciana.

In the foyer they were greeted by a Jamaican in jeans and a food-splattered sport shirt. He had a blunt, brutish face, narrow eyes and a jagged scar that ran from his left eyebrow to his chin.

"Hey," he said to Reitman. "Glad to see you, mon. Been waiting for you." He looked at Lisa and frowned.

"This is Miss Collier." Reitman took her arm. "Lisa, this is Benjamin."

Benjamin said, "Yeah." Lisa didn't say anything.

"We'll sit out on the terrace," Reitman said. "Bring us a couple of rum punches, will you?"

"Sure you need another one?"

Howard let go of Lisa's arm. In a voice that sent a chill down her back, he said, "Rum punches, Benj. Right now."

The black man's face went still. A muscle jumped in his cheek. "Yeah, mon. Sure." He gestured toward the terrace. "Sit wherever you want."

There were six tables out on the terrace. A flight of rickety-looking stairs went down to the jungle below. None of the tables was occupied. Reitman held a chair for Lisa. "Guess it's not the season," he said. And laughed.

She didn't say anything.

A different waiter brought the drinks. He was tall, slat-thin, with sharp cheekbones and a nose that looked as though the end of it had been whacked off. A moustache and a stringy goatee completed the unsavory picture.

"How you be?" he asked Howard Reitman.

"Great. You?"

"Be fine. How things in Miami?"

"Hot." Reitman laughed. "You know." He took the glass from the man's hand and drank half of it in one gulp. "Long as you're here you might as well bring us a couple more."

"No more for me," Lisa said.

"You haven't even tasted your drink. Believe me, sweetie, one taste and you'll want more." He winked at her. "That goes for a lot of things, doesn't it?"

She looked down at her drink without answering.

By the time the waiter returned with two more drinks, Reitman had finished his first. Lisa had only sampled hers.

"Tell me when you're ready to eat," Tall-and-skinny said.

"Sure, sure. But we're in no hurry, are we?" Howard reached across the table and patted Lisa's hand. And when the waiter left, he said, "You need to loosen up, sweetheart." He grinned. "You ever smoke ganja?"

"What?"

"Jamaican marijuana. Great stuff. Stronger than you get in the States. A couple of drags and you haven't got a care in the world." He leaned forward. "This place is like, you know, like a private club. They've got a room in the back where you can get any kind of a fix you want. Nobody around to hassle you. You get too high, there's a couple of cabins out back where you can spend the night."

"I don't do drugs," Lisa said.

"Everybody does drugs, babe." He finished his second drink and reached for the one she hadn't yet touched. "You have a couple of smokes, maybe take a hit or two of coke. Doesn't mean you're an addict."

This time she didn't even bother answering him. She knew now that she was out of her element. All she wanted to do was get away from this place and Howard Reitman.

"There's something new everybody's been talking about," he went on. "Something sorta between coke and heroin. They call it splat." He chuckled. "Hell of a name, isn't it? Maybe because after you use it you go splat. Going to turn the world upside down, Lisa. Hell of a lot of money in it. Millions to be made. And not just for the top brass or the dealers. Even the mules, the carriers, will be making big bucks."

He drained the third rum punch. "For instance, Lisa, somebody like you—you know, somebody here on vacation—could carry a bag back to the States in their makeup case. Make maybe ten grand for one trip."

She was too appalled to do more than stare at him. And yes, she was scared out of her wits. My God, the man was into drugs! Not only that, though he hadn't come right out and said it, he was suggesting she carry drugs back into the United States!

She wished she knew how to hot-wire a car. She didn't even know what hot-wiring entailed, but she'd seen movies on television when somebody would reach under the dashboard, fiddle around and start the car. It looked easy. If you knew how. She didn't.

Tall and Skinny came to the table. "You be ordering now?" he asked.

Reitman waved him away. "Couple more drinks first."

"Somebody wants to see you."

"Yeah? Like who?"

"You know."

"Oh." Reitman sat up a little straighter. He started to pick up his glass, hesitated, then put it down. His hands were shaking, but he forced a smile and said to Lisa, "I'll be right back, dear. Why don't you order for both of us? The steaks are good. Make mine medium, will you?"

He left. Lisa didn't move, but sat there, staring out into the dense, junglelike growth of trees and tropical shrubs. Dumb, she told herself. This was really a dumb thing to do. You've gotten yourself into a mess and now you've got to figure a way out of it.

She wouldn't let him drive while he was drunk. She would insist he give her the keys and let her drive them back to the hotel. If he objected, she'd damn well walk.

She wished Sam were here. Then wished she hadn't wished for him. But she couldn't help it. Sam was a take-charge man, somebody you could depend on. He'd know what to do in a situation like this. She could almost hear him whispering, "Get the hell out of there, Lisa. Walk if you have to."

With a sigh, she picked up her purse and went to stand near the railing. Everything was so quiet. She could hear the call of jungle birds, the rustling of a night animal through the bushes. The low murmur of voices. Then not so low. Someone shouted, sounding loud and angry. And Reitman's voice, apologetic, scared.

Curious, she moved farther along the railing and looked in the direction of the voices. Three men were standing in the doorway of what looked like the kitchen. She couldn't quite see them, but knew that one of them was Reitman. The angry one waved his arms and shook his fist. He moved under the overhead light and she could see his face. He looked familiar. But where had she seen him? Was he someone she'd met in Miami? Another friend of Philip's?

A name came to her. Montgomery? Montana? Mon— Montoya? Yes! Montoya! But he—he was wanted for murder. She'd seen his picture on the front page of the *Miami Herald*. Juan Montoya. Drug king. Escaped murderer. The Miami police had tried to arrest him, but he'd gotten away before they could. A few months later he'd been arrested in New York and indicted for murder. There'd been a trial. He'd killed a guard and escaped.

He was here, standing less than thirty feet away from her.

"¡Estúpido!" he shouted. "Why the hell you bring a woman here? You know how important this deal is. What the hell you thinking of?"

"I—I'm sorry," she heard Reitman murmur. "I wasn't thinking. I had a couple of drinks—"

"A couple! *¡Borracho, pendejo!* I ought to kill you...."

"We got to get rid of her," another man said.

"*Sí, sí.* You are right. We cannot take a chance...."

Lisa didn't wait to hear any more. She ran for the stairs. Behind her the man named Benjamin called out, "Hey, where you goin'?"

She didn't answer, didn't stop.

"The woman!" he cried out. "The woman be running away!"

Montoya shouted an obscenity. Someone else cried, "Stop her! Stop her!"

She ran down the stairs, grabbing onto the wooden railing to propel herself along. She had to get to the shelter of the trees and bushes. They wouldn't be able to find her there. Heart hammering hard against her ribs, gasping with fear, she struggled for breath. God, oh God, oh God. Help me. Help me.

Footsteps sounded behind her. She reached the bottom step and headed for the trees. Into the trees.

The man chasing her grabbed her shoulder. She pulled away. He grabbed the back of her jacket, yanked hard and whirled her around. She struck out at him. He ducked the blows and seized her shoulders. She brought her knee up hard, got him between his legs. He woofed in pain and doubled over.

She ran as hard as she could through the trees. Had to get away. Had to hide. Had to—

Somebody grabbed her from behind. When she cried out, a hand was clamped over her mouth. She struggled, but it was like trying to fight a bulldozer. He pulled her back into the dense bushes. And there wasn't a damn thing she could do about it.

Chapter 7

"**S**top it!" It was Sam's voice. "Be quiet."

He pulled her farther into the bushes, his hand still over her mouth. Terrified, Lisa struggled, but he wouldn't let her go.

"Have you found her yet?" someone shouted from above.

"Not yet." The voice was alarmingly close. Underbrush crunched a few feet away.

"Don't move," Sam whispered close to her ear.

Move? She was paralyzed with fear.

The steps moved off.

"I'm going to take my hand away. Okay?"

She nodded and he let her go. "He's over there." Sam jerked his head to the right, and through the darkness and the overhang of trees, she saw the Jamaican, Benjamin, six feet away. Then the beam of a flashlight broke through the underbrush, and she saw the other one, the tall, skinny one.

"Where the hell she be?" the man whispered.

"She has to be here, mon. We gotta find her."

"We don't, it be bad for us." Tall-and-skinny sounded scared. "That Cuban be one mean dude. We don't find her, he liable to kill us. I'll look over there. You keep looking here."

He turned away, and the other man stayed. She could see him through the trees, gun leveled as he turned and came toward where they were hidden.

Sam shoved her down. She gave one fleeting thought to her new white suit and hugged the ground.

"Did you find her yet?" Reitman called down from above.

"No," Benjamin shouted back.

"Joseph and Stanley are coming down." Fear and urgency raised Reitman's voice to a hysterical pitch. "You've got to find her!"

Other footsteps came crashing through the underbrush. Sam's hand was on her back, holding her still. She heard the hushed voices, steps close by. Steps receding, far enough away so that she could whisper, "Sam, there's a man up there. . . ." She struggled for breath. "His—his name is Montoya."

"Montoya's up there?" He raised himself, looking at her, his face twisted with anger. "So why'd you run away, Lisa?" he whispered. "Things go bad? Your take not big enough?"

She stared up at him, not understanding. "What? What?"

"Don't play dumb. If you want me to help you, now's the time to tell the truth."

She tried to struggle away from him, but he held her pinned to the ground, his body half over hers. He could hear the voices of the men who were after her, searching in the other direction now.

"Tell me," he rasped. "Tell me or so help me God..."

In the shadowed moonlight that slanted through the trees, he saw the fear in her eyes, the bewilderment.

"Dammit, Lisa. Tell me the truth."

"His picture..." Almost incoherent with fear of the men who were looking for her, and of Sam, she said, "In the newspaper... I saw his picture in the *Miami Herald*, on the front page, when he—when he was arrested. He's—he's wanted for murder, and Howard—Howard is mixed up with him. I heard them talking and then I ran." Her eyes wide with shock, she looked up at Sam. "My God," she whispered. "You think—you think I'm—"

"Keep quiet."

Montoya's voice called from above, "We're leaving. Joshua, you stay. Benj and the rest of you, come on."

There was the clatter of footsteps running up the rickety stairs.

Sam scrambled to his feet. He couldn't let Montoya get away, couldn't lose him. "Come on," he said to Lisa, pulling her up beside him.

Her anger almost overcame her fear. "You thought I was mixed up with those people. You thought—"

"Shut up," he growled.

"No!" Raising her voice, so furious she wanted to strike out at him, she cried, "No!"

A gun exploded. A bullet whistled over their heads. Sam shoved her down, drew his own gun, crouched low. Lisa looked up, saw the Jamaican at the same time Sam did. The Jamaican swung around, gun raised to fire. Sam hit him hard with the butt of his weapon and he fell without a sound.

Sam grabbed his ankles and pulled him farther into the bushes, then yanked a piece of hanging vine off a tree and quickly tied the man's arms and legs together behind his back. "Come on," he said to Lisa.

"I'm not going with you."

"Oh yes, you are."

He heard the sound of a motor starting up. A cry, *"¡Vamonos!"*

Dammit to hell, Montoya was getting away! Sam grabbed Lisa's wrist and started running with her. She tried to get away from him and he turned on her, furious because there might still be some of Montoya's men around. He didn't have any choice; he couldn't leave her here.

"I don't have time to argue with you," he said between clenched teeth. "You're coming with me." Before she could answer, he started running again, pulling her behind him. She tried to get away, but he wouldn't let her go. He ran with her, slipping and sliding down the side of the mountain. She stumbled and fell. He pulled her to her feet and kept running, ignoring her protests. Only one thought raged through his mind: he had to get Montoya. Get him before he slipped away.

It started to rain. The ground was wet. Lisa said, "Wait. Wait, I . . ."

He paid no attention. They broke out of the underbrush, cut across a path and ran into the edge of trees. His motorcycle was there. He got on, pulled her up behind him, said, "Hang on," and zoomed out of the forest.

She hung on because she didn't have any choice, because she was stunned by what had happened, terrified. At the same time she wondered what in God's name she was doing here.

The moon was obscured by clouds. In the darkness Lisa could barely discern the overhang of trees, the long tentacles of vines that swept down, threatening to ensnare them. Branches and leaves slapped against their faces; the rain almost blinded them. This was little more than a rutted path. How could Sam see where he was going? Where *was* he going? Dear God, this was so dangerous, so frightening.

He whipped out onto what looked like the road she'd been on with Howard. Peering ahead over his shoulder, she saw the red taillights of a car.

Sam hit the accelerator. She pushed her head against his back and tightened her arms around his waist. What would he do when he reached the black sedan? How many men were in the car? Montoya, Reitman, the waiter Benjamin. How many more of them against Sam on an unprotected motorcycle?

The rain came harder, pelting down on them. Wet hair was plastered to her face and she rubbed against Sam's back, trying to get it out of her face so she could see.

He hit a thick patch of dirt, skidded to the side, fought for balance, then righted the motorcycle and sped on. They were headed into the mountains, barreling around curve after curve. She was scared to death, but there was nothing to do except hang on. Automatically she leaned when Sam leaned, and prayed like she had never prayed before.

She had no idea how long they'd been riding. She was tired, wind-whipped, windblown. The white suit was soaked through and she was cold. It had been warm when she'd started out tonight, but it wasn't warm now and her hands were cold. She wanted to beg Sam to stop, but knew he wouldn't as long as he could see the red taillights.

She looked around Sam's shoulder and saw ahead the lights of a village—a few houses, nothing else. A dog barked. The black car sped on. The red taillights disappeared around a curve in the road. She wanted to tell Sam to slow down, but knew he wouldn't. The motorcycle bumped, speeding full-out, onto the rutted street of the village. They raced through it, left it behind. Rounded a curve. Suddenly a black shape loomed in front of them.

She screamed.

Sam veered the motorcycle to one side and shot into a field. She hid her head against his back, felt his muscles contract as he fought for control. The motorcycle skidded and she knew they were going to crash.

As though she'd been shot out of a cannon, Lisa flew off, sailed through the air for a split second, then hit the muddy ground fanny first, rolled and came to a stop facedown.

Except for the whir of the still-spinning wheels, there was silence.

"Lisa?" Sam was on his hands and knees beside her. "Lisa?"

She rolled onto her back.

"Are you all right?"

She sat up, dazed. Mud squished through her fingers. She'd lost a shoe.

"Are you all right?" he asked again.

"I—I think so. What did we hit?"

"We didn't hit anything. A cow stepped out in front of the motorcycle. I swerved to miss it."

"You swerved all right." He helped her up. She felt dizzy, disoriented. "I lost my shoe," she said.

The motorcycle was on its side in the mud. Sam heaved it up and looked it over.

"It's too dark to see if anything's broken," he said. "I'll have to take it back to the village and check it out in the daylight." He propped it up and went looking for her shoe. Found it hanging from the branch of a bush.

"It's wet," he said when he handed it to her.

"Everything's wet." She put it on. "Are you all right?"

"Couple of bruises. Nothing serious. I'm sorry we took a spill. Lucky we're near a village."

It was raining. She was covered with mud from one end to the other. Her shoes were ruined and so was her suit. And he had the nerve to say they were lucky.

She dragged the hair out of her eyes and glared at him through the rain. He ignored the look. "C'mon," he said. "Let's get going."

He wheeled the motorcycle; she trotted alongside him. And cursed the day she'd come to Jamaica.

He knocked at the first house they came to. A minute or two passed before somebody called out, "What you want?"

"We've had an accident," Sam said. The door opened an inch or two and a man, sleepy-eyed, wearing only undershorts, peered out. He opened the door a little wider. When he saw the motorcycle, he said, "What happened?"

"A cow ran across the road."

A woman appeared behind the man. "A cow?" she said. "Oh, Lord! Lord! It be the calf. I know it be the calf." Her voice rose. "Did you see his eyes? Eyes like balls of fire?" And without waiting for a reply, she put her hands to her head, moaning, "He be back again, bringing the evil with him."

"You hush that talk," her husband said.

"But he's here," she wailed. "He turn his eyes on them and made them have the accident."

"You being silly. Now get out of here and go back to bed 'fore I swat you good."

She peered around the man. "You be careful," she whispered to Sam. "Night like this, with the devil cow wanderin', there be duppies, too. Get you if you don't be watching."

The man pulled her back and gave her a shove. "Git!" he said. And to Sam, "Don't pay her no mind. She be talking about duppies all the time."

Duppies? Lisa looked behind her, then moved farther up the steps, closer to Sam.

"We can't go on tonight," Sam said. "Is there a hotel in town?"

"There be no hotel, sir, but Miss Rebecca Adams..." He pointed down the street. "She be living two houses down. She rents rooms. You go right on down there. This be a mighty bad night to be out."

Guess so, Lisa almost said. Cows with balls of fire for eyes, duppies—whatever they were, rain and mud and maybe a broken motorcycle.

Sam thanked the man and they stepped off the porch back into the rain. Two houses down they stopped before a house that was bigger than the man's had been, but even more ramshackle. "The Jamaica Hilton," Sam said. He propped the motorcycle against the porch railing, then climbed the stairs and knocked on the door.

Five minutes went by before it was opened. A woman wearing a wraparound housecoat and a turban and holding a lantern above her head peered out.

"What you be wanting?" she asked.

"Mrs. Adams?" Sam asked. "We've had an accident. The gentleman two doors down said that you sometimes rent a room."

She looked past him to Lisa who was by the cycle. "I only got one to rent. She be your wife?"

"Yes, ma'am."

Rebecca Adams stood aside and motioned to Lisa. "You be looking like a drowned muskrat," she said as Lisa drew near. "Gotta get outta those clothes before you be catching your death." She motioned toward the motorcycle. "You got a suitcase on that contraption?"

Sam shook his head. "'Fraid not."

"Then I'll be giving the lady something of mine. Don't have nothing for you, mister. But best take off your clothes anyway." She chuckled. "Being as you're married I don't guess that matter much."

"Married?" Lisa looked at the woman, then at Sam.

"Three years last week," he said.

Lisa opened her mouth to say something, then clamped it shut when the other woman said, "This way," and led them through a small living room and down a narrow hallway. She stopped in front of an open door. "There's a shower out back, next to the outhouse," she told them. To Lisa, she added, "I'll bring you a couple of towels and something to put on after you shower."

She went into the room and told Sam to hold her lantern while she lit the one on the dresser. When it was lit, Lisa looked around. There was a cement floor, a bed and the dresser. Nothing else. Not even a chair. She glanced at Sam, saw him looking at the bed, and frowned. If he thought he was going to sleep here, he had another think coming!

Rebecca went out and returned in a moment with two thin towels, a minuscule bar of soap and a Mother Hubbard housecoat for Lisa. "The rain be stopping. You go on back now and take your shower, missus."

Lisa took the things the woman handed her, said, "Thank you," and started out of the room.

"Better take a flashlight," Sam said, and took one out of his pocket.

She nodded her thanks, followed the woman's "That way," and went through the house into the backyard. The shower was a boxlike contraption. There was an open shed next to it. She put the Mother Hubbard-style dress on the bench there and stepped into the shower clothes and all, because it seemed simpler to wash the mud off them that way. She pulled the chain to release the water, and when she thought her clothes were reasonably clean, she stripped and, naked, reached out and threw them over the bench.

Back in the shower, she gave the chain another pull and washed her hair. When she finished, she dried herself with the thin towel, reached out for the Mother Hubbard, put it on and, flashlight in hand, hurried back to the house.

Sam was standing in the middle of the room. He'd stripped down to his briefs. The rest of his clothes were rolled into a bundle on the floor. Lisa stared at him, horrified. "What do you think you're doing?" she said indignantly.

"Trying not to catch pneumonia." He looked her up and down. "Some outfit," he said.

She glared at him, handed him what was left of the soap and turned her back.

"The flashlight," he said.

She gave it to him and he started out of the room. At the door, he turned back and said, "Take whichever side of the bed you want," and before she could answer, went out and closed the door.

Damn the man! If he thought for one minute he was going to sleep in the same bed with her, he had better think again. On the other hand... She looked around the room. There simply wasn't any other place to sleep except on the cement floor. Maybe if he put a blanket down... But there wasn't a blanket on the bed, only a thin cotton bedspread and a sheet.

Muttering under her breath that if she ever got out of here she'd never leave Miami again, Lisa took the comb out of her purse and combed the snarls from her hair. Then she got into the bed and pulled the sheet over her.

Twenty minutes later Sam came in. She peeked at him through half-closed eyes. He had the wet towel wrapped around his waist, but as she watched, he took it off. Her eyes flew open. "What do you think you're doing?" she cried.

He reached for the bedspread and wrapped it around himself, toga-style. "Going to bed." He started to turn off the lantern, but she said, "Leave it on."

He almost smiled. "You want to keep an eye on me?" he asked, and when she didn't answer, he turned the lamp lower, but not off. He crossed the dimly lit room and, pulling back the sheet, got in beside her.

Lisa turned on her side, as far away from him as she could manage in the narrow bed. This was too impossible, too incredible. She was somewhere in the middle of Jamaica in bed with a man she'd known for less than a week, a man who thought she was mixed up in something terrible. The more she thought about it, the madder she got. She couldn't sleep and it made her angry when she heard his even breathing to know that he could.

She sat up and, reaching over, poked him in the chest. "Wake up," she said.

"Wha...?" he mumbled. "Wazza matter?"

"I want to talk to you."

He swore. "I'm sleeping. Can't it wait?"

"No, it can't. I want to know what this is all about and I want to know now."

He swore again and sat up. "All right. I'm awake. Shoot."

"I'd like to." She shifted so she faced him. "I want to know what you meant back there at the restaurant when you asked me about my take. My take of what? What were you talking about?"

"You knew who Montoya was," he said uncomfortably.

"*Everybody* knows who Montoya is if they're able to read a newspaper. He's been accused of murder and dealing drugs. He's a wanted criminal. A..." She stared at Sam. "My God," she said. "You think I'm mixed up with him. With some kind of a drug deal. Drugs!" She stared at him, horrified. "That's why you've paid attention to me, romanced me." She swallowed hard. "That's why you kissed me."

"Hang on a minute. I—"

"Hang on! Hang on? I'd like to smack you!"

"Look," he said. "I'm sorry, okay? We know that Reitman's involved and—"

"We? Who's we?"

"The Jamaican police."

"So they're after me, too."

"Not after you. Not exactly. But they know who you are. They know Philip is a friend of Reitman's." He sounded defensive. "Both you and Reitman are from

Miami. You come to Jamaica, he shows up a couple of days later, and right away you're buddy-buddy."

"So they thought—*you* thought that because I'd known him in Miami, I was mixed up in this—this whatever it is?"

"Lisa, I—"

"Is Howard a part of it?"

"Yeah. So we thought..." He was beginning to feel ashamed of himself. "We thought you were in on what's going down."

"Which is?"

"It's better you don't know."

"Oh, really? Because of your suspicions I'm in this up to my eyeballs, riding on the back of that damn motorcycle with you, landing in a mud puddle with you, here in the middle of Jamaica with you. In *bed* with you!"

That struck him as funny and he made the mistake of laughing. When he did, she smacked him.

The blow landed on his arm. He ducked when he saw another one coming and grabbed her wrists. "Dammit, that hurt," he said.

"I hope so!" This was the first time in her life she'd ever fought back. She'd been too terrified of her father, too intimidated by Philip. But now she was angry enough to let loose the pent-up rage she'd held in for so long.

Sam O'Shaughnessy, the man she liked, the man who made her feel all kinds of excitingly wonderful things when he kissed her, had only been pretending. He hadn't cared about her. Every kiss, every touch had been make-believe because he thought she was mixed up with a murderer, that she was a part of the filth that dealt in drugs.

She wanted to hit him, wanted to hurt him the way he'd hurt her. She struggled against him, and when he shoved her down on the bed and pinned her arms, she bit him. He yelped, let her go and, without thinking, drew his hand back.

Her eyes went wide. She held her hands up over her face, shrinking down, cowering in terror.

"Don't hurt me! Don't hurt me!" she cried, her voice pitched little-girl high. "Please, please, please. I'm sorry. I won't do it again."

"Lisa? My God! Lisa..." Sam reached out for her and she tried to scoot away. "It's all right, honey," he said. "I won't hurt you, Lisa. I'd never hurt you."

She shrank away from him, terrified, trembling. He put his arms around her and, though she struggled, drew her closer into his embrace.

"Shh," he whispered against her hair. "Calm down, baby. Nobody's going to hurt you. Take it easy, Lisa."

He held her close and felt the frantic beat of her heart against his chest.

"Let—let ..." She could barely speak. "Let me ... g-go."

"In a minute, sweetheart. Let me hold you like this." He lay back down, bringing her with him, and cradled her in his arms. He whispered soothing words and little by little the terrible shaking stopped. But her breathing came in painful gasps and her hands were as cold as ice.

When at last she stopped fighting, she lay stiff and still in his arms. He held her as gently as though she were a child. He rubbed her back, he kissed her forehead and eventually she relaxed against him. Finally her breathing evened out and he knew she was sleeping.

But still he held her, there in the dimly lit room, held her and soothed her and brushed soft kisses across her forehead.

Sam knew now that what he had suspected was true. Someone had hurt her, and the thought of it, of someone laying a hand on her as a child or as a woman, sickened him.

She was a small woman. How tiny, how defenseless she must have been as a child.

Had it been Philip who'd abused her, or a parent? Someday he would ask. But not now. Now it was enough to hold her.

Her hand lay on his chest. He picked it up and gently kissed her fingertips. "Sleep," he said. "I'm here, little Lisa. Nothing's going to harm you now."

Chapter 8

It had been one hell of a day. Everything that could go wrong *had* gone wrong. Montoya had been within grabbing distance, but he'd gotten away, and the thought of it was like ground glass in Sam's stomach.

He wasn't sure what he would have done if he'd caught up with Montoya tonight. He had the Beretta on him. The .44 Magnum, along with enough ammunition to sink a ship, was safely tucked away in the saddlebag. But a couple of guns weren't enough to take Montoya and Reitman. He had to have a plan; he couldn't go charging in on a bike, especially with Lisa along.

In retrospect, it was just as well they'd taken the spill. It gave him time to sort things out, make a plan. He didn't want to put Lisa in danger. Had to get her somewhere safe. On the other hand, if he let the trail get cold, he might never catch up with Montoya.

It was a hell of a fix. He didn't want her along, but would it be safe to leave her behind? If he took off after

Montoya and Reitman, missed them, and they doubled back and found her... He swore under his breath because, as dangerous as it was, Lisa would probably be safer with him.

He was sure now that she wasn't involved with the drug operation. He almost wished she had been. In a screwy kind of way that would have been easier to deal with than trying to sort out how he felt about her.

How he felt was all mixed up in a cockamamy jumble of irritation that she had to be here, attraction, desire, and most of all an overwhelming need to protect her. When he'd seen the fear in her eyes tonight, when she'd spoken in that scared, little-girl voice, he'd felt sick in the pit of his stomach because he knew he'd caused it.

It wasn't just a suspicion now, it was a certainty that somebody had physically hurt her. Somebody... She stirred in her sleep, murmured something unintelligible and nuzzled her head against his shoulder.

He could feel the warmth of her body through the god-awful Mother Hubbard. Made sleeping hard... No, skip that word. Don't think *hard*, think *difficult*. Made sleeping *difficult*.

But the word didn't help the ache in his groin. He wanted her, wanted to ease himself up over her, into her before she knew what had happened. She'd responded to him before. Just because she'd pulled away didn't mean she didn't want him. He could... No, he couldn't, not now when she was scared and vulnerable, not when she was emotionally and physically exhausted.

She lay with her head on his shoulder and, though she was asleep, every now and then her body quivered and jerked with remembered fear. "Shh," he said then. "It's okay, honey. You're safe. Nothing's going to hurt you."

He held her gently, and at last, warmed by her, strangely at peace with her beside him, he, too, slept.

Half-asleep, Lisa stretched. She felt the warmth of a leg against hers, the line of hip, the solidness of a shoulder against her cheek. She sighed and tightened her arm around the naked waist. Waist? Her eyes flew open.

"'Morning," Sam said.

"What are you...?" She gasped. "What are you doing here?"

"Waking up." He stretched, arms reaching above his head, and yawned. She averted her gaze, but not before she caught a glimpse of flexed shoulder muscles and broad chest with a V-shaped patch of hair that ran straight down in a narrowing line and disappeared below the sheet.

He was bare from the waist up. Was he from the waist down? She scooted away from him, confused, disoriented, frantically trying to sort things out.

He saw her confusion, briefly wondered what she'd do if he said, "Was it good for you?" but didn't because he was afraid if he did she'd jump out of bed and head for the hills. Instead he asked, "Did you sleep well?" And without giving her a chance to answer, he added, "I've gotta go check on the motorcycle."

The bedspread had slipped down over his body. He reached down to wrap it around himself again, and when he'd more or less succeeded, threw the sheet back. "Rest for a while if you want to," he told her. "I'm going to try to find a mechanic."

"Very well." She sounded as prim and proper as if she were at a lady's tea instead of in bed with a half-naked man.

He stood and, holding the bedspread around him, said, "I'm going out to get my clothes."

"Uh-huh."

With her hair tousled and her cheeks pinked by sleep, she was so damn appealing it was all he could do not to jump back into the sack with her. And because the thought of how it would be made his teeth ache, he headed for the door.

Lisa lay back in the bed and tried to reconstruct everything that had happened the night before: the discovery that Howard knew Montoya, that Montoya was here in Jamaica and that Howard was working with him. She wasn't sure what they would have done to her if Sam hadn't arrived. But he had arrived, racing in on his motorcycle instead of on a white charger.

They'd ridden at breakneck speed after the big black car, zooming around the hairpin mountain curves in the dark, racing along until the black figure of an animal had loomed in front of them and she'd gone spinning through the air.

She wondered if Philip, because he knew Reitman, was connected in some way to the drug business. She'd fallen out of love with him a long time ago, but he had been her husband. She hoped he hadn't anything to do with all of this.

With a sigh, Lisa sat up and swung her legs over the side of the bed. That's when she remembered her sudden bout of hysteria, her fear when Sam had pulled back his arm as though to strike her. How she hated having him, having anyone, see her like that. Would the fear she had known as a child ever go away or would she always be plagued by the memory of the way it had been?

After her marriage to Philip she had been tempted to go back to Ohio, back to the farm. She had thought that if she faced her father as an adult she might be able to put the past behind her. But when she'd suggested it to Philip, without telling him why she wanted to go back, he'd said, "Good Lord, Lisa. Why would you want to go there?" He emphasized *there* as though Tipp City and the farm were at the other end of the world, a world he wanted no part of.

Because she didn't have the courage to go alone, she put the idea of returning out of her mind. But she knew now that she had to go back. It was time to put the past behind her; she could only do that if she faced her fear. Facing her fear meant facing her father, and that, though she hated to admit it, still frightened her.

When she opened the door of the bedroom, she smelled coffee and suddenly realized how hungry she was. She followed her nose to the kitchen and found Rebecca Adams standing at the wood-burning black stove.

"Good morning," Lisa said.

"'Morning." Rebecca turned and smiled. "You like a cup of coffee and something to eat?"

"If it's not too much trouble."

"No trouble. Sit you down. Your husband already be eating." She poured Lisa a cup of Blue Mountain coffee and said, "I be fixing you some eggs and breadfruit. Got some fried plantains left over from yesterday, too."

"That'll be wonderful." Lisa took a sip of her coffee and after a moment's hesitation asked, "What are duppies?"

"Duppies?" Rebecca frowned. "Who be telling you 'bout duppies?"

"The lady two doors down. We almost hit a cow last night and when Sam, Mr. O'Shaughnessy, told her husband about it, she said something about a calf with balls of fire for eyes. Then she said something about dup-pies.''

Rebecca rolled her eyes. "That be Matilda. She shouldn't be telling you 'bout duppies. Just because she be a'scared of everything that moves don't mean she should be scaring you." She put a plate with two fried eggs in front of Lisa and sat across from her. "She be right 'bout duppies, though.''

Lisa paused, fork halfway to her mouth.

Rebecca leaned closer. "Duppies be ghosts that walk at night and bring evil." She looked around, as though afraid someone might overhear, and lowering her voice, went on. "The way it is, every man has two spirits, one from God and one not from God. When a man or a woman die, the good spirit fly up to a tree, then right on to heaven. But the evil spirit, it stay on earth and be-come a duppie.''

A bite of egg stuck in Lisa's throat and she took a sip of coffee to wash it down.

"Sometime the bad spirit live in the silk-cotton tree, sometime in the almond tree. But most often he be in the grave during the day and come night he gets up and wanders around. The way it works, if somebody don't like somebody, he go to the grave at midnight, scoop a small hollow in the ground and put in some rice. He sprinkle that with sugar water and whisper the name of his enemy." Rebecca shook her head. "I tell you, mis-sus, it take a strong obeahman to make the spell go 'way.''

Half-afraid to ask, Lisa said, "What's an obeah-man?''

"Voodoo man with strong magic." Rebecca leaned closer and whispered, "Matilda be right 'bout one thing.

Worse kind of duppie be a rolling calf. What scared her was hearing how you and the mister almost hit it."

The rolling calf with fireball eyes? Duppies and obeahman? Nonsense, Lisa told herself. But somehow that didn't stop the shiver from running down her spine.

The village didn't look much better in the daylight than it had last night in the rain. There was an open market, a small, old-fashioned general store and a one-pump gas station.

Because it had taken the spill in soft, rain-soaked mud, the Harley seemed to have come through the accident more or less intact. The man at the gas station Sam took it to washed the mud off, checked it out, revved the engine and said it was good as new.

"Is there a phone in the village?" Sam asked.

"No, sir. Won't find no phone for maybe ten, eleven miles."

That was bad. He needed to talk to Hargreaves, tell him where he was and let him know he'd spotted Montoya and was going after him. He could go back down to Ocho Rios, probably should because of Lisa, but if he did the trail would be cold.

"Where does the road out of the village lead?" he asked.

"Up to the mountains, sir. Up to the Cockpit Country. Be bad place, sir. There be giant forests where you be lost, big swamps where men go and no return. You better go back the way you came. Go down to Ocho Rios, to Kingston, Montego Bay or Port Antonio. All be nice places, sir. Big hotels and fancy tourist ladies looking for gentleman dude like you. You have fun there."

Sam shook his head and, with a grin, said, "Last thing this gentleman dude wants is another tourist lady." He pointed to the Harley. "Gas me up. I've got to get going." He took a pound note out of his pocket. "Are there other gas stations along the way to Cockpit Country?"

"No stations, sir. But there be places where you can get gas. If you be determined to go."

"I be determined," Sam said.

He rode the Harley back to Rebecca Adams's home. When he knocked, Rebecca let him in. "Your wife be in the bedroom," she said.

His wife. The words gave him a nervous tic. The day his divorce from Margaret had been finalized he'd taken an oath that he'd never go through the pain of another marriage again, at least not for another forty or fifty years. The words *wife* and *marriage* weren't in his vocabulary. They never would be.

He knocked. Lisa opened the door. She'd put the white pantsuit back on, but after last night's roll in the mud it would never be the same again. He looked her up and down and said, "You'd better go buy yourself a pair of shorts."

"I've got shorts back at the hotel."

"We're not going to the hotel."

She looked at him, surprised. Before she could ask why, he said, "I can't waste time taking you back. We're going after Montoya."

"We?"

"That's right." He sounded impatient. "There's a store in the village. Go buy yourself a pair of shorts and a shirt. If they don't have shorts, get jeans."

"I'm not going with you."

"You don't have a choice."

"Yes, I do. There has to be a bus that comes through here."

"There isn't."

"Then I'll walk back to the main road and hitch a ride to Ocho Rios."

"No, you won't." Sam took some money out of his pocket. "I'm going after Montoya," he said. "Unfortunately, I don't have any other choice except to take you with me."

"Well, I have a choice." Hands on her hips, Lisa faced him. "I'm not going with you and that's final."

"And what if Montoya and Reitman decide to double back? What if they come looking for you?" He shook his head. "Whether you like it or not, you're in this now. I don't want you with me any more than you want to be, but it's the only way. I'll do my best to keep you out of danger and I promise you that as soon as I can get you to some place where I'm sure you'll be safe, I'll let you go. Until then you stay with me."

She didn't want to go with him. If she absolutely refused, there'd be very little he could do about it except tie her up and throw her over the back of the Harley. She didn't think he'd do that, but she didn't want to take the chance. Besides, the thought of being taken by Montoya or Reitman scared her a lot more than the thought of being with Sam.

She took the money. When he said, "Hurry it up," she gave him a dirty look and marched out of the room.

There wasn't much of a selection in the way of clothes in the general store. She found a pair of boys' cutoff jeans, a T-shirt and a jeans jacket. When she left the store, she started back to Rebecca's house, then hesitated and walked down to the open market, where she bought some bananas and mangoes, a bag of hard rolls and a round of cheese.

Buying food before setting out on a motor trip was something she started doing as soon as she left home. In case she was ever marooned, by flood, fire or snowstorm, she wanted to be prepared. So whenever she started out, whether for a two-hour trip to Palm Beach or a longer trip to Atlanta, she always had something along in the car—a few apples, a package of crackers. Something.

Sam was waiting on the porch steps when she returned to Rebecca's home. "Hurry up and change," he said, playing the tough guy again.

But when she came out fifteen minutes later, his tough-guy facade faded. In the cutoffs and T-shirt she was a knockout. He remembered how it had been last night in bed with her, the feel of her body so close to his. His pulse raced; his palms felt sweaty. He said, "C'mon, we gotta get going," and turned away from her.

Rebecca came out and handed Lisa a brown paper bag. "Sugar yams," she said. "'Case you be hungry."

"I'm always hungry." Lisa smiled and hugged Rebecca. "Thank you for everything," she said, and handed the bag of yams to Sam, along with the things she'd bought in the market.

He wheeled the cycle around and headed it toward the road out of the village that led up into the mountains.

"You be going to Cockpit Country?" Rebecca's face wrinkled into a frown. "You be taking the missus up there?"

Sam nodded. To Lisa he said, "Time to get rolling."

"Wait." Rebecca turned and ran back into the house. Lisa raised her eyebrows in question, but didn't say anything. Five minutes later, the woman returned. "You take this with you." She pressed a smooth round stone into

Lisa's hand. "Obeahman give it to me. It be warding off the duppies."

"Rebecca, I—"

The Jamaican woman folded Lisa's fingers around the stone. "Keep it," she said.

"Well . . . well, thank you." Lisa put the stone in the pocket of her cutoffs.

Sam, already on the Harley, held his hand out to help her onto the back. "Maybe we'll see you on the way back through here, Mrs. Adams," he said. "Thanks for everything."

"Welcome, sir." She stepped closer. "You take good care of the missus, yes?"

"Sure." He gunned the motor and, with a wave of his hand, turned onto the road.

Lisa, with one arm around his waist, looked back and waved a a goodbye. But the other woman didn't wave back. She only stood there in front of her house and, as Lisa watched, quickly made the sign of the cross.

They rode for over an hour before they came to another village. Sam stopped and had the gas tank topped up in front of a store that sold lukewarm beer.

He bought a beer and then said, "Friends of mine have gone along ahead of us. They were driving a big black car. Did you see them?"

The man nodded. "They stopped for gas. Maybe one, two in the morning. Wanted to know if there was a place to stay once they got up into the Cockpit Country. I told them there be a place, Orangefield, 'bout an hour from here."

Orangefield. They'd probably stopped there to spend what was left of the night. Sam paid, took a sip of the warm beer and handed the bottle back to the man.

"Ready?" he asked Lisa, who'd gotten off to have a soda and stretch her legs.

"I suppose." With a sigh she climbed back onto the Harley. She hated the motorcycle, but she'd gotten used to it. She leaned into the curves without Sam telling her to now, and though she still kept a firm grip on his waist, she no longer dug her fingernails into him.

There was something about riding behind him like this, with the wind whipping her hair and the smell of the tropics filling her senses, knowing Sam was in control and that all she could do was hang on. There was an intimacy, an awareness of his body so close to hers that was exciting. Her thighs were around his, pressed close as though in an embrace. And when they leaned into the curves it was as though their bodies were welded together and they moved as one on the big, hot machine.

The mountains they were driving through held a proliferation of plants and trees: poinciana, banana and papaya and mango, West Indian cedars, mahogany and pimento. Golden trumpet vines added color, along with amaryllis, spider lilies, yellow hibiscus and wild orchids.

The air was cooler the higher they went and Lisa was glad she'd worn the jeans jacket instead of cramming it into one of the saddlebags. The sky was a clear, clean blue, and though they were far above the sea, it seemed to her that the salt smell mingled with the good rich smells of mountain vegetation.

She wished she could relax and enjoy the scenery, but how could she when she knew they were going into dangerous country, chasing a murderous drug lord? Maybe

Sam had been right when he'd said Montoya and Reitman might double back to look for her, but did he honestly believe she'd be safer with him?

What would happen when—if—he found Montoya and Reitman? Did Sam really think he could take them on, them and their Jamaican henchmen? One man against four or five? She wasn't a gambler, but the odds didn't sound too good from where she stood—or rather, from where she sat.

They rounded a curve. She leaned into it and gasped at the three-or-four-thousand-foot dropoff. Below lay fertile valleys and rolling plains. And in the distance the line of the sea, turquoise green in the late-morning sun.

Sam slowed the Harley. "Pretty, isn't it?" he called back over his shoulder.

"Yes."

"You tired?"

"No, I'm all right. How much farther?"

He lifted his shoulders in an I-don't-know gesture, and she felt the muscles of his back flex against her breasts. "We'll stop at Orangefield," he said.

And then? Lisa wondered. What if Montoya and Reitman were there waiting for them? Involuntarily her arms tightened around Sam's waist. She knew how badly he wanted to find them, but she wasn't sure she did. She wasn't even sure what she was doing here. She wanted to be safely back in Miami having a hot corned beef sandwich at Wolfie's. This . . . this riding on the back of a motorcycle, going higher and higher up into the dangerous Jamaican mountains with a man who until only a few days ago had been a stranger, seemed like a bad dream.

They rounded another curve and over Sam's shoulder she saw a village, bigger than the one they had passed through an hour before.

Sam slowed the Harley. There was a scattering of shacklike houses here, an open market, a stand that sold beer and soft drinks, a two-story wooden building with a sign that read Orangefield Hotel. Welcome.

Sam stopped the motorcycle. There was no sign of the black car. "Wait here," he said to Lisa.

He went in. A fat man in a sweat-stained shirt was fanning himself behind the desk. He looked up, surprised, and said, "You be wanting a room? Something to eat?"

Sam shook his head. "No room, but maybe we'll eat." He leaned against the desk. "I think maybe some friends of mine stayed here last night—a Cuban, an American and a couple of Jamaicans."

"They were here."

"How long ago did they leave?"

The man glanced at the clock that hung on the wall over the desk. "Maybe two hours ago."

"Have you got a phone?"

"Yes, sir, we have. But it not be working."

Sam muttered a curse. Montoya was only two hours ahead; he shouldn't hang around. On the other hand, Lisa needed something to eat and so did he.

"What's for lunch?" he asked.

"Pepper-pot soup, sir."

Sam hesitated. "Okay," he said. "Tell the cook to heat it up."

He went out and motioned to Lisa. "We'll have lunch as long as we're here," he said.

She climbed off the Harley and, opening the saddle-bag, took her purse out and slung it over her shoulder. He watched her come toward him, windblown and sexy. Keep your mind off her and on the job you've got to do, he told himself. But when he motioned her ahead of him he made the mistake of looking at her—trim figure, great legs and the sauciest bottom this side of Albania.

Damn, he thought angrily. A man doesn't stand a chance against odds like that.

Chapter 9

The pepper-pot soup was hot, the bread was crisp, the beer cold.

"That was all right," Sam said when they'd finished. "You ready to roll?"

They'd had little to say while they ate, but ever since they'd left this morning, Lisa had been thinking about what they were doing and what could happen if and when they caught up with Montoya.

"No, I'm not ready," she said. "We have to talk about this."

Sam raised an eyebrow. "This?"

"Your going after Montoya alone. Dragging me along with you. Why don't you notify the police?"

"Because so far I haven't been able to find a phone."

Lisa lowered her voice. "What you're doing is too dangerous. You're one man against Montoya and Reitman and the men who work for them. Suppose you do catch up with them?"

"I damn well plan to."

"On that blasted motorcycle?"

He allowed himself a smile. "You don't like the hog?"

"Let me put it this way, Sam. It's not exactly a Mercedes."

"I'm not a Mercedes kind of guy." He took the last sip of his beer. "I suppose Philip was."

She looked startled.

"He have a Mercedes?"

"As a matter of fact he did."

"Figures."

Her mouth tightened. She tapped impatient fingers on the tabletop. "I think we should go back to Ocho Rios and notify the police."

"I'm the police."

"Not in Jamaica."

"I'm working with them. They know what I'm doing and they're as anxious to get Montoya as I am." He leaned forward, his voice serious. "I know it's dangerous, Lisa, and I'm sorry that you're along. I'd take you back if I could. I'd get in touch with the police if I could. But I can't. If I turn back now I'll lose the trail. Somewhere along the way there's got to be a phone. As soon as we find one I'll—"

"Sam?" The color drained from her cheeks. "Sam. That—that man."

"What man?" He swiveled around, didn't see anybody. "What's wrong?"

"He's here. The—the skinny one with—with almost no—no nose. I saw him in the doorway."

"Who? Who're you talking about?"

"The waiter, at the restaurant with Howard." Without thinking, she reached for Sam's hand. "Maybe they're here. Maybe Montoya..."

He shoved his chair back, took off running toward the door and collided with the waiter who had served them. "Where's the other guy?" Sam roared.

The man's eyes grew big and he tried to back away. "I be the only waiter, sir."

Sam shoved him aside and, gun in hand, started toward the kitchen. Two steps behind him, Lisa cried, "There he is!"

Sam turned just as Tall-and-skinny sprinted through the lobby and made for the steps. Sam ran after him, gun drawn.

The man dashed into the bushes. A motor roared and a motorcycle came out, going fast, straight at Sam. He jumped to the side and raised his gun, but the Jamaican turned and fired first. Sam heard the whomp of the blast, felt the heat of the bullet graze his thigh. The force of the shot spun him around and drove him to his knees. He fired and missed.

"Come on!" he yelled, scrambling up, limping, holding one hand around his leg.

"Wait!" Lisa cried. "You've been hit. Let me—"

He grabbed for her arm and hauled her onto the Harley behind him, gunned the motor and swept out onto the road in time to see the other motorcycle disappear around a curve.

Sam took the same curve at a forty-five-degree angle. Lisa cried out and tightened her arms around him. There was a straight stretch of road ahead. He gave it all he had and watched the speedometer climb to eighty, ninety. A hundred and ten. Her face pressed hard into his back.

Had to catch the son of a bitch. Make him talk, make him lead them to Montoya. He slowed for a curve, barely managed to balance the Harley, heard Lisa's muffled scream, righted the cycle and pressed down on the accelerator. The man ahead of them slowed, swung back, raised his gun and fired. Sam swerved hard to the right and kept going. He saw another curve ahead, the sheer dropoff to maybe five thousand feet of empty air, and slowed down. The man in front didn't. Keeping the same fast speed, he swung around to take another shot.

Sam veered the cycle, this time to the left. The Jamaican fired again, turned back just as he rounded the crest of the curve and tried to slow. But it was too late. He spun out of control, skidded toward the edge of the road, lost it and went over, arms flailing, screaming, the motorcycle cartwheeling after him.

Sam slowed and stopped.

"Oh my God!" Lisa cried.

He swung his leg over the seat, shouted, "Wait here!" and ran to the edge of the road. He looked down. Below him a thousand feet or so he saw the motorcycle smashed against a pile of rocks, wheels still spinning. And the sprawled body of the man he'd been chasing.

He turned away and walked back to Lisa. She stood beside the Harley. "Is he—is he dead?"

"Yeah."

"What are you going to do?"

"Keep going."

"But..." She swallowed hard. "Shouldn't you do something?"

"Like what? The man's dead, Lisa. There isn't anything I *can* do."

He started to get back on the cycle. She saw the blood on his leg. "You've been hit," she said. "I forgot."

"It's nothing."

The jeans were torn; the skin had been grazed. "Have you got a first-aid kit?"

"Yeah, but—"

"Get it," she said, suddenly sounding like a top sergeant.

He got it out of the saddlebag. She took the small scissors and cut away enough of his jeans so that she could see the wound. She cleaned her hands with a towelette from her purse, then spread ointment into the cut, put a square of no-stick gauze over the wound and adhesive to hold it in place.

"Thanks," he said.

"You're welcome." She handed the kit back to him and they climbed onto the motorcycle.

They rode higher and higher into the mountains. The air grew cooler, the shadows lengthened and it was as though they were enclosed in a tunnel of trees. This was Cockpit Country, and Lisa knew from the brochures in her room and the things she'd read before she made the trip, that it was here in this wild and impenetrable terrain that the runaway slaves had come so long ago.

They called it the Land of Look Behind because the soldiers who had tried to capture the runaways had had to keep an eye in all directions against unexpected attacks from the slaves, who had vowed to fight to the death.

The descendants of the Maroons, who mingled their blood with the surviving Arawak Indians, still lived in the small towns and settlements that were scattered through this strange, wild country. As Lisa looked at the lengthening shadows of encroaching night, she thought about how it had been, and of the slaves, so brave and defiant, ready to fight to the death for their freedom. This had become their homeland, their "Island in the Sun." Here in this Land of Look Behind they had taken the step to freedom.

Lisa leaned her head against Sam's back and closed her eyes. In this tired, drowsy state, with her arms around his waist, her body close to his and his thighs pressed against the inside of hers, she became a part of him. Their two bodies were welded together in an intimate embrace as they moved as one on this big, black machine.

She sighed, and he felt the whisper of her breath against his back. Felt her breasts brushing against him like a soft, hot caress when she moved. He raised his head and felt the wind against his face. He wished there had never been a Juan Montoya, that he wasn't a cop on an assignment, but simply a man, a tourist, riding through the fading afternoon with a beautiful woman who had her arms around his waist. He wished they had all the time in the world, that the only urgency was the urgency to lie together in the shelter of the trees, to hold and be held, to share long, lazy kisses.

But that was a dream. A man had died today; other men would die before this was over. That was the reality. He had to think tough and act tough. This wasn't a time for daydreaming.

He slowed the Harley and turned back to Lisa. "It's getting dark," he said. "We'd better stop."

"There's a town up here," she said. "Accom—? Accom something. Maybe there's a hotel there, or a guest house."

"Accompong," he said. "But we're not going to stay there. Montoya knows we're looking for him, Lisa. He's waiting for us—that's why he left one of his men behind. If we'd decided to stay at the hotel in Orangefield tonight, Tall-and-skinny would have sent word. We'd have been sitting ducks." He shook his head. "We're better off camping out in the forest."

She'd never camped out in her life, but apparently she didn't have anything to say about it. Sam stopped and climbed off the Harley, and giving her his hand, helped her off.

He wheeled the machine off the road, up a small embankment and into the trees. An overwhelming assortment of ferns grew here, along with wild orchids, Jamaican ackee and sweet-scented frangipani and Indian cedar.

"This'll do," Sam said when he found a place under the trees. He took a blanket out of one of the saddlebags and spread it out. "Hungry?" he asked.

Yes. Hungry and so tired her bones ached. She wanted to sit in a tub of warm soapy water, soak her poor bruised-from-riding bottom, ease the strained muscles in her arms, wash her windblown hair, sip a glass of cool white wine.

"Lisa?"

She sighed. "Yes, I'm hungry."

She didn't sit down. When he took a knife out of his pocket, opened it and cut a mango in half and handed part of it to her, she ate standing up. He didn't. He sprawled out on the ground and leaned his back against the trunk of a tree. "Glad you bought 'em," he said when he took a bite. "Guess it wouldn't have occurred to me to bring any food."

"I always travel with food, even when I know there's probably going to be a restaurant somewhere along the way."

He raised an eyebrow. "Any particular reason?"

"No, I—I just like to know that I've got something to eat if I want it." Then, though she didn't know why, she said, "My father used to punish me when I was a little girl by taking food away from me. He'd make me sit at the table, most of the time through supper and the next morning's breakfast. I had to sit there while they ate and I couldn't touch anything because I knew if I did..." She lowered her head, ashamed now, wondering why she'd told him. "I didn't mean to say all that," she said in a voice so low he could barely hear. "I don't know why I did. I've never told anyone else."

For a moment or two Sam didn't say anything, but finally he said, "Last night and a couple of other times you acted as if I was going to hit you, as though you expected me to hit you. I knew somebody had probably abused you. I thought maybe it was Philip."

"No, it wasn't Philip." She wet her lips. "It was my father. He..." Her voice started shaking and the sickness of remembered fear rose in her throat. "The—the strap hung on the back of the kitchen door. If I did something bad..." She stopped, unable to go on.

"He beat you."

"Yes," she said, not looking at him.

He stood. "Come here," he said, and there was an expression on his face she'd never seen before, a look of pain, of compassion and understanding. "Lisa," he said, holding his hands out to her.

She hesitated, then like a sleepwalker went to him. He put his arms around her and she leaned her head against his shoulder.

He held her without speaking, and thought of the child she had been. Sickness and fury tightened his body. He wanted to go after the man who had hurt her, to beat him with his bare hands, pound him until he was senseless and bloody so that he'd never be able to hurt anyone again.

She raised her head and moved as though to step away from him. But he said, "No, let me hold you like this."

In a little while she stopped shaking. He kissed the top of her head and held her close, but he didn't say anything. His body warmed with need, but over and above the physical need was a stronger need. He wanted to protect her, to take away everything bad that had ever happened to her and tell her that she was safe because he was here.

He felt her breath against his throat and the slight relaxing of her body against his. He put a finger under her chin and raised her face. He kissed her, gently at first because he didn't want to frighten her.

She let him kiss her, but she didn't respond. Not at first. But little by little her lips softened and parted under his and her arms crept up around his neck to hold him as he held her.

Her mouth was soft and warm. He urged her closer. He put one hand against the small of her back, but when he brought her tight against him, she stiffened.

"It's all right," he whispered against her lips. "I won't do anything you don't want me to do." But he didn't take his hand away.

Warmth flooded through her, and though she told herself she should resist, when he pressed her closer she didn't. She wanted to be close to him, needed to be close to him.

He sank to the ground on his knees, taking her with him. Their arms were around each other, their bodies pressed together.

He cupped her face between his hands. He kissed her closed eyes, her cheeks, her mouth. His lips caressed her throat, her ears, and he took the lobe of one between his teeth to gently nibble. He said, "I want to taste you, all of you. I want... Lisa, oh, Lisa."

He lay back and brought her down beside him. He kissed her again. He touched her breasts and slowly began to caress them. He felt their softness through the T-shirt, the small nipples rising to the touch of his fingers. And knew he wanted more. Lifting her to a sitting position, he pulled the T-shirt over her head and reached to unfasten her bra.

She started to protest, but he stopped her words with a kiss. He kissed her until she couldn't think, couldn't reason, couldn't stop. Kissed her until her lips felt bruised and heated, until she moaned into his mouth and said, "Sam. Oh, Sam."

He left her mouth to kiss her breasts. He put one hand under her back, raising her so that he could better taste and sample. He gripped one pebbled tip between his teeth and in feverish haste ran his tongue back and forth across it. And when she cried out and her body arched up against his, he moved to pull down the zipper of her cutoffs.

"No," she gasped, and reached to stop him.

He captured her hand and silenced her with a kiss. He eased his hand inside the cutoffs and she felt the heat of his skin through her silky panties.

In the twilight gloom and fading light that shimmered through the leaves of the giant trees, he looked at her. Her lips were full and softened by his kisses. He thought she was the most beautiful woman he had ever seen. He kissed each breast again. And because he knew that if he didn't stop now he wouldn't be able to, he said, "Do you want me to stop?"

For the barest heartbeat of a moment she hesitated. "No," she said. "No, Sam. I don't want you to stop."

A sigh shuddered through him. He eased the shorts down over her hips, then the panties, and she lay naked before him. Her body in the afterglow of sunset was a perfection of golden ivory skin, of form and texture, of swell of breast, curve of hip, long lovely legs. Without taking his eyes off her, he began to unbutton his shirt. He folded it and put it beneath her head. He unfastened his belt, unzipped his jeans, yanked his boots off, pulled the jeans down over his hips and snaked out of his briefs. Then he lay down beside her and gathered her in his arms.

Lisa shivered with nervousness. He felt the beat of her heart against his chest and said, "It will be all right, Lisa. It will be good between us."

And though his body tightened with a terrible urgency, he forced himself to wait. He kissed her and gently caressed her breasts, and when her breath came fast, he leaned to take one tender nipple between his lips. He scraped it with his teeth, teased it with his tongue, and when she began to tremble and her body warmed to his, he ran one hand lightly down over her belly and hips, down to the apex of her legs. He held her there and, when she didn't pull away, began to stroke her. She was soft, warm and moist, and he wanted her with an urgency he'd never known before.

But still he waited, though he thought his body would explode, waited until she said, "Yes, Sam. Oh, please."

He kissed her mouth. He came up over her and brought that throbbing essense of himself between her parted legs, against her heat and her softness. She urged him closer. Her body lifted to his.

"Oh, yes," he said against her lips. And with an agonized gasp he thrust into her.

She cried out, not in pain but in pleasure, and clung to him, clung with her arms and with those marvelous legs, lifting her body to his, whispering, "Oh, Sam. Sam."

"Is it good? Do you like . . . ? Ah, Lisa . . ." Words uttered in mindless passion while he moved against her like a man possessed, afraid it was too much for her but unable to hold back because nothing had ever been as good as this. He ground his body against hers as though by the force of it he could make her a part of him. He wanted it to go on forever. Knew it couldn't because he was close . . . so close to the edge.

He heard her whispers of pleasure and raised himself so that he could look at her. It was almost dark now, and he could barely see her face. She moved her head from side to side as though in agony, the same sweet agony he was feeling.

"Tell me," he said. "Tell me."

The sound started low in her throat. A muffled groan. A murmur, a small whimpering that grew into a frenzied moan. "Sam? Oh please, oh please . . ."

She thrilled him, inflamed him with her need. He thrust hard, withdrew, thrust again and she cried, "Oh! Oh, yes. Ohh . . ."

He took her mouth. He took her cry, and his body thundered over hers, riding higher and higher toward that moment of glory, taking her with him on this trip into ecstasy. He joined his cry to hers, primitive and wild here in the denseness of forest where no one could hear.

When at last their breathing slowed, he said, "I'm too heavy for you. I'd better move."

She tightened her arms around him and held him close. "In a minute. I—I like to feel you like this, Sam."

He kissed her eyelids and her lips. He said, "Are you all right? Was I too rough? I didn't mean to be." He kissed her again and again. "It was so good, Lisa. You're so beautiful, so fine." More kisses. "I didn't hurt you?"

"No," she said against his lips. "It was . . ." She nuzzled her face against his neck. "It was wonderful," she whispered.

"I didn't mean it to end so quickly. Next time . . ." He tried to see her through the gathering darkness. "Next time we'll go slower," he promised.

"Next time?"

"You bet." He chuckled, then the chuckle died because when he thought of how it had been and how it would be again, he began to grow.

She felt it, too. "Looks like next time is just about now," she whispered.

He moved against her. "Do you know how you feel to me?" he asked, and in his voice there was a low purr of contentment. "Do you know how good it is to be inside you like this?"

She touched his face and shivered a sigh of pleasure.

They moved together slowly, sensuously, relishing every new sensation, every touch. He stroked her breasts, drawing out the peaked and pebble-hard tips, rolling them between his fingertips, teasing, teasing. And when she moaned, he kissed her mouth and his tongue stroked her lips as that other part of him stroked the warm and hidden heart of her.

She caressed his face; he kissed her palm. She ran her hands over his shoulders and loved the feel of his skin. Loved this time and place here in this dark forest with him, surrounded by the scent of frangipani blossoms and the call of night birds.

The pace quickened. "So good," he whispered. "So good."

She sighed with pleasure, lost in this sweet, hot loving, pressing closer, wanting to be enveloped by the arms that held her, by the legs that pinned her to him. She sought his mouth. She kissed him softly and deeply and whispered of the pleasure he was giving her. But in the telling, her passion grew feverish, hurried, urgent.

He knew.

Clasping her bottom, he ground his body against hers and his movements quickened. "Yes?" he said. "Yes?"

But there were no words, for she was beyond rational thought, lost in all the pleasurable sensations that gripped her.

"Lisa..." he moaned against her lips. "Lisa."

And when it happened for him, and for her, they held each other, heart beating against heart. He stroked her back. Again and again he told her what this meant to him, how good this was for him.

"I've wanted you since the first moment I saw you standing at the edge of the road," he said. "And when we kissed that first time it was all I could do not to take you." He kissed her with gentle kisses and called her his precious girl.

At last they grew sleepy. He curled himself around her back to hold and warm her. He kissed the back of her neck and her shoulders, he cupped her breasts, he rested that still-quivering part of himself between her legs.

And when at last he heard her even breathing and knew that she slept, he leaned his head against her and he, too, slept.

Chapter 10

It was the song of a bird that woke Lisa, a song as clear and sweet as any music. She lay listening, drowsy and contented, more relaxed than she'd been in years. But when she stretched she felt the stiffness in her bones from sleeping here on the hard ground. And something else, the pleasant lassitude of a body well used by loving.

She lay there thinking about how it had been with Sam, the fierce tenderness of his lovemaking. Of how, afterward, he had held and caressed her, and of how, exhausted, they had gone to sleep in each other's arms. In the half sleep of morning, she smiled. Sometime in the night she had felt his hands on her breasts, and before she came awake, he had eased himself into her. No words had been exchanged; none were needed. He had moved lazily, sleepily against her. He'd kissed the back of her neck, then reached around to touch and caress her, whispering, "Sweet Lisa, darling Lisa."

She remembered the gasp of his breath against her skin and her own smothered pleadings for release before her body spiraled to a climax that left her shuddering with reaction as he stiffened and moaned against her shoulder.

He'd held her and told her how she made him feel, how he loved making love with her. She felt protected and cherished, and had gone to sleep to the sound of his murmurings and his tender kisses.

It had never been like that with Philip, not in the almost-seven years she'd been married to him. Making love with him had been... She tried to think of a word and all she could come up with was *orchestrated*. He'd arranged their lovemaking. Almost ceremoniously he'd lighted the candles, poured champagne into crystal fluted glasses, put Mozart on the CD and used his breath spray.

It had all been so antiseptic, so quickly over that it hardly seemed worth the trouble. While she lay there, unhappy and frustrated, staring up at the ceiling, he would murmur good-night, turn his back and go immediately to sleep.

She hadn't known lovemaking could be the way it was with Sam. It was as though she'd suddenly discovered a delicious secret that nobody else in the world knew about. She wanted to hug herself because at last she had discovered what making love was all about.

Soon after she had met him she had told herself that he wasn't the kind of man she'd ever be interested in. She'd thought, God help her, that he was like her father. But he wasn't. He might be as big and brawny as Matt Collier, but there the resemblance ended. Sam, for all of his tough, rough attitude, was a gentle man. He made her feel like a woman, treasured and cared for.

The sun shone through the trees to dapple the morning with sunlight. She had no idea where they were, but it didn't matter. She didn't want to think about yesterday, or the man who had died, or the danger that lay ahead. She had today, and for the moment that was all that mattered.

She stretched again, luxuriating in her nakedness, then sat up and ran her fingers through her hair.

"Hey!" he called out from somewhere in the trees. "Are you decent?"

"No," she answered, and reaching for her T-shirt, pulled it over her head.

He came through the bushes, wearing his briefs, looking momentarily disappointed that she'd put something on. He took a bite of the mango he was eating and with a grin said, "Get up. I've got a surprise for you."

"What is it?"

"You'll find out." He reached down, pulled her to her feet, eyed her thoroughly, and said, "You look pretty good in the morning. Tousled and well loved, but good."

She blushed and pulled the T-shirt as far down as it would go.

He offered her a bite of mango. She took it, and when the juice dribbled down her chin, he licked it off and kissed her. "Taste pretty good, too," he said.

She backed away. Her cheeks were flushed and he knew she was embarrassed. But that was okay. Nothing could bother him this morning because he felt so good. Good? Hell, he felt like a million bucks. Wanted to grab one of the vines and swing through the trees. Beat his chest, yell some kind of primitive male cry that would tell all the birds and beasts in the forest what kind of a man he was—invincible and ready to take on the world. Because of Lisa. Because of the way she made him feel.

He picked her up in his arms and started running with her through the trees. When she squealed, he stopped long enough to silence her with a deep, satisfying kiss and say, "Time for your bath, madam."

"A bath?"

He moved past a stand of ferns, past flowering red hibiscus, wild orchids and cup-of-gold vines. He motioned with a nod of his head and, in a clearing, Lisa saw a pool of clear, clean water and a rushing waterfall cascading down from the mountain into one end of it.

"It's beautiful," she said when Sam put her down.

"Yeah. Right out of *South Pacific*." He took her hand and led her to the edge. There he looked her up and down and said, "Well?"

"Well what?"

"Off with the shirt."

"I—I can swim with it on."

"Aw, c'mon. Take it off."

She shook her head. For a minute he thought she was acting coy, waiting for him to take it off for her. Then he realized she was embarrassed and maybe shy, which struck him as strange after what they'd shared the night before. Strange, but maybe a little endearing, too.

"The shirt will be wet when we leave," he said reasonably.

"That's all right." She looked down at her toes instead of at him. "I can wear the jacket."

He shrugged. "But I don't want to wear wet briefs, so if you don't mind..." He stepped out of the briefs and turned to hang them over a bush.

Her first thought was that he had absolutely great buns! Then he turned and she headed for the water.

It was surprisingly cool. She swam fast to warm up, aiming for the waterfall. Swam into it, under it and laughed aloud with sheer pleasure. When Sam came up beside her she said, "I don't suppose you have any soap?"

He offered curled-up fists. "Which one?" he asked.

Going along with the game, she touched his left hand. He opened it and offered her a bar of soap. "Found it in the saddlebag this morning," he said. "Put it in the bushes along with my clothes. If you'll take your shirt off, I'll wash your back."

"No, thanks. I can manage." She soaped her hair, rinsed it under the waterfall and bathed as best she could without taking the shirt off.

When she finished, she handed the soap to him and said, "Your turn."

"Why don't you do it?"

She raised an eyebrow.

"Okay, just my back." He handed her the soap and turned around.

Lisa hesitated. This, too, was different. Sam, unlike Philip, seemed totally at ease with his body. She and Philip had never bathed together. He'd worn pajamas to bed, even when they were making love, and he'd expected her to keep her nightgown on. Once, when their air-conditioning had gone off in the middle of July, she'd gone to bed without a gown and he'd said, "Really, Lisa."

Sam wasn't like that. He was totally uninhibited, comfortable in his skin. And no wonder! He was well built, with the football-player shoulders she'd always thought she disliked. His skin was tanned and smooth and he had muscles, not the weight-lifting, bulging muscles that turned her off, but firm smooth ripples of toughness beneath his skin. Nice.

She liked the feel of him against her hands, liked the way his shoulders tapered down to a slimness of waist and tempting roundness of buns. She wanted to touch them, knew she shouldn't, but found her hands going lower. They hesitated at the small of his back before, as though with their own volition, they slipped lower.

Sam didn't move. She soaped his buns. They were tight and firm and well shaped. She'd never done anything like this before and it fascinated her. Round and round her hands moved, trailing soap bubbles, rinsing and soaping again.

He said, "I suppose you know what you're doing to me."

She felt him shudder, felt her own response—a kindling flame, an inner trembling. She ran her fingernails over his skin and heard the sharp intake of his breath. She touched the tender skin at the bottom of his backside close to the apex of his legs. He turned. Her eyes widened and she said, "Oh, my!"

Before he could catch her, she dove under the waterfall and started swimming toward the center of the pond.

He came after her. She was fast; he was faster. "Oh no, you don't," he said, and grabbed her.

"Oh yes, I do!" She pulled away, splashed the water with the flat of her hand and started swimming.

He muttered a curse, chased her, and this time when he caught her he hauled her into his arms. She laughed and the sound of it in the morning air was free and joyous and full of fun. He gripped her waist and raised her, still laughing, up out of the water. She was as light as a water sprite, as young as springtime. The sun shone on her face and he knew he had never seen anyone as lovely as she was.

He brought her closer. The laughter stopped. She looked at him, her head cocked to one side as though puzzled. He let her down slowly so that she slid along the length of his body. The T-shirt pushed up; their wet nakedness touched. Her eyes went wide, then sleepy with desire.

Still holding her like that, he kissed her. Her lips parted under his. His hands slid around to cup her bottom.

"I can't wait," he said, and holding her like that, he thrust into her.

"No," she protested. "We can't... What if somebody..."

He pressed her closer, moving hard against her, caught up in the wildness of it, the craziness of a desire so intense that he couldn't have stopped if a platoon of Florida alligators had come after them.

He plunged and withdrew to plunge again, and each time he did she made little puffing sounds, like he was pushing the breath right out of her. She clung to him, her legs wrapped around his, holding him the way he held her. Then suddenly her head went back and the little puffs of breath became frenzied cries of helplessness. There was sun on her face and passion in her eyes, and with the knowledge that it was as good for her as it was for him, he lost it. He wrapped his arms around her, hanging on as though if he didn't he'd shoot right up out of the water.

It had lasted maybe four minutes—the best four minutes of his life. When he eased her down into the water, she slumped against him, her heart racketing against his chest.

"Open your eyes and kiss me," he said.

She opened her eyes. She kissed him, softly, gently, and something deep inside him, an emotion so new it scared the living hell out of him, stirred to life.

He said her name, "Lisa?" with a sense of unreality. What was happening here? This wasn't the way he usually behaved. He was a realist, a meat-and-potatoes man. He didn't believe in sunlit pools or waterfalls or summer mornings or being so moved by beauty that it was all he could do not to bawl like a baby. This dame had bewitched him. He wasn't going to let this happen.

She touched the side of his face. "What is it, Sam?" she asked. "Darling, what is it?"

"Damned if I know," he said, trying to sound tough. But he made the mistake of looking at her again. His insides turned to mush. He held her, his face against hers, not sure what was happening to him, not even sure that he liked it.

"Let's get out of here," he said.

Without a word she swam beside him to the shore. He planned to cut this short, tell her they had to get going.

She came up out of the pond, sluicing the water from her body, slicking back her hair, unaware that the T-shirt showed every curve. It clung to her breasts and her nipples and hiked up over her thighs.

"Oh, hell!" he said, giving in. And with a wicked growl, picked her up and headed for the grassy place beside a bed of ferns.

"What are you doing?" she asked.

"Losing what's left of my mind." He laid her down and stood glowering at her.

"Take that damn shirt off," he said, his voice made harsh because of all of the conflicting emotions churning inside him.

She started nibbling on her lower lip.

He knelt beside her. "Want me to do it?"

She raised her arms above her head.

He couldn't figure out why his hands were shaking. He pulled the shirt up and off. She hugged her knees, partially hiding her breasts.

"Uh-uh." He drew her hands away and rolled her back onto the grass. He tried hard to remember she wasn't his type, that he liked tall brunettes, not pocket-size blondes. She was pocket-size, all right, and absolute perfection from the top of her curly head right down to her red toenails.

He laid one hand over her breast. "You affect me in strange and pleasurable ways," he said. "I didn't want to get involved with you. I told myself that from the beginning."

"Because you thought I was involved with Howard Reitman." She nodded. "I know it's different now, but in the beginning, the night we went out to dinner and afterward we kissed and—"

"Couldn't stop kissing."

"Yes." She looked up at him. "Did you kiss me then because you thought I was a part of this terrible thing with Howard and Montoya? Because you thought if you got close to me you might find out something about them?"

"No, Lisa. I kissed you in spite of what I thought. I kissed you because I couldn't keep my hands off you. I couldn't then, I can't now."

He kissed her, a long, deep kiss, and when he let her go he lay beside her and nuzzled his head against her breasts. She threaded her fingers in his hair and held him there, soothing him as though she understood all of his inner turmoil. He felt the sun on his back, warming him as she warmed him. In a little while he parted her legs and rested that throbbing part of himself against her.

"This is how much I want you," he said.

Her body shifted, enclosing him. Slowly, slowly, he moved against her, feeling his excitement build, hearing the harsh sound of his own breathing as she moved with him. This is madness, he thought. We did this only a little while ago. How can I want her again? Why do I want her again? Then all thought faded and he kissed her. He touched his tongue to hers. He kissed her breasts, and when she moved beneath him and he knew she wanted it as much as he did, he joined his body to hers.

He went deep into the very heart of her. He felt her warmth close about him and listened to her sweet sounds of pleasure. She wrapped him in her arms and in her legs. She sought his mouth and whispered, "Oh, Sam. Oh, Sam."

She made him feel like a conqueror, a pirate, a king of the forest. But most of all he felt like a man, a man who would live and love forever. He could hold nothing back from her, he would give his all, everything he was, everything he had ever hoped to be. Because with her everything seemed possible.

He wanted to possess her, to become a part of her, to stay like this forever with her, in her. She lifted herself to him and they did become one as they raced together toward that final moment. She clasped him to her breast, and when he said, "Tell me! Tell me!" She surged against him.

"Yes, yes, yes, yes..." she whispered.

Heart racing, body on fire, he plunged into her, again and again, crying out each time, unable to stop himself because he could not hold back the joy and the wonder of it. He clasped her face between his hands and rained kisses over her closed eyes, her cheeks, her mouth. He said her name again and again, and held her as though he would never let her go.

He knew they should get up and get moving, but Lord, it was heaven to lie here like this with her. He'd never been more content. He was happy as a sixteen-year-old with his first girl, as weak from their loving as a ninety-year-old man after a twenty-six-mile marathon.

Her eyes were closed; her head was resting on his shoulder. Sun streaked down through the trees and across her body, making shadowy patterns on her breasts, turning her skin to gold. In a little while they would get up and get on the Harley to pursue Juan Montoya. But for now, for this brief space in time, they could hold each other in this sweet aftermath of their lovemaking.

"Are you sleeping?" he asked.

"No." She opened her eyes. "But I may never move again, and if I do, I'll probably walk funny." She grinned. "You've ruined me, O'Shaughnessy. I'm weak as a newborn kitten, depleted, exhausted..." She hesitated, and raising herself on one elbow, said, "And happier than I've ever been." She ran a finger down the length of his nose to his lips and traced them with the tip of her finger. "I didn't know anything could be like this...like it is with you."

His eyes stung. And because he didn't want her to know what her words meant, he said, "Yeah, it was all right...." But he couldn't go on, couldn't pretend that it wasn't everything he'd ever hoped and dreamed making love with a woman could be. He pulled her back into his arms and pressed her head against his shoulder. "I didn't know, either," he said. "Not until now."

They held each other like that, but in a little while, because she wanted to know everything there was to know about him, she said, "Tell me about you, Sam."

"What do you want to know?"

"Everything. Where did you grow up?"

"Chicago. Well, Chicago and Detroit." He shifted and brought her closer so that she rested with her head in the hollow of his shoulder. "My parents were killed in a bus accident when I was thirteen and I went to live with my mother's brother in Detroit. Uncle Frank was a really weird guy. I don't think he drew a sober breath the last thirty years of his life.

"He wasn't a mean man, and I suppose in his own way he did the best he could for me. I had enough to eat, money for clothes and books, but he really didn't care whether I went to school or not."

"But you did? Go to school, I mean?"

"Yeah, because I figured it was the only way out of Detroit. I graduated from high school and a couple of days later joined the navy. I was a tough kid, but they straightened me out. I liked it and I stayed in for eight years. When I got out I bummed around New York for a while, then joined the NYPD. I got interested in criminology and took night courses at NYU. A couple of years ago I was promoted to lieutenant."

"My brother, Jimmy, joined the navy when he was seventeen, too," Lisa said. "Only he didn't wait until he graduated. He left home before that."

"Where is he now?"

"I don't know, Sam. I haven't seen him since he left. He sent a card to my mother from the Brooklyn Navy Yard after he joined up. My father wanted to have him arrested and brought home, but the navy recruiting officer in Dayton just laughed at him."

"How old were you when you left?"

"Seventeen."

Seventeen and alone. Little girl lost, fending for herself. He tightened his arms around her and wondered what she'd do if he told her he'd checked up on her. At the time it had been the right thing to do, but now he wished he hadn't. And because he didn't want there to be any lies or secrets between them, he said, "I've got something I have to tell you. I don't like telling it and you won't like hearing it."

She peered up at him, puzzled. "What is it, Sam?"

"When I thought you were involved with Reitman I had you checked out."

"Checked out?" She looked like she didn't even know what that meant.

"I asked Hargreaves—he's the captain of police in Kingston—to run a check on you. He contacted Tipp City. There was an old, outstanding warrant for your arrest."

Lisa pulled away from him and sat up. "For my arrest? What for?"

"I don't know. It was for a long time ago, eleven or twelve years."

For years she'd looked over her shoulder, afraid that someday there'd be a knock on the door and it would be her father. Or she'd feel a hand on her shoulder and when she turned he'd be standing there.

"My—my father. He...must have tried to find me. To bring me back."

Fear choked her. It didn't matter that it was unreasonable, it was there, deep inside her. It scarred her mind just the way his belt had scarred her legs.

She stared at him. He saw the terror in her eyes. "My God," he said. "You're still that afraid of him."

"I—I guess I am. I wanted to go back to see him and I...I asked Philip to go with me. I didn't tell him why I wanted to go. I thought if I faced my father, if I asked him why he'd treated me the way he did, maybe I'd be able to put the past behind me. But Philip wouldn't go with me and I..." She shook her head. "I'm ashamed of this, Sam, but I honestly was afraid to go alone."

"We'll go together," he said. "When this is over I'll take you. I'll be right there beside you."

And when you're not there, he told himself, I'll go back and beat the hell out of the son of a bitch.

In a little while they went back into the water, and this time Lisa didn't put her T-shirt on. They swam, and when they came out, they dressed and had a breakfast of the sweet yams Rebecca had given them, along with some cheese and a piece of hard bread.

Just before they left, Sam looked back at the place where they had slept together, a slice of paradise here in this jungle setting.

He put his arms around Lisa and held her close. "We'll always remember this, and how we were together here." he said.

Then, because he knew he must, he took her hand and they went back to the Harley.

Chapter 11

The gravel road narrowed the higher they went. Sam didn't go as fast as he had the day before and it was pleasant to ride along with the wind in her face, enjoying the countryside, waving to the farmers in their fields or the housewives puttering in their yards. Smoke rose from braziers in front of the few houses they passed; the smell of farm animals and roasting corn filled the air. When they passed a farmer leading a small herd of goats, Sam stopped.

"Afternoon," he said. "I wonder if you could tell me how far we are from the next town?"

"That be Maroon Town, sir. No more than five mile from here." He poked at one of the smaller goats with his stick. "You want to buy her?" he asked. "Tie her there behind the lady. Make you mighty fine dinner."

"Don't think so," Sam said.

The man looked at Lisa, and with a wink said, "I trade you my ten best goats for her."

"Ten?" Sam shook his head. "Sorry, friend, no deal. If you want to double it—"

Lisa pinched him and he laughed. "Guess not," he told the man as he rolled away. "But thanks for the offer."

The man laughed, too, and waved until Sam was out of sight.

"Twenty goats?" Lisa said. "You'd trade me for twenty goats?"

"Woman, I wouldn't trade you for a whole herd of goats, with a couple of million bucks thrown in."

"Okay," she said, and reached up to kiss the back of his neck.

He wished he wasn't a cop, wished he was an insurance man—just a guy on vacation with a great-looking gal. Here in Jamaica for a little fun in the sun, and when it was over he'd go back to selling life insurance.

But Lisa wasn't just a good-looking gal and he wasn't in life insurance. He was here on a job and he couldn't rest until the job was finished and Montoya was safely back in a cell. As for Lisa . . . there'd be time to think about that when all this was behind him.

He wanted to tell himself that he'd made a mistake by becoming intimate with her. Maybe before he'd thought that if they made love he'd get her out of his system. But he knew he hadn't, wasn't sure he ever would.

He'd try to find a way to send her back from Maroon Town, maybe get her to Kingston and have Hargreaves put her in protective custody. He had to know she was safe so that he could concentrate on Montoya. Couldn't concentrate unless she was out of harm's way.

Maroon Town was a small place with a couple of stores, a fruit-and-vegetable market, a one-pump gas station, an open-air restaurant and a hotel. He parked the Harley in front of the hotel.

"Let's see if there's a phone," he said as he helped Lisa off.

There was one on the registration desk in the lobby. Sam approached the man behind the desk. "I'd like to make a call to Kingston," he said.

The man indicated the phone. "Certainly, sir."

"It's a private call."

"Then perhaps you'd like to step into our private office," the man said. "There's a phone there you can use. If you'll give me the number, I'll be glad to get it for you."

"I can't dial direct?"

"I'm afraid not."

He didn't like it. He'd have no way of knowing if the desk clerk listened in. But he had to make the call.

"Okay." He wrote the number of the Kingston police on a piece of paper and handed it to the clerk. "Do you have a dining room?"

"Through that door, sir."

"Why don't you go in and have something to drink?" Sam said to Lisa. "I'll join you when I'm through."

The clerk indicated another room. "You may go in there," he said.

Sam went in and closed the door behind him. Five minutes went by before the phone rang. He picked it up and somebody said, "Kingston Police. May I help you?"

"I want to talk to Hargreaves."

"Who may I say is calling?"

"Sam O'Shaughnessy."

"A moment please, Mr. O'Shaughnessy."

Sam tapped impatient fingers on the table. Another five minutes went by and finally Filoberto said, "Sam? Where are you? I've tried for three days to get you."

"I'm in Maroon Town."

"In Cockpit Country? What are you doing there?"

"Following Montoya and Reitman."

"Good Lord! Why didn't you call before?"

"Couldn't get to a phone."

"You're sure they're there? In Cockpit Country?"

"They were yesterday. I chased one of them. He took a couple of shots at us, missed a curve and went over the mountain. So yeah, I'm sure."

"Do you have any idea where..." Hargreaves paused. *"Us?"* he said. "Did you say *us?"*

"Yeah. I'm with Lisa Collier."

"What in the world are you doing with her?"

"It's a long story. But I can tell you one thing for sure, she's not involved with Montoya or Reitman. They know she knows about them, though, and she can testify that Reitman is mixed up in the drug operation. I want her somewhere safe. I'd like you to put her in a hotel in protective custody with a twenty-four guard."

"Yes, all right. I'll arrange it. Now what about you?"

"All I've got is your Harley, a couple of guns and some ammo. I don't know for sure where Montoya and his boys are, but when I catch up with them I'm going to need some backup."

"Yes, of course. Look, Sam, why don't you stay where you are until we get there. It'll take me a little while to arrange things. Let's say we'll be there sometime within the next three or four hours."

Sam thought for a minute. He didn't want to wait. On the other hand, he knew it was the smart thing to do. One of Filoberto's men could take Lisa back to Kingston, then he and Filoberto's group could continue the chase. He needed backup; it was best to wait.

"Okay," he said. "We're at the hotel. We'll wait here."

"One other thing, Sam. We're running out of time. I found out from one of our men who's been working on the docks that the shipment of drugs is going to take place any day now. Once it goes down, Montoya and Reitman will hightail it out of the country. Our source thinks they've arranged for a boat that will take them to South America. Word is it's going to pick them up somewhere near Port Antonio."

"Dammit!" Sam exploded. "If they get away—"

"They won't, now that we have an idea where they are and what they're up to. But we'll have to work fast."

"Maybe I should keep going, stay on their trail. I could leave Lisa here—"

"No, you hold on until we get there, Sam. That's an order."

Sam swore. "Okay, okay," he said. "But hurry it up. I've got a feeling time's running out."

"Three or four hours," Hargreaves said, and hung up.

Sam stared at the phone a couple of seconds before he put it down. He heard a click that could've been the Kingston operator, or the guy at the desk. There was a feeling in his gut he didn't like, the slight prickle of hairs on the back of his neck. Something was going to happen, but he didn't know what.

Lisa was the only one in the small hotel dining room. There wasn't any air-conditioning, only a ceiling fan near the kitchen to stir the air.

A waiter appeared and she smiled up at him. He didn't smile back. He looked surprised, nervous. His jeans were dirty and so was the supposed-to-be-white apron tied around his waist. He wore a spot-stained blue kerchief around his neck.

She ordered coffee and stuffed *chochos,* a tasty concoction made with riced coco, cinnamon and brown sugar. And absently wondered if the man was upset because she'd interrupted his lunch break.

The food was good and the Blue Mountain coffee was strong, maybe strong enough to keep her awake. She wasn't complaining, but she hadn't had much sleep last night. Her muscles were sore from sleeping on the ground and from riding the Harley. She'd have given anything for a few hours on a soft bed.

With Sam.

Just the thought of him made her knees go weak. She felt as if she were on a merry-go-round, going round and round, spinning out of control. She'd spun out of control last night and she wasn't sorry she had. What she'd shared with Sam had been special and wonderful. She was crazy about him, half in love with . . . *Half?* Uh-uh. She *was* in love.

Maybe that scared her a little; maybe she didn't want to be because she wasn't sure how Sam felt about her or if he was the kind of man she wanted to spend the rest of her life with. But she'd fallen for him, head over heels, end over applecart, and there wasn't a thing she could do about it.

She didn't know what would happen or where they'd go from here. But for now she was sticking with him. Whither he went, so did she. Yesterday, when they'd pursued the motorcycle and the man on it had started shooting at them, she'd been scared out of her wits. Nevertheless, she didn't want to leave Sam. She'd stay with him until this was over, then they'd talk about . . . well, about whether or not they had a future together.

Smiling to herself, Lisa picked up the cup and took a sip of coffee. A man, not the waiter, stood in the kitchen doorway watching her. She froze. Dear God. God. God. God. Benjamin! The one who'd run after her the night she got away from Howard Reitman. He of the brutish face, the narrow eyes and the jagged scar.

She didn't move, didn't even breathe. She looked away, took the last sip of her coffee and put a few coins on the table. With studied nonchalance she stood and, with her bag over her shoulder, started toward the door. Before she'd gone more than a step or two he blocked her way.

"Why you be in such a hurry?"

"Let me pass."

"Don't think so. I think it be nice if you come with me."

She tried to shoulder past him. He didn't move. Too quickly for her to escape, he grabbed her and pulled her into the kitchen. When she tried to cry out, he slapped a hand over her mouth.

She came back with her elbows. He grunted and hit the side of her head with his open hand. She staggered and would have fallen if he hadn't been holding her.

"You gotta get her out of here, mon," the waiter said, sounding scared, looking scared.

"I'm goin' to."

"What 'bout that dude she be with?"

"He'll come after her. When he does, we got 'em both."

"Where's the Jeep?"

"Just outside the door."

"I'll help you."

''No. You stay here, wait till the big dude come. If he ask about her you pretend like you don't know nothin'.'' Still holding Lisa, he reached into her bag and fished around until he found her lipstick. He handed it to the other man. ''Put it beside her plate. That way he know she been here. I'm gonna wait in the Jeep with the motor running. Soon as he sit down and ask you 'bout her you say, like you was real nervous, somebody grab her. Wasn't nothin' you could do.''

Sam! He'd come after her. They'd trap him. Kill him. She struggled, but Benjamin held her in a viselike grip with one arm, his other hand over her mouth. She bit him. He smothered a yelp and hit her again.

''Gimme something to tie her with,'' he told the waiter.

The waiter looked around, then yanked at the piece of cord that had been holding the kitchen curtain back. He grabbed Lisa's hands and tied them. He took the spot-stained bandana from around his neck and stuffed it into her mouth. She gagged and he said, ''That'll keep her quiet.''

''I gotta do one more thing.'' Benjamin shoved Lisa against the stove, then turned and, before the waiter could dodge, hit him square in the mouth with his doubled-up fist.

The other man staggered back. ''What you do that for?'' he cried.

''It's gotta look like you ain't in on this. When he sees you he be knowin' there's some bad stuff going down.'' Benjamin shoved Lisa out the door. He held a finger to his lips. ''I hear somethin','' he whispered.

The waiter peered into the restaurant. ''It's him coming. The big American dude.''

Lisa fought the gag and tried to scream. All that came out was a throaty, desperate moan.

Benjamin grabbed a handful of hair and yanked her head back. "You try that again," he whispered, "I kill you."

He shoved her out the door and down the steps in front of him, pushed her onto the front seat of the Jeep and started the motor.

She thought about hurling herself out of the vehicle. Her hands were tied in front of her; she could break her fall, roll away.

Benjamin took a gun out of his belt, laid it between his legs and, with one hand on the steering wheel, inched the Jeep forward.

She had to do something. What? Dear God, what? Grab the gun, shoot him. Or the keys. Pull them out of the ignition and throw them away.

She turned and saw Sam at the kitchen door. He dashed down the steps, gun drawn, crying, "Lisa! Lisa!"

Benjamin gunned the motor and wheeled out of the yard. Sam ran after them. He got off a shot. It hit the dust just in front of the back tire.

"Hang on!" Benjamin cried. She had no choice; they were going too fast. She grabbed the side of the Jeep with her bound hands, looked back, saw Sam running around the side of the hotel toward where he'd parked the motorcycle.

Benjamin swerved around a curve so fast she came up out of the seat. He yanked her back. She tightened her grip on the side of the Jeep, saw the speedometer climb to fifty, sixty, sixty-five. All she could do was hang on and pray.

Lisa! Oh my God! The man had Lisa. He was out of breath, heart thudding hard against his ribs by the time he reached the motorcycle.

He swung his leg over the seat, gunned the motor and spun out onto the road. Ahead of him he could see the cloud of dust from the Jeep. The vehicle was going fast. Too fast. Dangerous on the curves...

If anything happened to Lisa... Had to get to Lisa. Had to. But how? If he shot the tires out, the Jeep would swerve, might go over the edge of the three-thousand-foot drop... or smash into the side of the mountain. He couldn't risk it. All he could do was keep going, keep the Jeep in sight and wait for his chance.

Ahead lay a straight stretch of gravel road. Sam got the bike up to eighty-five and held it there. He could see the top of Lisa's head, see her swaying, knew how dangerous this was for her.

He shouldn't have left her alone, but who in the hell would think that one of Montoya's men would have been in Maroon Town? That meant Montoya knew he was after him. He'd sent Tall-and-skinny after them yesterday, and now the guy who had Lisa. Who was the pursuer, who the pursued? Was Montoya playing a cat-and-mouse game with him?

Sam was a cop. He lived with danger every day of his life and he'd come to Jamaica knowing and expecting that there'd be a certain amount of risk. But Lisa had nothing to do with this, wouldn't have been here if he hadn't suspected her of being involved with Reitman. If he'd played square with her in the beginning she wouldn't have given Reitman a second look. If anything happened to her it would be his fault.

There was another curve ahead. The Jeep slowed to maybe forty; Sam went to sixty. He took the curve fast, leaned hard into it and gained on the vehicle. They were almost out of the curve when the Jeep slowed again. Ahead Sam saw a pile of rocks from a landslide practically covering the road. The driver of the Jeep had no choice but to slow even more to find a way around the rocks.

"Jump, baby," Sam muttered. "Jump!"

And as though she heard him, Lisa half jumped, half fell out of the Jeep. She hit the ground, rolled and pushed herself to a sitting position. Sam gunned the Harley, raced up alongside her, stopped long enough to reach down with his left hand and grab the back of her shirt to lift her up behind him. She swung her leg over the seat and he half turned to help her.

"Hang on!" he cried, wheeling the motorcycle around to go back the way they'd come.

A shot rang out. He looped to the right and felt her grip tighten on the back of his belt. Her hands were bound, it was the only way she could hang on to him.

Another shot was fired. Another. The Jamaican had turned the Jeep around. He was coming after them.

"Lean into me," Sam shouted. "I'm heading up the mountain."

She clutched his belt.

"Now!" he cried, and zoomed off the road onto a path between the trees.

Behind him more shots rang out. He steered the cycle among the trees as fast as he dared. Branches scraped him, slashed at his face. He ducked, but he didn't slow down because he had to get out of firing range, had to lose the bastard.

Finally he slowed the bike and listened for the sound of the Jeep. He'd lost it! But he kept on until he was in a density of wooded growth, just to make sure. At last he stopped, swung off the Harley and lifted Lisa down.

The first thing he did was pull the wadded-up kerchief out of her mouth. She gagged, then coughed. "Easy, baby." He reached into the saddlebag for the canteen, opened it and held it to her lips. "Take a swallow," he said. "It'll help."

She drank. "Okay," she said. "I'm okay."

He got a knife and cut the cord that bound her wrists. She wasn't okay. The side of her face was scraped and bloody from where she'd hit the gravel when she jumped. There was a long scratch on her right arm, a bloody cut on one hand. Her T-shirt was ripped and so were the cutoffs.

He picked her up and carried her to a flat place under the trees, laid her down gently and ran back to the motorcycle. He returned with the first-aid kit, the rest of the bar of soap and the canteen. He felt her arms and her legs to make sure nothing was broken.

"Hurt anywhere?" he asked.

"Everywhere."

"We've got to get you cleaned up."

He took a piece of gauze and wiped the blood from her face. She flinched. He said, "Easy, Lisa. Easy, sweetheart."

God, this was tearing him apart. She was hurt, hurting, and it took every ounce of his willpower to keep his cool.

Bits of gravel were stuck to her skin. He picked them out. She clasped her hands, but didn't say anything.

"I'm going to rub a little salve on the side of your face," he told her. "It'll hurt."

"Okay."

He touched her skin as gently as he could. She sucked in her breath, but didn't move.

He took care of the cut on her hand next, knew it hurt when he had to pick the gravel out. This time she gasped in pain and turned her face away.

"Almost done," he said, and felt her pain as if it were his own. Sweat dripped down his face; his stomach was in knots. "Hang on, Lisa. Couple of minutes more."

He cleaned the cut with the soap, rubbed on some antiseptic cream and bandaged her hand.

Her face was pale and pinched. "Just the arm now," he said, trying to sound matter-of-fact. "It's only a scratch." He cleaned the dirt and cinders away. "It's not too bad, Lisa. It won't take long. Hang on."

He wiped his sweat away with the back of his arm, and rubbed the antiseptic cream across the scraped skin. Finally he said, "All done."

"Thanks." She took a deep breath to steady herself. "I guess we'd better get back on the road," she said.

"Not until you rest."

"I'm all right."

"Sure you are." He eased her back against the trunk of a tree and she closed her eyes.

"They know you're after them," she said.

"Yeah."

"And they're after us."

Us. Like they were a team. She was scared, hurt, and she still said us. A couple of minutes went by before he could say anything. When he could, he said, "I talked to Hargreaves. He's captain of police in Kingston. He's coming with some of his men. It'll be three of four hours before they get to the hotel."

Lisa opened her eyes. "But we can't go back there."

"No."

So what in the hell was he going to do? Hide out until Hargreaves and his men showed up at the hotel and then try to contact them? But who could he trust? How many of them were in on it? Would Hargreaves be walking into a trap? Hargreaves wouldn't be going in alone, of course, he'd have four or five of his men with him. Montoya's thugs wouldn't dare try anything.

But him? Yeah, he had a feeling both he and Lisa were at the top of their hit list. Montoya had already sent two of his men after them. How many others were looking for them?

Sam mulled things over for a couple of minutes. Finally he decided he'd better try to find a place to hole up. He'd get a message back to Hargreaves, let him know where they were and arrange to have Lisa taken back to Kingston.

She'd closed her eyes again. The pallor of her skin looked stark against the scrape on the side of her face. She'd done the right thing by jumping out of the Jeep, but she could have been killed—could have hit her head on a rock or had the back wheel run over her. The thought sickened him. She was mixed up in this because of him. If anything happened to her he'd never forgive himself.

He let her rest for a while before he said, "Lisa? We'd better hit the road."

She opened her eyes. "Where are we going?"

"I don't know." He helped her up and put his arms around her. "Somewhere safe," he said. "I'll send a message back to Hargreaves. Don't worry, Lisa, we'll get you back to Kingston."

She rested her bruised face against his shoulder. Back to Kingston? Away from him? No, not as long as he was in danger.

She wouldn't tell him now, but when the time came, when they finally caught up with Hargreaves, she'd refuse to go. For as long as Sam was in this, she was, too. She wouldn't leave him. He couldn't make her.

Chapter 12

He found a mountain path and followed it, driving as slowly as he could, all the time aware of what the bumps and jars were doing to Lisa. She needed medical attention. He doubted they'd find any in the direction they were going, but he didn't dare go back to the hotel. The best he could hope for now was to find a settlement of some kind, a place where Lisa could rest. Then he'd worry about sending word back to Filoberto Hargreaves.

The captain of police would arrive at the hotel in Maroon Town in a few hours, expecting to find him there. He'd be upset, worried and furious. But there wasn't anything Sam could do about that. He didn't dare go back.

He stopped twice to let Lisa rest. Each time he did she slumped to the ground. The scrape on her face looked red and painful, and blood had seeped through the bandage on her hand. She said very little, but he knew how tough this was for her.

If they didn't find a village or a house soon he'd have to stop, and they'd camp out the way they had last night. But Lisa needed more than that. She needed a clean bed and medical attention.

Almost an hour went by before Sam caught the scent of wood smoke. The path widened and in a little while he saw a cluster of houses. Maybe there'd be a doctor here, a small clinic, a place where Lisa could get the attention she needed.

He wheeled the bike into the settlement. A man was sitting on the steps of the first house, smoking a cigarette. He looked up, startled, when he saw the motorcycle. "Lord 'a mercy," he said. "Where'd you come from?"

He was tall and rail-thin, with blue eyes, dark skin and curly white hair. He got up and started down the steps.

"We've had an accident," Sam said. "My wife's been hurt."

The man peered around Sam's shoulder and looked at Lisa. "Lord, sir, she need some tending."

"Is there a doctor in the village?"

"No, sir. There be no doctor here in Trinity."

"A clinic? A nurse?"

The man shook his head. "Hereabouts when folks be hurt they mostly tend to themselves. Where were you headed?"

"Maroon Town. Took a wrong turn, I guess." He stopped and swung off the bike. "Is there a guest house in town? A room I can rent?"

The man shook his head. "No guest house," he said, and offering a hand added, "I be Horatio Appletree."

"Sam O'Shaughnessy."

The man looked at Lisa. "Best you come up on the porch outta the sun and sit a spell, missus."

Exhausted, hurting as she was, it was all Lisa could do to murmur, "Thank you."

Sam helped her off the bike. Appletree offered a hand to help. "We got a bedroom," he said. "I guess you could rent that. Me and my missus could make us a pallet in the other room."

The house looked ready to cave in. The front-porch steps were broken and pieces of tin were missing from the roof. But if there was a bed and running water, it would be better than camping out in the forest the way they had last night.

"That's mighty nice of you," Sam said to Appletree. "We'd like to stay if you're sure it's all right."

"I be pretty sure." He turned and called out, "Delight?"

A woman almost as tall and skinny as Horatio appeared in the doorway. She had on a blue cotton dress and her hair was tied up in a red bandana. She came out on the porch, letting the screen door bang behind her.

"These people need a place to stay the night. I told them they could rent our bedroom."

Hands on her hips, she frowned, first at Horatio, then at Sam. But when she saw Lisa, she said, "Oh, my Lord, what happened?"

"We had an accident with the motorcycle," Sam explained. "My wife had a bad fall."

The woman came down the steps and put an arm around her. "Come in," she said. "You gotta lay down 'fore you fall down, girl. I be Delight. You come along with me."

Lisa felt weak in the knees. If she didn't lie down she was going to collapse.

By this time curious neighbors had gathered near the house. They stared at Lisa and murmured among themselves. Two boys of nine or ten looked at the motorcycle with big, inquisitive eyes.

"Be damn big machine," one of them said.

"Go like hell." The other one touched the handlebars.

Horatio slapped his hand away. "Don't you be touching that."

Lisa started to smile, but her face hurt and she gasped in pain. Delight said, "Your wife look in bad shape, sir. I'm goin' to take her inside."

"Thank you. I appreciate it." Sam rested a hand on Lisa's head. "I'll be along in a minute," he said.

She nodded, wanting to tell him she was okay, that he didn't have to look so worried. But she couldn't summon the words. She leaned against Delight. Funny name. Pretty name.

The woman led her into the house. Lisa saw a sagging sofa, two straight-backed chairs, a rocker. They went into a bedroom. Here there was a bed, a couple of shelves that served as a dresser. Clothes hanging from nails on the walls.

"Best you get outta them clothes," Delight said. "I bring you something to sleep in and some water so's you can rinse off."

Lisa slumped down on the bed. She hurt all over, hurt too much to move.

Delight closed the door behind her. Sam came in with the first-aid kit. He looked around and shook his head. "Sorry, Lisa. I'm afraid this was the best we could do."

"It doesn't matter." She bent down to take her sandals off, but he said, "No, I'll do it."

He took them off, then the torn cutoffs. One hip was scraped.

Delight knocked and came in carrying a pan of water, a washcloth, a towel and a bar of yellow soap. She had a long cotton gown over her arm. "My, oh, my," she exclaimed, giving Lisa the once-over. "Look like you been chewed up and spit out."

That brought a smile. "That's the way I feel," Lisa said.

"Horatio be bringing the motorcycle up on the porch," Delight told Sam. "Won't nobody steal it, but those rascally boys be curious. 'Fore you know it they break something."

"Good idea." He hurried out of the room. He and Horatio carried the Harley up, then he went back to Lisa. She was pale and her hands were starting to shake.

Delight said, "You want me to help you?"

"I can manage," Sam said. "But thanks."

When Delight left, he took Lisa's torn T-shirt off and checked her out, running his hands over her shoulders, down her back, her chest. He tilted her face up to the light. The scrape on her face wasn't as serious as he'd first thought, but now he saw the bruise on the other side of her cheekbone. He touched it and she flinched.

"Benjamin hit me," she said.

Sam swore. That was another score he had to settle. He wet the washcloth and bathed her face as gently as he could, then both her arms.

"I must look awful," she said.

"Like you've been run over by a truck." He took the bandage off her hand, wiped the blood away, put more antiseptic on and a clean bandage. He had her lie down while he tended to the scrape on her hip. She was already starting to bruise. By tomorrow she'd be hurting really badly.

He helped her into the flour-sack nightgown. "I'm sorry as hell I got you into this," he said. "I shouldn't have left you alone."

"It isn't your fault."

"Yes, it is." He kissed the bruise on the side of her face. "You shouldn't have become involved in this, Lisa. It's my fault you did. If I hadn't suspected you, if I'd trusted you in the beginning and admitted to myself how I was beginning to feel about you, you wouldn't have gone with Reitman and none of this would have happened. You'd be safely back on the beach at the Poinciana drinking a planter's punch."

Lisa pulled back so that she could look at him. "But I want to be with you, Sam, not on the beach at the Poinciana."

Something clutched at his insides. He looked at her, then away because he knew she was getting to him, stealing into his heart, making him go all weak inside when she looked at him like this. He wasn't ready for this kind of feeling. He might never be.

He eased her down onto the bed and pulled the sheet up over her. "Get some rest," he said.

She closed her eyes. "Think I'll sleep for a little while."

He leaned down and kissed her. "I'll be here if you need me."

She smiled. "I know," she said.

A little before nightfall Sam wakened her long enough to eat some chicken soup. He propped her up in bed, said, "Open your mouth," and spooned the soup in.

When she said, "Enough," he wiped her chin, gave her two aspirins, eased her back down onto the bed and tucked the sheet around her as if she were a child. She was asleep before he left the room.

He'd asked Horatio about a phone. No, the other man told him, there wasn't one in the village. The nearest one was in Maroon Town.

He couldn't go there. He had a feeling the waiter in the dining room had been in cahoots with Benjamin. Probably the guy at the registration desk was, too. If he was, he'd listened in on the call to Kingston.

When Horatio said, "Gotta go fetch my cows," Sam sat out on the front porch and thought about what to do next. He was pretty sure that for now he and Lisa were safe. This was a small settlement; these were nice people. But he'd stick to the story that he and Lisa were in Jamaica vacationing.

He didn't want them to know he was a cop because very likely some of these people grew ganja. Probably most of them grew just enough for themselves, but there were others who grew it for big distributors. He didn't blame them. They were poor people trying to put food in their children's mouths any way they could. He wasn't after them, but after the big boys, the men at the top who bought and sold the stronger stuff, the ones who made their fortunes out of getting kids hooked.

He knew very little about this Cockpit Country, but he had a feeling it was here that most of the grass was grown. He had to be careful because very likely, as in Colombia and Bolivia, there was a head man in the village who reported to one of the big honchos, who in turn reported to the head drug guy in the district. All of them could be working with Juan Montoya.

He thought about asking somebody here in the village to carry a message to Hargreaves at the hotel, but he couldn't take the chance. If he picked the wrong man, a man whose living depended on working with the drug people, the guy might lead Montoya's men back here. He had to depend on his own instincts now. When he could contact Hargreaves himself, he would; until then he was on his own.

When Horatio came back with his two cows, Sam went with him to the small corral in back of the house. Then he and Horatio each ate a bowl of soup. The old man asked him why he'd come to Jamaica and Sam said he and Lisa were here on vacation. He and his wife were from Wisconsin, he said. They'd come to swim and sun and drink some good Jamaica rum.

Horatio laughed, said "'Scuse me," and returned with a bottle of Appleton's. They each took a couple of swigs right out of the bottle. After the third swig Sam felt some of the day's tension easing out of his body. He thanked Horatio for the drinks, said "Good night," and went in to Lisa.

She didn't fully waken when he lay down beside her, but she moved closer. He put his arm around her waist and kissed the top of her head. "Go back to sleep, baby," he said.

For a long time he lay like that, just listening to her breathing, watching her face by the light of the moon shining in through the open window. His moonlight lady, so small and defenseless in his arms. Her body jerked as though in fear and he whispered, "It's all right, Lisa. I'm here, sweetheart. Nothing's going to hurt you now."

He knew now how much he cared about her. He wasn't sure he wanted to. They were different. He was a cop who'd been around the track a couple of thousand times. He'd done things and seen things he didn't even want to think about. She was as innocent as a babe, as delicate as a rose. What in the hell could she see in a big galoot like him?

Margaret hadn't been delicate as a rose. She was the tall-brunette kind of woman he'd always gone for. She did aerobics, lifted weights and knew karate. He had a feeling she could hold her own with a man, anytime, anywhere.

She'd hated his being a cop, especially after Danny was born. She didn't like him being away from home three or four days at a time and she'd accused him of sleeping with other women. He never had, not in the six years they were married. Which was pretty damn ridiculous considering that she had slept with other men.

The first time he discovered she'd been unfaithful, he'd left her. Then Danny got sick and she'd begged him to come back. So he had, not because of her but because of Danny. But it wasn't any good. He could forgive her, but he couldn't forget. He didn't want to touch her, and after a while she found somebody else—quite a few somebody elses.

Because of Danny, he let her file for the divorce. Only when she demanded full custody did he threaten to charge her with adultery. She gave in and he got Danny on holidays.

But it hadn't been enough; he hadn't been there for his son the way he should have been. He hadn't known until it was too late that Danny was on drugs. He'd never forgive himself for that.

He'd vowed after his failed marriage that he'd never marry again. And he sure to God didn't want another kid.

It worried him that he and Lisa had made love without using any protection. He didn't know whether or not she was on the Pill, but he had a hunch she wasn't. He broke out into a sweat. What if she got pregnant? What in the hell would he do? He didn't want to start another family. He'd been down that road and would never travel it again.

Sam laid a hand over her stomach. What if the seed had already been planted? What if even now his baby was growing there? He snatched his hand away as though he'd been burned and said a fervent prayer that it hadn't happened.

When Lisa awoke the next morning she could barely move. Every muscle in her body ached. She pulled herself up out of bed, hobbled over to the chair where her purse was and reached for her compact mirror.

She groaned. The place on her face where she'd been scraped looked awful. The skin beneath one eye had turned an interesting shade of purple and so had the bruise on her cheek where Benjamin had hit her. Her arm hurt, her hip hurt, her hand hurt. She was a wreck.

She looked around for her clothes. They weren't on the shelf, nor were they hanging on a nail. The nightgown of flour-sack material covered her so that she was decent enough. She opened the door and peered out, heard Sam on the porch talking to Horatio and called, "Sam?"

He came in. "Didn't know you were up," he said. "How do you feel?"

"Don't ask. I can't find my clothes."

"Delight washed and mended them. They're hanging on bushes in the backyard to dry." He turned her toward the light. "God," he said. "You look awful."

"Thanks a lot."

"How about a shower and something to eat?"

"There's a shower?"

"Like the one we had the night we almost hit the cow."

The cow with the rolling, fireball eyes. Lisa shivered. "A shower might help," she said.

"I'll show you where it is." He saw she was moving like a ninety-year-old granny and took her arm to help her. They went into the kitchen. Delight was standing in front of the sink.

"You're up," she said, smiling at Lisa. "How you be feeling?"

"Just about as bad as I look." Lisa smiled back. "Is it all right if I take a shower"

"You go right ahead, but your mister better be helping you."

"No, I can—"

"Yes, I'll help her," Sam interrupted.

"When you finish, breakfast be ready. Got mango and papaya and I be frying some plantains." Delight motioned toward the door. "You go ahead. It all be ready by the time you through."

"Listen," Lisa whispered to Sam when they stepped out into the backyard, "I can shower by myself."

"Maybe, but it'd be a lot more fun with me." Without giving her a chance to refuse, he pushed back the cloth curtain that served as a shower door.

He went into the shower stall with her, stripped out of his jeans, helped her take off the flour-sack gown and put everything on a bench outside before he turned the water on.

Her body was covered with bruises that were purple and green against the paleness of her skin. He bathed her as carefully as he would a child, barely touching the scrapes and scratches. He washed her hair, rinsed out the gravel embedded there and examined her scalp for cuts.

When he'd checked her out and bathed her, he put his arms around her and held her there under the water. For a little while he forgot that he didn't want to make a commitment, forgot that she might already be pregnant. He didn't want to think about that. He backed away because he kind of wanted her. Well hell, a lot more than kind of. The urge was strong, powerful, but even more powerful was the need to protect and care for her.

He turned the shower off and gently patted her dry. "Easy, love," he said when she winced.

When he'd finished, she put her arms around his neck and leaned her head against his shoulder. "I'm crazy about you," she whispered.

"Yeah?" he said, trying to sound tough. Trying to act as though the words didn't make his knees turn to Jell-O.

"Yeah." She smiled. Then, because she knew how she was affecting him, she touched him, lightly, quickly. And before he could react, she stepped out of the shower, pulled the flour-sack gown back over her head and headed for the kitchen.

He stood there, hard as a rock, swearing under his breath. And knew there'd never been another woman who affected him the way this one did.

They were on the front porch shelling peas when Delight said, "You know 'bout voodoo?"

Lisa looked up, startled. "Uh, yes. I mean I've heard about it."

She knew it was practiced in some of the Caribbean islands, especially in Haiti, and that it was some kind of religious cult that believed in sorcery and fetishes.

"Voodoo be powerful stuff." Delight leaned closer. "Tomorrow night we goin' to have a voodoo night," she confided. "You and mister come and see. Yes?"

A little afraid, but excited, too, Lisa nodded. "If we're still here," she said. "If it's all right with Sam."

Voodoo. The word send a chill down her spine. A friend who'd been to Haiti had seen a voodoo ceremony, at least the kind of voodoo that tourists were allowed to see. "It frightened the life out of me," Patti had told her. "The participants in the ceremony went into a trance that I guess was supposed to help them communicate with the spirit of their long-dead ancestors. They went kind of crazy, writhing around on the ground, doing all sorts of weird things. It scared the living daylights out of me."

Nevertheless, Lisa wanted to see it. "I'll go," she told Delight. "If we're still here tomorrow, I'll go."

"Good!" Delight patted Lisa's knee. "I'm goin' to make up some poultices to put on your hurts so tomorrow you feel better."

Lisa certainly hoped so. Today she was one huge ache. Every muscle hurt and her face felt as though it had been steamrollered. And she was worried about Sam.

He'd told her he was supposed to meet Hargreaves at the hotel. Was Hargreaves still there waiting for them?

She knew Sam had to get to the police captain. She didn't want to hold him back, neither did she want him to leave without her.

In a little while she went into the bedroom to rest. Delight brought in evil-smelling poultices and put them on her face and her hip.

"You sleep now," she said. "When you wake up you goin' to feel better."

Lisa slept, and when she awoke, Sam was sitting next to her on the bed.

"What's that smell?" he asked when she opened her eyes.

"Delight's poultices." She took the one off her face, then the one from her hip and put them on the floor beside the bed. "I think they helped," she said. "I feel better." She yawned and stretched. "Have you ever seen a voodoo ceremony?

"Yeah, once in Haiti. Why?"

"Delight told me there's going to be voodoo here in the village tomorrow night."

"And you want to see it?"

"Of course I do."

"It'll scare the pants off you."

She grinned. "That's one way to get 'em off."

He grinned back. "Now I know you're feeling better."

"I'll be up and chasing you around the room by tomorrow."

"I certainly hope so." He hesitated, wondering how to tell her what he was going to do. But because she had to know, he said, "I'm going to take a little ride tonight."

Her heart gave an uncomfortable leap. "You're going back to the hotel?"

He nodded. "I've got to get to Hargreaves, Lisa. By now he's probably frantic, wondering what happened to us. I've got to get word to him."

She sank down onto the pillows. "The waiter at the hotel knew Benjamin, Sam. He helped him. Benjamin hit him so it would look like he wasn't involved, but he was. If he was, then maybe other people at the hotel are, too." She clasped her hands together. "It's dangerous, Sam. Please don't go."

"I can't just sit here and do nothing. I've got to get to Hargreaves." He took her hands. "You'll be safe here. If Hargreaves is still in Maroon Town and I find him, I'll bring one of his men back with me. I'll make sure he gets you to Kingston." She didn't want to go to Kingston, not without him.

"If Hargreaves isn't there, I'll be back," Sam went on. "It'll take me two hours at the most." He put his arms around her. "It's going to be all right, Lisa. So don't worry, okay?"

She wanted to tie him to the bed, sit on him, hold him, do anything she had to to keep him with her. But because she couldn't, she said, "Sure, Sam. I understand. Whatever you say."

They had dinner that night with Horatio and Delight, more fried plantains, roasted breadfruit and scrambled eggs. Sam and Horatio each had a Red Stripe; she and Delight had coffee.

"I'm going to ride over to the hotel in Maroon Town," Sam said when they finished. "Need to use the phone there."

"Be better if you wait till mornin'." Horatio wiped his mouth with the back of his hand. "Be mighty hard to find your way back in the dark."

"The motorcycle has a light. If I keep on the path I'll be all right." Then, thinking that if Hargreaves was still there he could come back for Lisa with one of the police captain's men, he said, "If I have too hard a time getting there I might have to spend the night. Will you look after Lisa while I'm gone?"

"'Course we will," Horatio said. "Come on. I'll help you get your machine off the porch."

The two men went out; Delight and Lisa followed. She wasn't happy about Sam's going back to the hotel. If anything happened to him . . .

He started to roll the Harley to the edge of the porch, but had trouble moving it.

He bent down and, using the flashlight, looked at the tires. The front one was flat. He looked closer and saw that it had been slashed.

"What is it?" Horatio asked. "What be the matter?"

"Tire's slashed."

"What?" Horatio bent down. "That can't be! No-body'd do that."

But somebody had. Somebody who knew who he was and why he was here.

He couldn't leave now; there was no way out.

Chapter 13

"Who would do such a thing?" Lisa closed the bedroom door. "My God, Sam, somebody knows who you are. We've got to leave. It's too dangerous for you here."

"We can't go anywhere until I get the tire fixed. Horatio knows somebody in the next village who has a repair shop. He'll take me there tomorrow."

"We could start walking right now."

Sam shook his head. In the shape Lisa was in she wouldn't last half a mile. And he couldn't leave her here, not when somebody was on to them. The smell of danger was in the air; he hated having her exposed to it. If he couldn't find Hargreaves, he'd take her to Kingston himself. If he could get the tire on the Harley fixed.

Hargreaves had said Montoya was probably headed for Port Antonio. As soon as he got Lisa safely to Kingston he'd ditch the Harley, get a car and head for the coast. But right now she was his first concern. Maybe she shouldn't be, but that's the way it was.

"Do you think it was Benjamin who cut the tire?" she asked. "Do you think he followed us here?"

"Maybe. Maybe not. He might have arranged for somebody else to do it."

"But how would he know where we are?"

"Jungle telephone," Sam said with a shrug. "These people have a way of getting news to each other. We're strangers, we stick out like a couple of sore thumbs. Word would get around that we're staying here."

He hesitated, wondering how much he should tell her about the way the drug business worked. And it was a business. Big business.

"A lot of these mountain people grow ganja," he said. "Kinda like the old-time moonshiners who used to make illegal whiskey. The difference is that ganja is grown for the big-time operators." Sam sat down on the bed, pulled off his boots and shucked off his jeans. "It works like a syndicate," he went on. "Small farmers like Horatio..." He shook his head. "I'm not saying Horatio is doing it, but probably a few of the village men are. They grow the stuff under the control of a district boss who works for somebody else, who works for the syndicate bosses. A poor farmer can make more money than he's ever made before by growing ganja."

He lay back on the bed, hands under his head, and montioned for her to sit beside him. "I don't blame the village farmers. Maybe they don't realize that by growing ganja they're hooking kids who eventually will try something stronger—coke, angel dust, crack or the new stuff Montoya and Reitman are going to ship out. It's a hell of a lot more dangerous than any of the other drugs that're currently on the market."

"That's terrible, Sam."

He nodded. "The dealers will peddle it to kids who'll peddle it to other kids, and they'll all try it because they're always looking for something new. Another thrill, another high. Some of them will OD. Some of them, like..." He stopped and looked away.

"Like who?" Lisa asked.

"Danny. My kid."

"Oh, Sam. I didn't know. I'm sorry."

"He was fourteen. I didn't know he was into drugs. Can you imagine that? I was his father, but I was so busy working for the DEA I didn't know my own son was using."

He swung off the bed and began to pace. "I'm not sure that Margaret—that's my ex-wife—knew, either. If she did, she didn't tell me." He shot Lisa an agonized look. "I don't blame her," he said. "It's my fault. If I'd been around more maybe it wouldn't have happened. I'd have spotted it, done something about it.

"I was working undercover with the Tijuana police, setting up a scam to stop a load of coke coming in from Colombia when I got word to call Margaret. She was at the hospital, but I talked to her sister. She told me that Danny had OD'd. I got a flight out of San Diego that night. He was unconscious when I got to the hospital. I sat beside him and held his hand. I told him he was going to be all right, that I was there and I'd take care of him. But he didn't hear me. He never regained consciousness. He died before I could tell him one more time how much I loved him."

Lisa reached for his hand.

"Margaret said it was my fault. She said if I'd been more of a father it wouldn't have happened. She said—"

"She was wrong." Lisa put her arms around him. "Kids take drugs, Sam. Most of the time it isn't anybody's fault."

"I should have been there for him. I should have—"

"Shh," she said, and drew him to her. She knew how hard it had been for him to tell her this, but she was glad he had confided in her. It helped her understand why he was in Jamaica, how important his work was to him.

"I don't know why I told you."

"I'm glad you did."

He reached for his jeans. "I'm going to take a walk."

She took the jeans away from him. "No," she said. "Come to bed with me."

He looked at her, his eyes bleak with remembrance. Then he sighed and tossed the jeans over a chair.

She took her clothes off, then slipped the flour-sack nightgown over her head. They lay down together. She put her arms around him. Tomorrow or the day after they would be on the move again, but for now they could be together like this, here in this humble room in this ramshackle house.

In a little while he said, "You'd better get some sleep."

"I'm not tired. Are you?"

"No."

She raised up on her elbow and looked down at him. "I'm feeling a lot better," she said.

"Oh?"

She heard the hint of a smile in his voice and waited for him to make the first move. He didn't. Instead he said, "You're still not in great shape, Lisa. You'd better get some sleep."

She knew then that he was still upset about his son and that it had been a mistake to think making love would help. But oh, how she longed to hold and comfort him.

But all she could do was rest a hand on his leg and say, "Good night, Sam. Sleep well."

"You, too."

He lay on his back and looked up at the ceiling, still thinking about his son. Danny would be sixteen now. In another two years he'd have been going to college. If he'd lived. If he hadn't taken drugs. Fourteen, with his whole life ahead of him. School dances and football games, girls to meet, women to love. But he hadn't experienced any of it; his life had been over before it had even begun.

God, how he hated every mother's son of the bastards who made a living off hooking kids like Danny. He'd promised himself when he sat there holding Danny's hand that he was going to devote his life to bringing every rotten one of them down. The DEA wanted him full-time. He'd been putting them off because he liked working for the NYPD. But when this was over, when Montoya and Reitman and all of the bums connected to them were behind bars, he'd turn in his NYPD badge and go with the DEA.

But first he had to get Montoya, take him back to New York to stand trial for murder, as well as for drug running. And he had to make sure that Lisa was safe.

Lisa. He'd promised himself that they wouldn't make love again until they had some kind of protection. That meant he couldn't touch her until all of this was over with and they were back in Kingston. Or Miami. Yeah, he'd see her in Miami in a few weeks. Until then . . .

He felt the brush of her leg against his and tried to think about something else. Baseball. He wondered if the Jays would take the series this year. It didn't help. Okay, think about tomorrow.

Finding the guy who'd slashed the front tire of the Harley. Getting it fixed. Tomorrow. Tomorrow... Finally all thought faded and at last he slept.

He came awake slowly. Lisa's arm was around his waist, her breast against his chest, one leg thrown over his. His body was tight as a drum, hard as a rock. He tried to remember why he'd thought they shouldn't make love. Didn't want to remember.

She sighed and moved closer, unconsciously rubbing against him when she did. He clenched his teeth. Couldn't. Shouldn't. Okay, maybe if he just held her and touched her it would be enough.

It wasn't.

He rubbed his hand across her breast, cupped it and ran a thumb over the tip.

She stirred, and he kissed her. "Lisa?" he whispered against her lips. "Lisa?"

"Umm," she said, stretching, leaning her body into his.

He squeezed the pebbled tip of her breast and the kiss deepened. He ran his hand down over her belly and hips and began to stroke her.

She nuzzled against his throat.

"Have to touch you like this," he said.

"Me, too," she whispered, and began to stroke him.

"I guess you know what you're doing to me," he said against her lips.

"Guess I do."

"You know what's going to happen if we don't stop?"

"Uh-huh." She moved her body so that she was lying half-under him. "I love it when you touch me, Sam. Love touching you like this."

He smothered his moan against her mouth. "Listen," he said, fighting for reason, "we haven't been taking any precautions. We don't have any protection. We..." All thought, all reason fled. There was only now and the terrible need.

He rolled her beneath him and she lifted herself to him, warm and ready and trembling with eagerness. She clutched his hips and took him inside her. She encircled his back with her legs and made him a prisoner of her body.

They moved slowly, silently together, both of them aware of Horatio and Delight, who slept in the other room. He wanted to tell her how he felt enclosed in her warmth this way, how her eagerness excited him, that he felt enveloped by her, a part of her.

He kissed her bruised face, her closed eyes, her cheeks and her lips. He whispered, "Ah, Lisa. Lisa." And moved slowly, deeply within her.

She caressed his shoulders and his back. She turned her face into his throat, whispering, "So good, Sam. So good." And held him close, luxuriating in this slow, sweet rise of passion.

Their cadence quickened and a whimper started low in her throat. Her body heated and she became like a wild thing beneath him. She rose and fell with him, gasping with pleasure, whispering urgent pleas against his mouth. When it happened, she buried her face against his shoulder to smother her cry, not even aware that in the throes of passion she nipped his skin.

It sent him over the edge. He reeled out of control, holding her close because he was afraid that if he didn't he'd spin right out into space.

They held on to each other. He kissed her again and again and at last, when their hearts returned to a normal beat, he made as though to move. "Don't leave me, Sam," she said. "Not yet."

"I'm too heavy for you, sweetheart."

"No. Stay. Please stay."

"Then this way." He rolled so that she lay on top of him. "Like this," he said. "Sleep like this, Lisa."

She burrowed into him. Already half-asleep, she kissed the shoulder she had nipped and whispered, "I love you, Sam."

"Lisa?" he said. "Lisa, listen." But she didn't hear him; she was fast asleep.

He hadn't counted on love. This between them was pretty great. Great? Hell, it was sensational. He was crazy about her. But love?

He'd been telling himself for the last couple of years that he didn't need or want love. He wasn't a guy who led with his chin, who rushed into something. He and Margaret had known each other for almost three years before he got around to asking her to marry him. Three years and he really hadn't known her at all.

He'd known Lisa for what? Almost a week? They were good together. He loved making love with her, and when they got back to the States he'd keep on seeing her even if it meant spending half his salary flying back and forth to Miami. But there was a catch to that: he didn't think she was the kind of woman who'd be content with a prolonged affair. She was little, she was sweet, but she was also feisty. If this went on too long she'd give him an ultimatum. Fish or cut bait. Put up or shut up. Marriage or adios.

The thought of marriage made him break out in a sweat. He wasn't ready; he might never be ready. He...
She wiggled against him, trying to find a more comfortable spot, and he felt himself grow again. What was the matter with him? Had he let himself be bewitched by a

pint-size dame who could turn him on with a look or a touch?

What was he going to do about her? What in the hell was he going to do?

Sam And Horatio left right after breakfast the next morning.

"The village is four or five miles from here," Sam told Lisa. "I'll be pushing the Harley, so it'll be harder than walking. Take us maybe two hours. Don't know how long it'll take to fix the tire, *if* it can be fixed. But don't worry, I'll be back this afternoon."

"Be careful."

"Always." He kissed her. "Stay inside today, Lisa. Don't even go out on the porch."

"I won't." She stood in the doorway while he and Horatio got the Harley off the porch, and watched until they disappeared through the trees at the end of the village. She'd said she wouldn't worry, but she would. Sam had to get the Harley fixed, but she hated his going off without her.

She helped Delight in the kitchen. She fretted in her room. By four that afternoon Sam hadn't returned.

"Don't you worry," Delight said. "They be back soon."

Five o'clock came. Six. And still there was no sign of Sam and Horatio.

Lisa paced through the small house. She didn't know what to do. What if something had happened to Sam? What if Benjamin had followed him to the next village? Or Montoya?

By seven-thirty even Delight was concerned. "This not be like Horatio," she said. "No matter where that man go, he always be home by dinnertime."

She fixed yams and breadfruit for their supper, but neither of them could eat. "Horatio know there goin' to be voodoo tonight," Delight said as she cleared their plates. "Never knew that man to miss voodoo."

"What time does it start?"

"'Bout ten, missus. Sure they goin' to be back by then."

But they weren't.

Lisa kept going to the front door and looking out. Finally, because it was dark, she went out onto the porch and peered through the darkness, hoping she'd see them coming past the houses. At a quarter to ten she heard the sound of drums.

"Voodoo be startin'," Delight told her.

Voodoo? Lisa had almost forgotten. "But I can't go," she said, remembering Sam's admonition not to leave the house. She wouldn't, anyway; she had to wait for him.

"I be goin' and it best you come with me. Don't do you no good waiting alone here. If your mister and Horatio haven't come by now they probably won't be back till mornin'. You better come to voodoo with me."

"But I have to wait for Sam."

"Won't do you no good to be sittin' here by your sad lonesome."

Lisa hesitated. Sam had told her not to leave. Whoever had cut the motorcycle tire might still be here in Trinity. The thought of that—of being alone in the house, knowing Benjamin might be out there somewhere in the darkness—spooked her. She'd rather be in a crowd with Delight than alone.

"All right," she said. "I'll go with you."

"Good!" Delight looked at Lisa's cutoffs. "Folk's goin' to be looking at you if you go like that. I got a skirt that maybe fit you."

She went into the bedroom and rummaged through the clutter of clothes on the shelves there. Finally she pulled out a blue-and-white-flowered skirt. "Try this on," she said. "It'll fit."

Lisa took off her cutoffs and hung them over the bed. Something fell out of the pocket and rolled across the floor. She bent to retrieve it and saw it was the small smooth stone Rebecca had given her to keep the duppies away. She picked it up, held it in her hand for a moment, and when she put the skirt on, put the stone in the pocket.

"It be time," Delight said.

"Maybe I should leave a note for Sam, just to let him know where we are. If he and Horatio return, they can meet us there."

"They won't be returning." Delight turned away so that Lisa couldn't see her face. "Leastways not to-night."

Lisa stared at the other woman. Delight's shoulders slumped; her whole body seemed dejected. Before Lisa could say anything, she sighed and said, "Come along. It's time we go."

Lisa followed her out of the room, but at the top of the steps she hesitated. The drums sounded louder than before—jungle drums repeating the same rhythm, over and over. *Tum* tum tum, *tum* tum tum. They were primitive, hypnotic.

Suddenly she wasn't sure she was doing the right thing. She was in a strange country, in unknown territory. She'd never seen voodoo before. She'd be the only white woman there. Would these people object to her being witness to this ancient religious rite?

Delight hurried down the steps. "It goin' to be startin'," she said.

Lisa had no choice, unless she wanted to stay alone in the house.

They walked to the edge of town. There were no lights in the windows of the other houses, no signs of life. Everyone had gone to the voodoo ceremony.

The sound of the drums grew louder, and finally through the trees and underbrush, Lisa saw a glimmer of light. Delight took her arm to hurry her along.

Dozens of lanterns and candles reflected on the faces of the people who had gathered and were sitting on the ground in a wide circle. Delight led her into the circle and they sat cross-legged. Only the people next to them looked curiously at Lisa. The others were intent on the empty space in the center of the circle. A few of them had soft drinks, others had glasses, whether filled with rum or water or a soft drink, Lisa didn't know.

Out of the darkness a young woman appeared. A white robe covered her from neck to feet; a white turban hid her hair. She walked barefoot to the center of the ring, then spun around and placed a lighted candle on the ground.

A man entered. He, too, was clad in a white robe.

"That be the voodoo priest," Delight whispered.

He carried a clay jar, and using something that looked like sand, began to spread it on the ground in a design.

"This be the symbol of the spirits that be coming," Delight said. "Now he be goin' to pour water on the four places the spirits goin' to enter."

The spirits? Goose bumps rose on Lisa's arm.

The drums stopped. There was a breathless moment of silent expectation. The voodoo priest led three women into the circle. A man began to shake a rattle, while another recited words in a language Lisa didn't understand.

The drums began again—first the smallest, then the second, louder, faster, and finally a booming explosion of sound as the third and biggest drum joined in.

The women in the circle began to move their shoulders and their arms, then their feet. They swayed to a curious rhythm, faster and yet faster, on and on to the hypnotic beat of the drums. Suddenly one of the women stopped. When she moved again her body jerked with every beat of the drums. As though propelled by an invisible force, she began to spin. She hurtled about, stumbling, falling, rising again, thrashing wildly with her arms. She raced around the circle in a terrible frenzy. Suddenly she stopped and snatched a glass out of someone's hand. She threw the liquid out and bit into it. As Lisa watched, the woman chewed and swallowed bits of glass.

She danced on, danced until a man brought her a live, squawking chicken. She grabbed the bird by its neck and whirled it around and around until she had twisted its head off. She lifted the headless and still-flapping bird above her head and drank its blood.

"Oh my God!" Lisa said under her breath.

Now the other two women began to dance. A man ran into the ring holding a torch over his head. He swung it round and round, then touched it to a pile of dried grass and twigs and pieces of wood. One of the women knelt before the fire, then began to whirl and spin over it, into it. She grabbed a burning branch from the flames and licked it.

Lisa turned away. She couldn't watch anymore. She wished she hadn't come; she wanted to leave.

"I'm not feeling very well," she said to Delight. But Delight didn't hear her. She was watching the dancers with glazed eyes. Lisa put a hand on her arm. "Delight?" she said.

But the woman didn't answer, only stared, mesmerized, in a trance.

Lisa looked at the people around her. They, too, were transfixed. Some had their eyes closed while they swayed to the heated rhythm of the drums. She was an alien, a stranger out of place and time. She had to leave, had to get out before she, too, was caught up in the dance and the dancers who hurled themselves around the circle, jumping over the fire, into the fire, their eyes rolled back, strange guttural cries coming from their throats.

She tried again to speak to Delight, but it did no good. The Jamaican woman was in another world, at one with those who watched, with the three women who danced, with the voodoo priest.

Should she leave? Go back to the empty house and wait for Sam? Or should she stay here and wait until this was over? No, she had to leave.

Lisa started to push herself up, and as she did, she turned a little to the right. And saw him. The leaping flames of the fire were reflected in the narrow eyes, shone on the jagged scar. For a moment she couldn't breathe. It was as if, like the others, she, too, was frozen somewhere in time.

But Benjamin wasn't. He was here, looking at her, showing his white teeth in a broad and terrible grin. The stone in her pocket hadn't kept the duppies away, after all.

He slowly rose and started toward her.

She jumped up and, frantic with haste, tried to step around those seated cross-legged behind her. She put her hands on strange shoulders, murmuring, "Excuse me, excuse me." It didn't matter; they were too entranced by the ceremony to hear or to help. She climbed over a prostrate woman. A man in the grip of the spirits that had claimed his body reached out for her. She ducked under his arms and kept going until she reached the outside of the circle. She looked over her shoulder and saw Benjamin striding toward her.

She ran, not toward town but toward the trees, into darkness.

"Come back, nice lady." The sound of his voice, laughing at her, was close, so close.

Terrified, heart thudding against her breast, Lisa ran into the woods. Branches tore at her hair and slapped into her face. It didn't matter. She had to get away.

A thin beam of light cut through the darkness. A dark object loomed in front of her. She screamed, and the sound she made cut like a sword through the night.

"Lisa? Lisa, is that you?"

Sam! She stumbled through the darkness toward the motorcycle.

"Missus?" Horatio asked. "That be you, missus?"

She looked up at him, past him to Sam astride the Harley. "He's here!" she cried. "Benjamin is here!"

"Get on!" Sam reached out for her and pulled her up behind him. "I'll be back," he said to Horatio. Then he gunned the motor and shot back into the darkness of the forest.

Chapter 14

Gunfire ripped through the night. A bullet snapped off the branch above Sam's head, but he didn't stop. He had to get Lisa out of the line of fire.

He switched off the light on the motorcycle and tried to see through the dark forest. Lisa clung to him, face pressed against his back. Another shot rang out behind them.

"Horatio?" he called out. "Horatio?" When there was no answer, he stopped and jumped off the bike. "Stay here!" He shoved a gun into Lisa's hand. "There's no safety. All you have to do is pull the trigger."

"My God, Sam . . ."

"I've got to see if Horatio's okay. Stay down out of sight."

"Sam, wait . . ." But he'd already turned and was running through the trees. She slid off the back of the Harley. The gun felt cold and hard in her hand. Was

Benjamin still out there? Somewhere in the forest? She closed her hands around the gun.

The drums had stopped. It was quiet now. Too quiet. Where was Sam? Had Horatio been shot? What was...?

A branch snapped. "Sam?" she whispered. "Sam, is that you?"

"Why, no pretty lady. It be me."

She whirled around, looking right and left, trying to see through the darkness.

The snap of another branch. Closer. The crackle of leaves. She couldn't see. She squeezed her eyes shut, and when she opened them she could make out the shape of the trees, huge and mysterious in the dark of the night. Fear choked her and she hunched down, her back against a tree.

Above her, clouds scudded across the night sky. As she watched, the moon slid out from the cover of the clouds and shone down through the trees like a pale yellow beacon.

"Pretty lady?" She heard a chuckle, low, insidious, more frightful than a shouted cry. "Pretty lady?"

Lisa froze. She couldn't breathe, couldn't move. Her gaze darted right, left.

"Peek-a-boo, I see you." The singsong voice was taunting her. "Peek-a-boo."

He stepped out of the bushes and came toward her, white teeth shining in a broad smile.

"Big dude fella leave you all alone? Now ain't that too bad? Just you and me and the motorcycle, and we be gone 'fore he come back. We be going to have us a fine time 'fore I take you down to Port Antonio. Maybe my boss want to kill you, but I goin' to say, 'No, no she come with us. Keep us happy all the way to South America.' "

Lisa shoved herself away from the tree. "Don't come any closer," she whispered.

"'Course, we goin' to have to dump you overboard soon's we get there. But I sure goin' to enjoy you 'fore we do."

The gun wasn't cold now, it was hot and wet with sweat from her palms. She gripped it in both hands.

"Lord-a-mercy," he said, mocking her. "The little lady has a gun. You goin' to shoot me, pretty lady?"

Her hands were shaking so badly it was all she could do to hang on to the gun. So was her voice when she said "I'm—I'm warning you."

"Sure you are." The words were spoken in a deceptively soft voice. "Sure you..." He leapt at her, arm outstretched, hand reaching for the gun, so close she could smell the rum on his breath.

She closed her eyes and squeezed the trigger. He stopped, stood where he was, his eyes as white as gravestones in the light of the moon. His fingers curled. He took a staggering step forward and reached for her throat.

She fired again, heard the *whomp* of the bullet hitting his body, watched him slowly fold and fall.

The gun slipped out of her hand. She slumped back against the tree.

"Lisa! Lisa, where are you?"

"Here." The word was no more than a whisper. "Here."

Sam crashed through the trees. "I heard a shot. What happened? Are you..." He saw Benjamin facedown among the fallen leaves and ferns. He bent down, shone his flashlight on the prone body, felt for the carotid pulse. "He's alive. Are you all right?"

"I—I never sh-shot anybody before."

"Where's the gun?"

"I dropped it."

He shone the flashlight on the ground, found the gun, pocketed it. "Horatio's hit. I've got to get him."

"But what about..." She pointed. "What about Benjamin?"

"We'll have to leave him here. I'll come back for him as soon as I take care of Horatio." He bent down and went through the fallen man's pockets, found a gun and shoved it into the top of his boot. "Sure you're all right?" he asked Lisa.

No, she wasn't all right. She was trembling inside, sick to her stomach. She'd shot a man, maybe killed him. How was she supposed to feel?

Sam didn't wait for her reply; he grabbed the bike and hurried back the way he'd come. Lisa followed. They found Horatio sitting with his back against a tree, holding a hand over the bandanna tied around his thigh.

"We're going to get you home." Sam motioned for Lisa to take the Harley, and when she did, he leaned down to pick Horatio up.

"You can't be carrying me," the man protested. "I be too heavy."

"You be too skinny." Sam hefted the man over his shoulder. To Lisa he said, "Stay right behind us."

Still in a state of shock, she did as she was told and awkwardly wheeled the Harley after Sam and Horatio. She'd shot a man. Not only that, she'd left him lying there. Sam had said he'd go back after him, but that might be too late. Benjamin might be dead by then. And she would have killed him.

They came out of the trees into the village. A few lights pricked the darkness, but no one was about. Everything was quiet now after the voodoo ceremony. When they reached Horatio's, Lisa propped the motorcycle against the steps and Sam carried Horatio into the house. Delight had been sitting in one of the straight-backed chairs, but she jumped to her feet when she saw them.

"Horatio!" she cried. "What happen?"

"He's been shot." Sam carried the other man into the bedroom and laid him on the bed. "I'm going to need a light," he told Delight.

But she stood there without moving, wringing her hands, saying, "Oh, Lord. Oh, Lord," over and over again.

"I'll get it," Lisa said.

She brought the lantern. Sam told her to hold it up so that he could see the wound. "Delight, get me a knife," he said. "I've got to cut his trousers." And when she still didn't move, he raised his voice. "Dammit, woman, get me a knife!"

Her eyes widened. She stood stock-still for a moment, then turned and ran out of the room. When she came back, she handed Sam the knife. "I put water to boil," she said.

"Good." To Lisa, he said, "Hold the lantern higher, please."

He cut into Horatio's pants. The bullet had entered the skin at an angle. He didn't think it had touched the bone, but it had to come out.

"I'll need some clean cloths," he said. "If you don't have them, tear up a sheet. Lisa, there's adhesive tape and a pair of scissors in the first-aid kit. And the antiseptic cream. Delight, bring me the water as soon as it boils. I'll need a bottle of alcohol, too."

"You goin' to take the bullet out?" Horatio asked.

Sam nodded.

"How 'bout a drink of rum 'fore you do it?"

"For you or for me?"

Horatio managed a laugh. "I be guessin' for both of us. You ever taken a bullet out before?"

"No, but once a year I take a brush-up course in first aid." Sam hesitated. "I can go to Maroon Town in the morning and try to find a doctor if you want to wait."

Horatio shook his head. "Don't even know if they got a doctor there. Better you do it. Just give me a swig of rum and I'll be fine."

Delight came back with a pan of boiling water. Sam put the knife and the scissors in it. Delight brought the rum and Sam handed the bottle to Horatio before he went out to the kitchen to scrub his hands and arms. When he came back to the bedroom he said to Lisa, "Your turn to wash up. I'll need you to help me."

She didn't think she could, but Sam wasn't giving her time to think. She handed the lantern to Delight and went into the kitchen and washed her hands. When she came back, Sam said, "Okay, here we go."

He sponged the blood away and cleaned the wound with alcohol. He said, "Hang on, Horatio. I'm starting."

Horatio tilted the bottle up. "Go 'head, mon," he said. "Do it quick as you can."

Sam made a one-inch incision. Above his head the lantern wobbled. "Easy, Delight," he cautioned. "Take it easy."

He probed for the bullet. Horatio hissed with pain, but didn't move. The knife touched metal. "Hold the skin apart with your fingers," Sam said to Lisa. And when she did, he went in, using the tip of the knife, and slowly brought the bullet out.

"Get a cloth," he said. "Sponge the blood away."

She moved like an automaton, holding herself together, doing what had to be done. When it was over, Sam said, "Hand me the tape."

He cut small strips and crisscrossed them over the wound, then put a folded patch of cloth over the tape. "Hold it," He said to Lisa, and put adhesive on to keep it in place. "All done," he told Horatio.

But Horatio, the bottle of rum still clutched in his hand, had lost consciousness. Sam wet a piece of cloth with alcohol and held it under Horatio's nose. The man sputtered and opened his eyes.

"All finished." Sam took the bottle and drank from it. "Get some rest now. Lisa and Delight will be here if you want anything."

"Where you goin'?"

"Gotta check something out, but I'll be back."

"You going back to where I got shot?"

"Yeah. I want to have a look around."

"You watch yourself, hear?"

"I hear." Sam rested a hand on Horatio's shoulder. "This is my fault," he said. "I've brought you trouble. I'm sorry."

"No need to be. We done had us a little adventure, that's all. That's . . ." His eyes drifted closed.

"Stay with him," Sam told Delight. He took Lisa's arm and led her out of the room. "I've got to go back for Benjamin," he said.

"Let me come with you."

He shook his head. "Delight may need you. Stay here. I won't be long." He put his hands on her shoulders. "What were you doing out in the woods?"

"I went to the voodoo ceremony."

He raised an eyebrow. "How'd you like it?"

"Don't ask."

"What about Benjamin? Where'd you run into him?"

"He was there, at voodoo. I saw him when I was leaving. I tried to get away, but he followed me."

He drew her into his arms. "It's been a bitch of a day," he said.

Lisa leaned into him. "I don't want you to leave."

"I can't leave him lying there, Lisa."

"What if he's…" She took a steadying breath. "I told him to stop. I warned him. I…" She covered her face with her hands. "I'm not sure I could live with myself if I've killed him."

He took her hands away. "Benjamin's a killer and a drug dealer, Lisa. If you hadn't stopped him, only God knows what would have happened. You did what you had to do. I want you to remember that."

"What are you going to do when you find him? I mean, if he's alive. If he isn't…" She shook her head, unable to go on.

"Bring him back here. Patch him up. Then try to find Hargreaves in the morning and turn Benjamin over to him."

"I'm afraid," Lisa said. "If anything happens to you—"

"Nothing will."

She touched his face. "Be careful, Sam."

"I always am." He kissed her. "But especially now, Lisa. Because I've got you to come back to."

"Yes," she said. "You've got me."

He went out and got onto the Harley. She stood at the door, watching until he was out of sight. Then she went back into the house and into the bedroom to see if there was anything she could do to help Delight.

Sam approached the wooded area cautiously. At the edge of it he stopped the Harley, got off and rolled it into the trees. He left it there and began searching for Benjamin on foot. The night sky was overcast and the smell of rain was in the air.

He went slowly. Using his flashlight, he found the tracks the motorcycle had made. He'd gone twenty, maybe thirty yards before he'd heard the shot that hit Horatio. If he followed the tracks, he'd find Benjamin.

He hoped for Lisa's sake that she hadn't killed him. He knew her pretty well now, knew that no matter how justified it might have been, the fact that she had killed a man would haunt her for the rest of her life. Besides, Benjamin was worth more to him alive than dead because he knew where Montoya was.

Sam moved silently through the trees just in case Benjamin hadn't been hurt as badly as he'd first thought. He reached the place where he was pretty sure he'd left Lisa. He stopped and looked around. There wasn't any sign of Benjamin.

He walked in an ever-widening circle around the area, sure he was close to the spot where Lisa had shot Benjamin. Could he be wrong? He went back to where he'd first looked, leaned down and, with his flashlight, carefully studied the ground.

The leaves had been flattened, part of a fern broken off. He held the flashlight closer. Some of the leaves were stained with blood.

Benjamin had been here, but now he was gone.

Either he'd walked out or someone had dragged him out. But who? My God, who?

Lisa was out on the porch waiting for Sam when he wheeled the Harley up to the steps.

"Oh, no," she whispered when she saw he was alone. "He was dead, wasn't he?"

He hauled the machine up onto the porch before he answered. "No, he wasn't dead."

"Then—then where is he?"

He wiped a hand across his face. "Damned if I know."

She stared at him. "What do you mean? What are you talking about?"

"He was gone when I got there."

"Maybe—maybe you were in the wrong place." Her voice rose. "He had to be there."

"He wasn't. He's gone." He gripped her arms. "Come back in the house, Lisa."

"If you looked...if he wasn't there, then—then somebody took him away." She stared at him, her eyes wide with fear. "There's somebody else here. Somebody who—"

"Stop it!" He put his arms around her and held her close. "If Horatio is all right, we'll leave in the morning. I'll find a phone so I can call Hargreaves. We'll get you somewhere safe."

"I won't leave you."

"You'll do what I say." He gripped her arms. "Don't you understand?" he said, anger and frustration catching up with him. "I couldn't stand it if anything happened to you. From now on you'll do what I tell you. You shouldn't have left the house tonight. If you hadn't, none of this would have happened."

"But Benjamin was here in Trinity," she protested. "If I'd been in the house alone he might have..." The thought terrified her. She swayed toward Sam and he tightened his arms around her.

"It's okay," he said. "It's okay, Lisa, baby." He held her close, then picked her up and carried her into the house and laid her down on the straw mat where Horatio and Delight had been sleeping. There was no lantern here, only the light from two candles.

"I'm here," he said. "Nothing's going to hurt you." He smoothed the hair back from her face. "I have to check on Horatio. Will you be all right for a couple of minutes?"

Lisa nodded. "Go ahead, Sam. I'm okay now."

"Good girl." He kissed her. "I'll be right back."

Horatio was asleep. Sam put a hand on his forehead. It was cool to his touch; there wasn't any fever.

"He goin' to be all right?" Delight whispered.

"Yes, I'm sure he will be." Sam handed her a couple of aspirins he'd taken out of the first-aid kit earlier. "If he wakes up, give him these."

"Thank you for helping him, Mr. Sam."

"You and Horatio took us in when we needed help. It's me who should be thanking you." Sam rested a hand on her shoulder. "Your Horatio's a good man," he said.

"That he is. We been together over thirty years. Couldn't hardly live without him."

"You won't have to."

He went out and closed the door. Lisa was sitting up on the mat, her back against the wall.

"How is he?" she asked.

"He's okay. No fever."

"Thank God." She patted the mat. "You'd better get some sleep, Sam."

"Yeah." He yawned. "It's been a doozy of a day. The guy that fixes tires wasn't there when we got to the village. We hung around for three or four hours before he showed up. Then it took him another couple of hours to fix it." He shook his head. "He did the best he could, but I'm not sure how long the tire will last." He stretched and yawned again. "I'm going to take a shower," he said, and with a grin teased, "Care to join me?"

"If you promise not to take advantage of me." She smiled. It was a weak smile, but the fact that she made the effort meant she was feeling better.

He poked a finger at his chest. "*Moi?* Take advantage of you? My dear, how could you think such a thing?" He reached down, pulled her up beside him, gave her a bear hug and said, "I kinda like you, little lady."

It wasn't a declaration of undying love, but it was something.

The water in the shower was still warm from the heat of the day. They stood under it for a few moments, just holding each other, before they bathed. He teased her a little, drawing soap foam out from the tips of her breasts and blowing the bubbles away. But that's all he did because he knew she was near exhaustion. So even though he wanted to fool around, he didn't. Instead he turned and said, "Wash my back."

When they came out of the shower, she put the floursack nightgown on and he wrapped a towel around his waist. "Feel like I could sleep for a week." He stretched, then draped his arm around her shoulder. "Hope you don't mind the accommodations tonight."

"They're fine," Lisa said. "Horatio and Delight have been sleeping on the floor ever since we arrived. If they didn't mind, neither will I."

They reached the front room and she lay down on one of the mats. Sam stood over her. "You going to take your nightgown off?"

Lisa shook her head. "Delight might come out. I'd better not."

"You could put it within grabbing distance. I like to feel you naked beside me, but if you don't want to..."

"It isn't that I don't want to."

"Then do it."

"You're a tough man to argue with." She pointed to the candles. When he blew them out, she took her gown off and they lay down together.

"This is more like it," he said when she came into his arms. He held her without speaking. "You've had a bad time, Lisa. I'm sorry."

"If only I knew that I haven't killed him."

"He was alive when we left him. Maybe he walked out by himself." Maybe, but he doubted it. Which meant that there'd been somebody else with Benjamin, somebody who knew that he and Lisa were here. If Horatio was all right in the morning, he and Lisa were going to get the hell out of Trinity.

"Sam." She sat up. "Sam, I just remembered something Benjamin said. He told me he'd take me to Port Antonio. He said maybe his boss would want to kill me, but that he'd take me with him on the boat so that—so that I could entertain them on the way to South America."

"Son of a bitch," Sam said under his breath.

She started shaking again. "I'd have jumped overboard before I let them lay a hand on me."

He put his arms around her. "It's all over, Lisa. You're safe."

She caressed his face. "Make love to me, Sam. Help me to forget everything that's happened tonight—the things I saw at the voodoo ceremony. Benjamin. And poor Horatio lying wounded in the next room. Let's pretend for a little while that none of it ever happened. I want—"

"I know what you want." He kissed her eyelids, her nose, her mouth. He trailed a line of kisses over her ears and down to her throat. And tightened his arms around her because he knew he never wanted to let her go.

He kissed her shoulders and her breasts. He nuzzled his head into her tummy and circled her navel with his tongue. She held his head as he rose to take one hard nipple between his teeth, and gripped his shoulders when he buried his head between her breasts.

She said, "Oh, Sam. Oh, darling."

She made as though to move under him and he said, "Not yet, my Lisa. Tonight is for you, sweetheart."

He feathered kisses along her ribcage and her belly and over the rise of her hips. He parted her legs and ran hot kisses along the inside of her thighs.

"Sam?" A whisper of sound. Of passion and uncertainty. "Sam?"

He gently cupped, then kissed her. "It's all right." He took the hands that might try to push him away and held them to her sides when he began to kiss her.

She tried to pull away, but he wouldn't let her. Not until she said, "I have to touch you. Let me touch you."

When he released her, she laced her fingers through his hair. "Oh, Sam," she said.

She'd never known anything like this before. She was on fire, whimpering in ecstasy, clutching his shoulders, whispering his name over and over again.

He reached up to caress her breasts and squeezed the tips between his fingers. Her body rose, yearning, straining. But he said, "Not yet, Lisa. Not yet, little love."

He stroked her hips. He made her wait. But when he touched her like that again it was too much. A shock ran through her. Her body lifted and soared. She pressed a hand over her mouth to stifle the scream that rose in her throat.

He came up over her. Into her. "Again," he whispered. "Again for me, Lisa."

"Sam!" His name was a strangled whisper in the quiet of the room. She was out of control, his to do with as he would. She lifted her body to his and held him as he held her.

Together they raced toward that final moment. She couldn't bear it, had to bear it because this was Sam and because she loved him. Loved him.

"Tell me." He moved against her. "Tell me, Lisa."

But there were no words, for this—this that was happening to her—went beyond words, beyond thought. There was only feeling, an emotion too big for words. She clung to him. She kissed him and, when she did, it happened for both of them, fast and hot and so unbearably good she wept.

He kissed her mouth; he kissed her tears. And held her as though he would never let her go.

Chapter 15

The following morning Horatio sat up in bed and declared he was hungry enough to eat a whale all by himself, but he'd settle for half-a-dozen fried eggs and a couple of plaintains.

Sam checked his leg. The small incision looked good and the skin around the wound was cool. He put a clean bandage on, told Horatio he'd better stay in bed for the day, and that he was almost as good as new.

"Lisa and I are going to head out this morning," he said when he finished.

"I be mighty sorry to see you and your missus go."

His missus. Sam wasn't sure how he felt about that. Sometimes, like last night, he wished she was, wished he could look forward to a whole forty or fifty years of the kind of wondrous joy they'd shared only a few hours ago.

Their bed had been a mat on the floor, but it hadn't mattered, not as long as they were together. He adored her warmth and her passion. Maybe he even loved her.

But he'd made a mistake about marriage once, and he didn't want to make the same mistake again. He was a cautious man, he told himself, not one to rush into things.

"We have to leave this morning," he said to Horatio. "I have some things to take care of."

"Uh-huh." Horatio raised his eyebrows. "I don't believe you be just vacationing. You act like maybe you be a policeman."

Sam nodded. "That's what I am, Horatio. I should have told you before. I had no right to involve you in this without telling you."

"You didn't involve me. I just happened to get in the way of a bullet." His blue eyes were curious. "Did you shoot the fella that was chasing your woman?"

"Yes." He didn't want Horatio to know it had been Lisa who pulled the trigger.

"He dead?"

"I don't know."

"You don't know? But you went looking for him last night."

Sam snapped the first-aid kit shut and went to stand by the window. "I found the place where he'd fallen when I shot him, but he wasn't there. I don't think he could have managed to walk out by himself. He had to have somebody working with him."

Horatio looked hard at Sam and after a moment's hesitation asked, "You with some kind of drug agency?"

Now it was Sam's turn to hesitate. But because he respected Horatio and owed him an honest answer, he said, "Yes, I am."

"'Cause some folks hereabouts grow a little ganja."

"No." Sam shook his head. "I'm after bigger game, an escaped murderer who's part of a group that's manufacturing something a lot more dangerous than ganja."

"This man you're after, he be killing people?"

"A lot of people."

"Then goin' after him be mighty dangerous business."

"I'm not alone, Horatio, I'm working with the Jamaican police. I was supposed to meet them in Maroon Town, but the man who shot you yesterday got there first. Lisa was injured, and I had to bring her here."

"You goin' back to Maroon Town when you leave?"

Sam nodded. "I have to." He counted out five twenties and handed them to Horatio. "I hope this is enough. I've got to keep some in case I need it."

"It be more than enough, 'specially since you had to sleep on the floor last night."

"It was okay. We didn't mind."

"Bet you didn't at that." Horatio chuckled. "'Peers to me with a pretty little missus like you got it don't matter where you sleep, so long's the two of you are together."

The two of them. Together.

He shook Horatio's hand. Lisa came in to say goodbye. She was dressed in the T-shirt and cutoff jeans Delight had mended. She looked as fresh and as beautiful as though she'd slept all night in a feather bed instead of in his arms on a mat on the floor.

She kissed Horatio's cheek and hugged Delight. These wonderful people had taken them in. She would never forget them.

Sam took her hand to lead her outside. "Ready?" he asked.

Ready, but reluctant to say goodbye.

Delight came out onto the porch with them. "You be careful," she told Sam. "You be taking good care of your missus."

"I will." Sam put his arm around Lisa and helped her onto the back of the Harley.

Lisa waved another goodbye. As they headed out of the village, she turned to look back one more time before they took the narrow path that led to the road that would take them back to Maroon Town.

There were only a couple of small trucks on the road this morning. Both of them were loaded with breadfruit and cassavas. "For the market in Kingston," Sam said.

This was wild and rugged country, hauntingly beautiful with all kinds of lush, green plants growing along the road and up the mountain slopes. Now and then on a turn in the road they could see the turquoise sea below, a cruise ship, a few fishing boats.

In spite of everything that had happened, Lisa didn't regret coming to Jamaica. It was beautiful, an island in the sun, and when this was over she wanted to come back. She wanted to lie on a beach with Sam, swim in the sea with him, dance under the stars with him. Make love with him.

He had never said he loved her. Perhaps for him the word did not come as easily as it did for her, or perhaps he hadn't fallen in love with her as she had with him. Maybe in time he would. Falling in love might be difficult for a man like Sam. He had his work, which meant so much to him. And he'd been married before. Maybe he'd decided he never would again.

And he'd lost a child. How terrible that must have been.

She wanted children. She'd told Philip that before they'd married, and he had agreed. "At least three," he'd said. But almost as soon as the minister had said the words uniting them as man and wife, he'd changed his mind. "Let's wait a few years," he'd said. A few years became seven.

She'd love to have Sam's children. The thought that she might already be pregnant was a little frightening, yet it excited her. She'd stopped taking birth-control pills when she and Philip separated. There hadn't been any need to take them because she'd had absolutely no intention of being intimate with anbody else for a very long time. She needed peace, time to search for direction. Time to rebuild her life.

This with Sam had happened so fast there hadn't been a chance to run to her friendly neighborhood pharmacy to refill a prescription. She wasn't a fool; she'd known the risk she was running. Yet she hadn't had the willpower to stay away from him.

She leaned her face against his back and tightened her arms around his waist. And wondered what he'd say if she really was pregnant. Would he blow a fuse? Head for the hills? Or would he make an honest woman out of her?

The Harley slowed and she saw that they had almost reached Maroon Town. Ahead, under the shade of bamboo trees, was a roadside stand that sold roasted corn and beer and soft drinks.

"I'll leave you there while I go into town," Sam said.

"No."

He pulled to the side of the road, climbed off the motorcycle and tried to look ferocious. "Did you say no?"

"You bet I did. If you think you're going to leave me sitting here while you go back to the hotel, you've got

another think coming. Every time you leave me alone
something awful happens to me. From now on I'm
sticking with you.''

"No, you're not." It was said with his chin thrust out
and his eyes narrowed angrily. "For all I know, Montoya and his men might be sitting in the hotel lobby.''

"And for all you know they might be sitting behind the
bamboo trees waiting to grab me." She shook her head
and, with a grin, said, "From now on I'm sticking with
you, Sam. Through thick and thin, till death us do..."

He stepped back as though he'd received a mortal
blow. Lisa didn't know whether to laugh or cry. Bullets
or bad guys didn't scare him, but the words *till death us
do part* made him blanch. She wondered what he would
do if she told him she was pregnant. Smite his chest and
faint dead away?

She had a few unpleasant thoughts about men in general, but managed to keep them to herself. "I'm staying
with you," she said. "And that's *final.*"

He'd been right about her. She might be little but she
packed a powerful punch. He had a sudden vision of her
squaring off, small fists doubled up at her hips, saying,
"Pick up your socks. Take the garbage out. Clean the
garage. And that's *final.*" God help him!

"Okay," he said, knowing he'd lost the battle. "But if
I tell you to stay put, you stay put. Got it?"

"Of course." She smiled, sweet as a piece of sugar cane
now that she'd gotten her way.

He was ticked off when he got back on the Harley, but
the minute she put her arms around his waist his anger
vanished. He didn't want to deal with his feelings right
now, but once this was over he had a lot of thinking to
do.

Ten minutes later they drove into Maroon Town. He parked the Harley at the open-air restaurant next to the hotel. There were other people there so he was pretty sure Lisa would be okay.

"I'm going into the hotel," he told her. "You go to the restaurant."

"You could pin a star on my chest and make me your deputy."

"I'd like to pin something on you all right."

Lisa stood on her tiptoes and kissed him. "Anytime, anywhere, partner."

"You're a shameless wench."

"Damn straight," she said. "If you need backup, holler out."

"Yeah, right."

He started to turn away, but she grabbed his arm. "Be careful, Sam."

"I always am."

They looked at each other, She snapped his a salute. He turned and walked quickly to the hotel next door. She watched him go, then went to the outdoor restaurant.

The man behind the counter looked up when she came in. He seemed to study her for a moment before he said, "Be with you in a minute, lady."

"That's all right," Lisa said. "I'm not in a hurry."

He left the counter and went into the back, where she couldn't see him. The three other customers, all men, looked at her curiously. She nodded, then turned her attention toward the hotel, hoping and praying that Captain Hargreaves was still there, and that, if he wasn't, he would have left one of his men.

But what if, instead of the Jamaican police, some of Montoya's men were there? What if Sam was walking into a trap? She wanted to be with him. He'd told her to

stay here and she would. For a while. Fifteen minutes. If
he wasn't out by then she'd go looking for him.

The counterman came back. "What you be havin'?"
he asked.

"Hot tea if you have it."

"I have it."

He went back behind the counter and Lisa turned to
watch the hotel entrance again. It was all she could do not
to get up and go after Sam. When the man returned with
the tea, she asked for a piece of lemon.

"We got lime," he said.

"That's fine."

He brought it, and she squeezed some of the juice into
the cup. The man didn't move. He just stood there
watching her.

"You want anything else?" he asked.

"No, thank you."

He stood there a moment longer before he turned and
went back behind the counter.

She sipped the tea and worried about Sam, wanting
desperately to go charging into the hotel after him. She
wasn't comfortable here alone. The waiter kept watching her; the other three men whispered among themselves. She drank half of her tea. It was good, with an
odd flavor that she found intriguing.

A breeze came in through the open sides of the restaurant, but she was warm. From the hot tea, she supposed.
She took a tissue out of her bag and wiped her face.

Heat waves rose up from the street and everything began to look a little fuzzy.

She took another sip of tea. Suddenly her stomach felt
queasy and she felt dizzy. Maybe this was morning sickness. But it wasn't morning. Something was happening.
It was hard to... to keep her eyes open.

She looked toward the counter. The man behind it was staring at her, as though he was waiting for her to say or do something.

She said, "May I—may I have a glass of—of water?" Her voice was slurred. She looked down at her cup. The tea was all gone.

She pushed back the chair. Had to get to Sam. Sam could help her. Sam ... She tried to stand. Knees wobbly ... legs like wet noodles. She looked toward the three men. Their faces were indistinct. She said, "Oh," and felt herself starting to slip. She sank back down in the chair, whispered, "Help ..."

Then the darkness closed in all around her.

The same man was at the reception desk. He looked up, startled, when Sam strode in, and reached for the phone. Sam ran across the lobby, stretched his arm over the desk and grabbed the man by the front of his shirt.

"Let me go!" the man cried. "Take your hands off me."

Sam belted him across the face with the back of his other hand. "I'm looking for a man by the name of Hargreaves," he said. "Is he still here?"

"What are you doing? Let me—"

Sam hit him again. "Is he still here?" he repeated.

"He—he and his friends left two days ago."

"Anybody with him stay behind?"

"No." The man's eyes were wide and frightened.

Sam let him go and reached for his gun. "Put your hands on your head and stand right there where I can see you," he said. "You make one move and you'll be singing soprano for the rest of your life."

He picked up the phone and dialed Kingston. "Hargreaves," he said when somebody answered.

"Who shall I say is calling, sir."

"O'Shaughnessy. Hurry it up."

"Yes, sir. Right away, sir."

The desk clerk sidled toward the door leading into the private office. In a deceptively soft voice Sam said, "Stop right there."

The man froze.

Hargreaves came on the line. "Sam?" he yelled into the phone. "My God, Sam, is that you?"

"Yeah. Finally."

"Where are you?"

"At the hotel in Maroon Town. Just got here."

"Where have you been? Why didn't you wait for me?"

"Somebody nabbed Lisa. I had to go after her. I got her and headed farther up into the mountains. Knew I couldn't wait around until you got here." He looked at the man with his arms on his head. "The guy who works here behind the desk is in on it. So's the waiter in the restaurant. As soon as you can you'd better send some of your men to pick them up."

"Is the woman still with you?"

"Yeah, and I'm going to keep her with me until somebody from your office can get her to Kingston where she'll be safe."

"Let me think a minute."

"Take all the time you need." Sam leveled the gun at the desk clerk. "I'm not going anywhere."

"All right, Sam, here's what we'd better do. Time's running out. We've got to get Montoya before he sends the shipment and skips the country. Do you still have the motorcycle?"

"Yes."

"Then you'd better head toward Port Antonio. I'll meet you there with backup. Fort Royal Hotel. Meantime I'll send a couple of men to Maroon Town to clean out the hotel.'' Hargreaves hesitated. "I don't like the idea of the woman being with you. It could be dangerous for her.''

"I can't leave her here.''

"All right then. As soon as you get to Port Antonio I'll assign one of my men to her. How soon can you leave Maroon Town?''

"I'm leaving right away. Lisa's next door. I'll pick her up and we're on our way''

"Be careful, Sam. It's beginning to look as if there are more people involved in this than we first thought.''

"Don't worry. See you in a couple of hours.'' Sam put the phone down, ripped the cord off it and said to the clerk, "Okay, bozo, hands behind your back.''

"You can't do this,'' the man protested. "You don't have the authority.''

"Wanna bet?'' Sam came around the counter to jerk the clerk's hands behind his back. When he'd tied them, he pushed the man toward the private office. Before he could open the door he heard a footstep, a scraping sound. He turned and saw the waiter, saw the gun in his hand. He shoved the desk clerk to the side just as the waiter fired. He heard the *whomp* as the bullet meant for him hit the clerk.

Sam crouched down. He got off a shot. The waiter stumbled back, clutched his shoulder and fired again. So did Sam. This time the man went down for good.

Two down. He wasn't sure how many more might be around, just knew he had to get the hell out of here.

He put the gun in his pocket, but kept his hand on it. A couple of dozen men were standing in front of the hotel when he went out. Nobody said anything. He elbowed past them and strode into the open-air restaurant next door. Lisa wasn't there.

Dammit to hell! Why couldn't she just once do what he told her to do? He'd told her to stay put. Why hadn't she?

"There was a woman here," he said to the man behind the counter. "Where'd she go?"

The man shrugged. "That not be my business."

Sam's jaws clenched. He walked over to the man, slowly, deliberately. He'd had one hell of a morning. He wasn't in the mood to fool around.

"I'm going to ask you one more time, pal. If I don't get an answer, I'm going to climb over the counter and beat the crap out of you. Where did the lady go?"

The man backed away. "She—she ask me if there be a shop for ladies. Maybe she go look in the shops."

Sam swore under his breath. Lisa knew they were in a dangerous situation, but she hadn't listened. She'd gone shopping! He wanted to throttle her. Would as soon as he caught up with her.

He hurried out of the restaurant and looked up and down the street. There were two stores. One looked like it might be a general store, the other had clothing in the window. He went there first.

There were no customers, only a bored-looking young woman who gave him a stem-to-stern once-over when he entered.

"I'm looking for a young woman," he said.

She fluffed her curly black hair. "Nobody here but me. Will I do?"

He looked her over. Cute. Skin the color of polished mahogany. Tight red blouse, black skirt halfway up to her hiney.

"Sorry, honey," he said, "but I'm afraid not. My wife'd cut my heart out if I even looked at anybody else. Especially somebody like you." He glanced around the room. "She's small and blond. She was probably here in the last twenty minutes or so."

"Hasn't been nobody but me here all mornin'."

"Is this the only clothing store?"

She nodded. "But they sell some things down at the general store. Maybe she's there."

"Okay. Thanks."

"If she isn't you can always come back here. I got no plans for the rest of the day."

"I'll keep it in mind."

He muttered under his breath all the way to the general store. They had to get going. If they didn't they'd be stuck on the road to Port Antonio after dark. He didn't want that. Damn the woman! Where was she?

He pushed open the door of the general store. There were a couple of people at the counter. One woman was buying coffee. Lisa wasn't there. He went up to them.

"'Afternoon," he said. "I'm sorry to bother you, but I'm looking for my wife. She's a small blond woman. Has she been in here?"

"No, sir," the man behind the counter said. "No lady like that been in today."

Where was she? His anger was all mixed up with fear now. What if something had happened to her? This was the middle of the day. She'd been in an open-air restaurant. What could have happened?

He said, "Thanks," and went out of the store. He looked up and down the street. Where could she have gone? Where was she?

"Hey, mister!"

He turned and saw the young woman from the clothing store hurrying toward him.

He waited until she caught up with him. "What is it?" he said when she did.

"A man came into the store almost soon's you left. He gave me this envelope and told me to give it to you." She handed it to him. "He said it was important."

"Thanks." The young woman started to turn away, but he said, "Wait a minute." He tore open the envelope and pulled out the folded paper inside.

We got your lady. She's our insurance. You plan on seeing her again you take the first plane out of Jamaica. Sooner you be gone better it be for everybody, most 'specially for the lady. It be real shame if we gotta cut her throat.

He felt like the wind had been knocked out of him. As though his insides were made of mush. He stood there, crumpling the note in his hands. Lisa. My God, they had Lisa!

"Are you all right?" The girl was looking up at him. "You feeling bad?"

Sam tried to focus. "Who gave this to you?"

"Mean-looking dude."

"Jamaican?"

She nodded.

"Have you got a phone?"

"Yes, but—"

He grabbed her arm and hustled her down the street. "I've got to use it," he said. "It's important."

"Somethin' bad happening?"

"Something real bad."

They went into the store and she handed him the phone. He called Kingston. "This is O'Shaughnessy. Has Captain Hargreaves left yet?"

"A moment, sir. I'll see if I can catch him."

Sam went silently crazy while he waited. Lisa had been right: he shouldn't have left her alone. He should have taken a chance on keeping her with him, no matter how dangerous it might have been.

They were using her to get at him. Get rid of him. If anything happened to her he'd never forgive himself. She'd been through hell because of him. They'd grabbed her because of him. They might—

"Sam?" It was Hargreaves's voice. "What's happening?"

"They've got Lisa."

"Good Lord!"

"I just got a note telling me to leave the country. They said if I didn't . . ." For a minute Sam couldn't go on. "They said they'd kill her." He gripped the phone so hard his knuckles popped. "I'm going after her, leaving now."

"Maybe you'd better let us handle it."

"But they've got Lisa!" he shouted.

"Yes, yes, I understand. We're leaving now, Sam. We'll be in Port Antonio before you. Check in with my men as soon as you get there."

"Yeah, sure. But listen, wait till I get there before you go in."

"If we can."

"Filoberto?"

"Yes?"

"I know you've got a job to do, but Lisa's life is at stake. She . . ." Sam stopped. "She means a lot to me."

"I understand, Sam. Believe me, we'll do everything we can to keep her from getting hurt."

"Okay. I'm on my way. See you in Port Antonio." He put the phone down.

The young woman was staring at him. "You be a policeman?" she asked.

"Yes."

"Something bad happen to your wife?"

His wife. The word brought a knot to his throat so big he couldn't swallow. "Yeah," he managed to say. "She's my wife."

He handed the girl a twenty. "For the phone call," he said.

She followed him to the door. "You be careful."

He leaned down and kissed her cheek. Because she was a good kid; because she'd been kind.

He headed for the motorcycle.

There was a small group of men and boys around it. He pushed through them and they fell back, afraid of the cold, white fury they saw on his face.

He got on the Harley, turned the ignition and gunned the motor. The men and the boys cleared out of the way. He saw the shop girl standing in her doorway. She waved. He waved back and rode down the street toward the road to Port Antonio.

"Lisa," he said when he got on the road. "Hold on, baby. I'm coming."

Chapter 16

Voodoo drums were beating in her head. *Tum* tum tum, *tum* tum tum—they were pounding against her skull. Sick to her stomach. Bed rocking. Had to tell Sam to make it stop. Sam? She tried to reach out for him, but something was the matter with her hands.

"Sam?" she said again, and when he didn't answer, she opened her eyes. She was in a cubbyhole of a room she'd never seen before. Dizzying shadows wobbled back and forth from a swaying lantern that hung from a chain at one end. Were lanterns supposed to sway?

She tried to sit up, but she couldn't seem to move her hands, couldn't pull them apart. She tried to focus and saw that her wrists were tied together. Tied? Her wrists were tied?

"Sam!" she cried out in panic. "Sam, where are you?"

There was no answer; she was alone. But where? My God, where was she?

She closed her eyes and took a couple of deep breaths. Calm down, she told herself. Try to think. If only her head didn't ache. No, forget your head. Try to remember. You and Sam went back to Maroon Town. He went to the hotel but he wouldn't let you go with him, so you went into an open-air restaurant and had a cup of tea. Okay so far. But what happened after that? You drank the tea and ... and what? She didn't remember anything after that.

She stared up at the swaying lantern. What made it sway? Why was she in bed? No, not a bed. Too narrow for a bed. A bunk bed? Yes, a bunk. Like on a boat.

She was on a boat. Sam wasn't here. She was alone and her hands were tied. Panic stunned her; fear choked her. She tried to sit up, tried to put both hands to her side to push herself up. When that didn't work she bent her knees and rolled to a sitting position, feeling dizzy, disoriented when she did. Lisa took deep breaths. She couldn't be sick, wouldn't be sick. If only the drums inside her head would stop! No, don't think about that, think about getting away.

There was nothing in the room except a bolted-down chair. Some clothes were wadded up on the floor in the corner. The round porthole, basketball-size, was closed.

She struggled with the rope that bound her wrists and twisted her hands back and forth to loosen it. She pulled at the knots with her teeth, but stopped when she heard footsteps outside the door. Somebody coming.

She tried with every bit of willpower she had to quell the sheer terror that threatened to overcome her.

Howard Reitman opened the door and came into the cabin.

He said, "Are you all right?"

"No!" Lisa cried. "Help me! Untie me."

"I—I can't, Lisa." He forced a smile and in what seemed like a too-cheerful voice said, "But I've brought a bottle of water. I thought you might be thirsty. Would you like a drink?"

She wanted to tell him to take his water and get out. But she was too thirsty to resist the offer. "Yes," she said. "Yes, please."

He held the bottle to her lips and she took a small sip, not sure it would stay down. When it did she drank more. "Okay," she said. "That's enough."

He put the bottle on the floor beside the bunk. "I'm sorry about this," he said.

"Are you?"

"I didn't want you to get involved. You wouldn't have if you hadn't been running around with O'Shaughnessy. It's his fault you're in this mess."

"His fault? He's not the one who's smuggling drugs." Lisa glared at him. "How could you get mixed up in this, Howard? How could you be associated with a man like Juan Montoya? You're Philip's friend. How could you..." She stopped. "Is—is Philip mixed up in this?"

"Philip? Of course not. I bought art and Philip helped me choose things that would go up in value. I don't know anything about art—what's good, what's bad. Philip did. We needed him."

"We. So even then you were working for Montoya." She tried to keep her anger—no, more than anger, her disgust—from showing. She had to stay calm, to think clearly. Even though he was mixed up in this, Howard was Philip's friend. He liked her. She had to convince him to help her. But it was hard to control her indignation.

"All those times you came to our house for dinner, you were mixed up in the drug trade," she said. "The paintings Philip helped you to buy were bought with drug money. You didn't give a damn about art, did you? You were only interested in laundering—is that what you call it?—laundering dirty money."

"Everybody's got to make a living." Reitman lowered his voice to a conspiratorial whisper. "You don't have any idea of the kind of money we're talking about. Hundreds of thousands of dollars, Lisa. Millions. A man can make a fortune in a couple of years. You just don't understand the way it works. It's just a business. I'm not hurting anybody."

Lisa thought of Sam's son dying of an overdose, of other kids, of crack babies, of men and women whose lives were ruined because of the drugs men like Howard and Juan Montoya dealt in. All the money in the world wouldn't buy back a lost or ruined life. A million dollars wouldn't return Sam's son to him.

"You're right, Howard," she said. "I don't understand."

"I feel read bad about this, Lisa. About you, I mean. I wish you hadn't gotten mixed up in it."

"But I am mixed up in it." And because she had to know, Lisa asked, "What's going to happen to me?"

"That—that isn't up to me. Montoya's the boss. He's hard to figure. I'll talk to him, though. Maybe because you're a friend of mine he'll..." He looked away, embarrassed.

"He'll maybe let me live? Is that what you're afraid to say?"

"This is a bad business, Lisa. You shouldn't have gotten involved."

"That's it? I shouldn't have, but I did, and so now somebody's going to kill me?"

He turned away.

"You could untie me," she said. "You could let me escape."

"And go where? Jump overboard?"

"That's better than sitting here waiting for somebody else to throw me over." She swallowed. "Please, Howard. With my hands untied I'd at least have a chance."

He shook his head. "I can't, Lisa. You're our insurance."

"What?" She looked at him and shook her head. "What are you talking about? I don't understand."

"We're holding you until we're sure O'Shaughnessy has left the country." He sat on the bunk beside her. "Look," he said. "We had to get him off our trail. If he knows we've got you, there's a chance he'll leave Jamaica. I know the Jamaican police are after us, too, but it's O'Shaughnessy that Montoya is worried about."

Howard covered her hands with one of his own. "I like you, Lisa. I always have. I told you before that if I'd known you and Philip were splitting, I'd have moved in on you like a grasshopper after a June bug. If I could talk Juan into letting you come with us—"

Lisa pulled away from him. "What are you talking about?"

"If you . . . you know. If you let me . . . I mean, if you and I were together, maybe Juan would let you go with us to South America." He put his arms around her and pulled her closer. "I'm nuts about you, Lisa."

"Howard, please . . ."

"There're two boats waiting for us in Port Antonio," he went on. "As soon as the shipment leaves, we'll set sail for Venezuela. You can come with me, Lisa. I'll take care of you. I'll buy you anything you ever wanted. We'll have a house, a boat, anything. Everything."

"Let me go."

"Lisa, listen—"

"No, you listen," she said, so angry she could barely get the words out. "I don't want you or your house or your boat. I'd rather be shark bait than ever have you touch me."

He recoiled as though she'd slapped him. He gripped her arms and shook her so hard she cried out and put her hands to her head to try to stop the pain there.

"You're not going to be shark bait," he said. "Not yet. We're saving you in case your boyfriend O'Shaughnessy shows up. If he cares anything at all about you maybe he'll think twice about trying to take us."

"You bastard."

He grabbed a handful of her hair and, with his face so close to her she could see a vein pulsing in his forehead, said, "It's your last chance, Lisa. I mean the difference between life and death for you."

His eyes were narrowed, his forehead damp with perspiration. She looked at the little, pursed mouth, the weak chin. Calmly, quietly she said, "There are ways to live and ways to die, Howard. I guess I'd rather die if living meant ever having you touch me."

He shoved her away with such force that her head hit the side of the bunk. The pain sickened her. He started toward the door.

"I—I can barely breathe in here," she managed to say, "Would you open the porthole?"

He looked at her for a moment. "Go to hell," he said, and left the cabin.

She leaned against the wall. Her eyes stung, but she didn't cry. Instead she said, "Sam," and drew comfort from the sound of his name.

Had he left Jamaica? Was he right now on a plane flying away from here, away from her? Somehow she didn't think so. He'd come here after Montoya and wouldn't leave until he caught him. Or until one of them was dead.

He would know, just as she knew, that Montoya was going to kill her whether he left Jamaica or not.

She wept then, not from fear of dying, but for what she would miss by dying. A life with Sam. Loving Sam. The children she would have had.

In a little while she stopped crying and tried to think. She wasn't dead yet, and while there was life, there was hope. She had to find a way to escape, a way to help Sam. She had to.

It was after dark by the time he reached Port Antonio. He went directly to the Fort Royal Hotel, parked the motorcycle and went to the front desk.

"Yes," the man there said. "Captain Hargreaves checked in several hours ago."

Sam used the lobby phone. Hargreaves said, "Come right up. I've reserved a room for you next door to mine."

He took the elevator to the third floor. Hargreaves opened the door when Sam knocked. They shook hands. "Glad you got here safely," he said, and motioned Sam into the room. He indicated the other three men. "Gilbert Fairfax, Cyril Winston, Victor Brimo. This is Mr. O'Shaughnessy, gentlemen."

They shook hands with Sam, and Fairfax, about five-eight and built like a prizefighter, said, "Glad you're on our team, O'Shaughnessy."

"We heard about the woman," Victor Brimo said. "Sorry."

As if he'd already lost her, as if she was already dead. Sam didn't answer the guy. Instead he turned to Hargreaves. "What's happening?" he asked.

"I've got a man working undercover on the docks. The drugs will be put aboard a fishing boat bound for New Orleans a little before midnight. The *Santa Cecelia* sails at one."

"South America?"

"Venezuela."

"How many men have you got?"

"The four of us, you, and seven others already down on the docks unloading bananas and working as long-shoremen. Enough uniformed officers to stop a revolution."

"Any sight of Montoya?"

"No," the man named Cyril said. "We think he's coming down the coast by boat. It's my guess he's got Miss Collier with him. Probably Montoya grabbed her on the off chance that once you knew, you might leave the country. But he's no dummy, Mr. O'Shaughnessy. I honestly don't believe he had much hope that you'd walk away. He'll keep her around in case there's a showdown. If there is she's his bargaining chip."

A bargaining chip. His Lisa. His moonlight lady.

It took every bit of his professional experience to say, "Are there any lookout points along the coast? Any chance of spotting them before they reach Port Antonio?"

"Maybe," Filoberto said. "But I didn't want to spare the men that it would take. I thought it better to keep an eye on the fishing boat and the *Santa Cecelia*. That way I know we've got them."

"What about Reitman?" Sam asked. "Any sign of him?"

"No," Brimo said. "He's probably with Montoya."

Reitman knew Lisa. Maybe he wouldn't hurt her; maybe he'd try to keep her safe. Maybe he'd try to... No,

Sam told himself, don't think about that. If you do you'll go out of your mind. He couldn't help her if he fell apart. He had to think like a cop. God, how he wanted to get this over with.

"Would you like a spot of rum, Mr. O'Shaughnessy?" Gilbert Fairfax went to the dresser. "For all of us," he said. "One for the road, yes?"

"Yes, indeed," Hargreaves said. "Good idea."

They had a drink. Sam looked at his watch. "It's eleven-fifteen," he said.

Hargreaves nodded. "Do you need anything, Sam?"

"More ammo."

Brimo opened one of the dresser drawers. "Help yourself."

Sam reloaded his two guns and shoved extra clips into the pockets of his jeans. He put the Beretta in his shoulder holster and shoved the Magnum in his other pocket. "Let's get the hell out of here," he urged.

"Another ten minutes," Hargreaves cautioned. "We don't want to get there too early."

Sam paced the room. He tried to keep cool, tried to concentrate on the way it would go down. But all he could think about was Lisa and the funny little salute she'd given him the last time he'd seen her. She'd been right; he shouldn't have left her, should have kept her with him. If anything happened to her...

"Time," Hargreaves said.

The other men checked their weapons: two nine-millimeter Uzi's, AR-15 assault rifles. Gilbert Fairfax crossed himself, and with Hargreaves leading the way, they left the room.

A Jamaican Lisa had never seen before unlocked the cabin and came in.

"Stand up," he said, and jerked her to her feet.

"What is it?" she asked. "What are you—"

"Shut up." He yanked her around. "You the woman who shot Benjamin, ain't you?"

Terrified by what she saw in his eyes, Lisa said, "I—I don't know what you mean."

"Shot him twice. Left him lying there."

"Is he—is he dead?"

"What the hell you be caring?" With his open hand he slapped her across the side of her head. She staggered back, but didn't fall.

"I care," she whispered.

"Sure you do." He grabbed her wrists and turned her around. "No," he said. "Old Benjamin not dead. He's hurt real bad, but the doctor say he's not going to die."

He pushed her through the door into a passageway. She looked around and tried to get her bearings. Ahead there were stairs leading upward. "I have to go to the bathroom," she said.

He jerked his thumb. "There. But be quick."

She held out her hands. "You have to untie me."

He hesitated, then took a knife out of the pocket of his jeans and cut the rope that bound her wrists.

She went in the door he indicated. There was a toilet and a washstand with a mirror over it. She went to the toilet, then washed her hands and face. Her wrists hurt and she let the water run over them.

The man who'd come after her pounded on the door. "Hurry it up," he said. "We be goin' to dock."

Dock. Where were they? In Port Antonio, where they planned to take the ship to South America? Did that mean...? She looked at herself in the mirror. Did that mean that before they boarded they would...what? Dispose of her?

Lines of the Dylan Thomas poem came suddenly to her mind. She looked at her reflection in the mirror and whispered, "I will not go gentle into that good night. I will fight with all of my strength against these evil men."

In an act of defiance she patted her cheeks to bring a bit of color into them and, shoulders back, went out to meet the enemy.

The boat rocked, jolted, and there was a scraping sound as it bumped against the dock. The man who had come for Lisa gripped her arm and pushed her up the stairs onto the deck.

They were at a wharf. There was a single light. Next to the boat she was on was a smaller boat. A fishing boat? On the other side of it was a ship. It was the *Santa Cecelia*, obviously the ship Montoya and Reitman were going to sail to South America on.

Montoya, wearing a seaman's cap, jeans and a *guayabera*, stood next to Howard Reitman. Both men had rifles. Next to them were two Jamaicans armed with what looked to her like machine guns. Men she hadn't seen before were running down the gangplank, boxes on their shoulders, hurrying to the fishing boat. Drugs, she thought. Those are the drugs.

Montoya spotted her. *"Oye, cabrón,"* he said in Spanish to the man who held her. "Why did you untie her?"

"She had to go to the bathroom."

"Do you want her to get away? Tie her hands."

"I didn't bring the rope."

Montoya slapped his own forehead. *"¡Estúpido!"* he shouted. "What kind of men do I have working for me? Get something. Tie her. What if—"

There was a crackle of sound. A voice boomed over a loudspeaker. "This is an arrest! Stop where you are and throw down your weapons."

Below her Lisa saw uniformed men running out onto the wharf, other men with machine guns and rifles. She heard police cars, the wail of sirens. The amplified voice repeated, "This is an arrest. Do not try to resist."

The men aboard the ship froze. Those carrying boxes on their shoulders started to run. Shots were fired. Two of them fell. Another two jumped off the wharf into the water.

Howard screamed. "The police! They're here! Oh, my God! What are we going to do?"

"Start shooting, you son of a bitch!" Montoya ducked behind an iron beam and began firing. The two Jamaicans next to him lifted their machine guns. The man holding Lisa let her go and pulled a revolver out of his pocket. A bullet pinged near her head. She ducked down behind a stanchion.

Uniformed Jamaican police jumped down onto the fishing boat. Others ran along the wharf toward the vessel she was on. There were other men, too, not in uniform.

Lisa looked frantically around. Could she make a break for it? No, bullets were flying; she had to wait. Behind her someone screamed, and when she turned, she saw the man who had come to the cabin to get her clutch his chest and fall. A man next to Montoya was hit. Montoya grabbed his gun and fired at the uniformed men below.

Two more of his men were next to him, firing at the police. An officer went down. More of Montoya's men rushed onto the deck, firing as they came. But still the police advanced.

Howard Reitman crouched behind the railing, screaming, "They've got us! They've got us!"

Montoya swung around. "Shoot!" he cried. "Before I shoot you!"

But Reitman had lost it. Eyes gone blank and wide with fear, he scuttled on his hands and knees for the safety of the stairs. Montoya raised his gun and fired. Howard's body jerked. He pitched forward, facedown.

Lisa stared, too horrified to move. In the beam of the spotlight she looked at Montoya. He saw her. His face was evil, menacing. As she watched, he curled his finger around the trigger. And she knew he was going to kill her.

A shot pinged just above his head. He whirled around and started firing.

She was hollow with fear. The men below were closer now, running toward the gangplank, firing as they came. Dark men. All but one. She cried out, "Sam! Sam!" But in the terrible confusion of noise, he couldn't hear her.

He charged ahead of the uniformed men. She stepped out from behind the stanchion and cried again, "Sam!"

He looked up and saw her. "Get down!" he shouted.

Montoya turned and rushed at her. He grabbed her, his arm around her waist, and held her in front of him in a viselike grip. He screamed words in Spanish she didn't understand.

Sam started up the gangplank.

Lisa felt hard metal against her temple.

"Stop!" Montoya said. "Stop right there."

Sam looked up. The spotlight was behind him; his face was shadowed.

"Call your men off," Montoya ordered. "If you don't, *señor*, you got a dead woman on your hands."

"Back off," Sam said to the uniformed men behind him.

They retreated a few steps, guns at the ready.

"Now you," Montoya said. "Get the hell out of here."

Sam shook his head. "I'm not leaving, Montoya. Let the woman go. Give it up."

The Cuban didn't answer. Instead, without taking his gaze from Sam, he called out, "Pedro? Are you there?"

"*Sí, capitán.*"

"Engine working?"

"*Sí.*"

"Get the boat going."

Lisa heard a clunk and a rattle. The purr of an engine starting.

"We make a deal," Montoya said. "You back off. You let me go, maybe I don't shoot the woman."

Sam didn't move. "Take me in her place."

"No, I keep the woman till we're out where it's deep. Then maybe I keep her. Maybe I feed her to the fish."

"I'll throw my gun away." Sam lowered his weapon and tossed it over the side. He held empty hands, palms up, out from his sides.

He was unarmed, vulnerable. He took a step forward and Lisa felt Montoya's body tense. The drug lord took the gun from her temple and leveled it at Sam. She knew he was going to shoot.

"Do not go gentle into that good night...." That dark night...

She brought her right elbow back, flung herself sideways to pull his arm out of the way, twisted, then turned and ran toward Sam, arms outstretched to shield him.

Something hit her. A fist in her back. She staggered, but kept running, legs pumping in slow motion.

Sam reached out for her. He cried, "Lisa! Lisa!"

But she couldn't see him. The good light was dying, the night was dark....

Chapter 17

"Miss Collier?" Someone patted her cheek. "Wake up, Miss Collier."

Her eyelids fluttered. She opened her eyes, then closed them because the light was too bright and because she was so tired.

"Open your eyes, Lisa."

She opened them and saw him standing above her. "Sam? Oh, Sam. You're all right. You're here." She tried to raise her arm to touch him, but it hurt, everything hurt, and she cried out.

"Easy," a nurse with nice brown eyes said gently. "Don't try to move, Miss Collier."

"What's the matter with me?"

A doctor in a white coat stepped forward. "You've been shot," he said.

She looked up at Sam. "Is it bad? Am I going to die?"

He leaned down and, so that the doctor and nurse

couldn't hear, whispered, "Yeah, on your ninety-second birthday in the middle of a fantastic climax."

She laughed, but it cost her and she yelped in pain.

The nurse said, "Really, Mr. O'Shaughnessy!"

The doctor frowned. "You have a shoulder wound," he told Lisa. "It entered from the back. We've removed the bullet and I assure you you're going to be all right."

"But you need rest," the nurse said with a look at Sam. "We're taking you to your room now."

Sam kissed her forehead. "I have to go," he said. "There're things I've got to take care of, but I'll be back in a little while."

"Is Montoya . . . ?"

"He's alive."

"That's quite enough conversation for now," the doctor said. "We're going to give you something to help you rest, Miss Collier."

She felt a prick of a needle in her arm. Then Sam kissed her again, this time on the lips.

Lisa awoke to find Sam sitting beside her bed. Groggy from sleep and from the shot they'd given her for the pain, she managed to say, "Hi. How long have you been here?"

"Awhile. How do you feel?"

"Okay, I think." She looked at the IV hooked up to her arm. "Everybody's taking good care of me."

"They'd better."

He sat on the edge of the bed and took her hand.

"I won't break," she said.

Very carefully he put his arms around her. But he didn't say anything because holding her close this way he remembered how afraid he'd been last night. He'd re-played those last moments on the boat over and over again in his mind. The way Montoya had used her as a shield. How she'd broken away from him because she'd known that Montoya was going to shoot him. He could still hear the terrible force of the bullet that hit her and see the puzzled look on her face as she staggered toward him. She'd taken the bullet meant for him. That humbled him. It brought him to his knees.

He kissed her and eased her back down in the bed. "I've got to go to New York this afternoon," he said.

"New York?"

"I'm taking Montoya back."

She bit her lip. "He's dangerous, Sam."

"Not anymore. One of Hargreaves's men got him in the leg before he could take another shot at you. He'll be handcuffed to a stretcher and when we get to New York there'll be plenty of cops waiting to greet him."

"Be careful."

"Always am." He brushed the hair back from her face. "The doctor says you'll be out of her in a few days, but you're going to have to take it easy. Hargreaves will drive you back to the Poinciana. You're to stay there—courtesy of the Jamaican police—until you're feeling better." He looked at his watch. "I'm sorry, Lisa. But I've got to go."

She didn't want him to, but there wasn't anything she could do about it. "How long will you be gone? I...I mean, how long will everything take?"

"Don't know. There'll be paperwork to do and the guys at the DEA will be asking a lot of questions." He smoothed the hair back from her face and wished he had the words to tell her how he felt. The doc had said she was going to be okay, but her face was so pale, she looked small and helpless lying here with her shoulder bandaged and an IV hooked up to her wrist.

He touched her face. "I was so damn scared," he said. "When I saw you running toward me, when you were hit..."

"It's over, Sam. I'm going to be fine."

"Sure you are." He tried to sound tough because he knew if he yielded to all the emotions churning inside he'd be bawling like a baby. So he looked at his watch again and said, "Got a plane to catch."

She looked up at him, wanting with all her heart for him to tell her he loved her. But he just stood there, uncertain, stumble-footed, a little embarrassed. Anxious to leave.

"I'll try to get back to Jamaica before you leave," he said. "If I can't I'll probably see you in Miami."

Probably.

He leaned down and kissed her. She touched his face, then, because she didn't want to see him leave, she closed her eyes. And kept them closed until she could no longer hear his footsteps in the hall.

Three days later Lisa left the Kingston hospital. Filoberto Hargreaves drove her to Ocho Rios, where an ocean-front room had been reserved for her at the Poinciana. When they arrived, he took her to her room and introduced her to a young woman whose name was Euphemia.

"Euphemia works here in the hotel," he said. "I've arranged for her to take care of you."

"But I'm fine now," Lisa protested.

"Sam wants to be sure you take it easy. Euphemia will bring you your meals and help you any way she can until you're stronger."

"I be quiet like a mouse and I won't be gettin' underfoot," Euphemia said. "I'll help you when you need help and skedaddle when you don't."

She smiled and Lisa was hooked. "All right," she said. "As long as you don't mother-hen me."

"Cross my heart and hope to kiss a buzzard if I do."

Lisa laughed. "You win," she told Filoberto.

"The clothes you left are in the closet. If you need anything, call me."

"I will." She offered him her hand. He kissed it, then sighed and let it go.

When he'd gone, Euphemia ran her bath and helped her into the tub. After the bath she asked Lisa if she would like to have lunch out on the balcony or in her room. Lisa said she'd prefer the balcony. Euphemia phoned the restaurant and, after consulting Lisa, ordered a steak, medium rare, and a green salad.

It was the best food Lisa had had in almost two weeks. She ate every bite, and when she finished, Euphemia helped her to the bed.

"You sleep now," she said. "I'll be back later. If you want anything you call number 5 on the telephone."

That became the pattern of Lisa's next few days. She slept late, and when she awoke, Euphemia ran her bath and brought her breakfast. And later her lunch and her dinner.

At the end of the week she told Euphemia she was well enough to take care of herself, that she really preferred taking her meals in the restaurant, and that, yes, she would call if she needed or wanted anything.

She spent the next few days at the swimming pool or taking long walks along the beach. Sam called to say he had no idea when he'd be able to return. There was a lot of paperwork to do, he said. Interrogations from both the NYPD and the DEA.

If he didn't come soon, Lisa decided, she'd go back to Miami. She had obligations at home, rent to pay, bills stacking up and work to do. She didn't have a lot of money, so couldn't be a lady of leisure much longer.

The past few weeks with Sam, in spite of the danger, had been the happiest of her life. With him she had felt complete, as though she had found the other half of herself. She'd fallen in love and for her nothing would ever be quite the same again.

Their love affair had been heightened by the danger they'd been in. Add to that the incredible beauty of Jamaica, palm trees swaying in the off-shore breeze, wooded glens and shaded ponds, a turquoise sea and nights that were made for love. It was a perfect place to fall in love, and she had.

But had Sam? He'd never said he loved her, maybe he never would. Perhaps he'd be perfectly happy with occasional weekend visits to Miami. But that wasn't her idea of till death us do part.

Sam flew into Kingston on Friday afternoon. He hadn't called Lisa because he hadn't been sure he could get away or that he'd be able to get a flight. He tried to call her from the airport.

The hotel operator rang her room. It rang for a long time before the operator said, "There's no answer, sir. May I take a message?"

He said yes.

She said, "One moment, please," and left him hanging while she answered another call. By that time they were announcing the last boarding call for the flight to Kingston. He had no choice but to hang up.

There were no rental cars available when he arrived. He called Filoberto and asked if he could borrow the Harley. Filoberto said, "Of course. I'll have someone deliver it."

When the motorcycle arrived, Sam stowed his gear on the back, thanked the guy who'd brought it, and took off for the two-hour drive to Ocho Rios.

It was after seven when he reached the Poinciana. He checked in, thought about calling Lisa's room but decided he'd clean up first. He'd gone directly from his desk at the NYPD to the airport and he'd been driving hell-for-leather on the Harley. He was rumpled and he needed a shave. He didn't want to look like a bum when he saw her.

After a quick shower and shave, he grabbed a clean pair of jeans out of his suitcase and a blue denim shirt. When he was dressed, he reached for the white dinner jacket that he'd bought yesterday at a men's shop on Madison Avenue. He'd never worn a dinner jacket before, but he wanted to look like a gentleman tonight.

He put the jacket on over the blue denim shirt and looked at himself in the mirror. "This is as good as it gets," he grumbled. Then he pulled his sneakers on, without socks, and placed a call to Lisa's room.

She answered on the second ring. "Hi," he said. "It's me. I'm here."

"Here? In Jamaica?"

"In the hotel. What's your room number?"

She told him. He said, "I'm on my way," and hung up.

She opened the door when he knocked and she was every bit as beautiful as he remembered. She had on a white dress with a low neckline and a short, full skirt. Her skin was tanned, her hair was sun-streaked.

"Hi." He kissed her and when he let her go, said, "You look great. How are you feeling?"

"Much better, thanks." She led him into the room. "Why didn't you let me know you were coming?"

"I tried to call from the airport in Miami. The hotel operator kept me hanging and my flight was called. I couldn't wait. I'm sorry."

"No, no, that's all right. Would you like a drink? We could order something."

"It can wait. I've got a couple of things I want to tell you."

"Oh?" Her heart gave a strange little lurch. She held her breath.

"Why don't we sit outside?" He took her hand and led her out onto the balcony.

Waves pounded against the shore. A full moon shone through the palm trees and music floated up from the dance floor. It was a perfect setting for what she hoped Sam was about to say.

He cleared his throat. "Lisa, my dear," he said. "I have something to tell you."

This was it. She held her breath.

"I found your brother," he said.

She looked at him, unable to understand. "Jimmy? You found Jimmy?"

"Through the Navy. He got out three years ago and moved back to Ohio. Back to the farm."

She stared at him. "With my father?"

"No, Lisa. Your father's dead. He died last year."

"My father's dead?" She knew she was repeating everything Sam said, but she couldn't take it in. His words ran round and round like a kaleidoscope in her brain. Jimmy. Her father. The farm.

"I talked to Jim," Sam went on. "He sounds like a nice guy. He spent a lot of years trying to find you while he was still in the Navy and since he's been out."

"Jimmy's alive," she said, and her eyes filled. "It's been over twelve years, Sam. I just... I just don't know what to say."

"I know." Sam squeezed her hand. "He said he'd fly to Miami to see you as soon as you get back. One other thing, Lisa. About the warrant. I checked with the local police. You were underage when you left home and your father had listed you as a runaway. The warrant should have been dropped from the books years ago. It has been now."

He moved his chair closer. "Now about us." He looked uncomfortable. "I've been thinking about us, about how close we got in such a short time. I realize a lot of . . . well, of what happened between us was because of the danger we were in and because . . . you know . . ." He made a wide gesture with his arm. "All of this, Jamaica, the trade winds, palm trees—"

"I understand," Lisa put in quickly, cutting him off.

He raised an eyebrow. "You do?"

"We've had an exciting time, Sam." She tried for what she hoped was a cheerful smile. "It's been an adventure I'll never forget."

One eyebrow shot up.

"But now it's time to get on with our lives. Yours. And mine."

"I see." He stood. "Have you had dinner?"

She looked startled by this change in the conversation. "Uh, no."

"Then let's go. I haven't eaten since breakfast."

Was that all he was going to say? Was he embarrassed? Relieved? Damn the man!

He started for the door. "Hurry it up," he said. "I'm hungry."

She barely had time to grab her purse.

They went down the stairs. In the lobby she started toward the door that led to the patio restaurant, but he took her hand and pulled her toward the door.

"Where are we going?" she asked.

"Out."

He led her to the motorcycle. She said, "I'm dressed! I'm wearing heels. I can't ride on *that*."

"Get on."

Hands on her hips, Lisa frowned. But he didn't seem to notice. He swept her up off the ground and plunked her down on the bike, then swung a leg over his seat and gunned the motor.

"Wait a minute..." she started to say, but he'd already roared out of the driveway and onto the road. His open white dinner jacket blew back in the breeze; her skirt was hiked up over her thighs.

She yelled at him to stop and take her back to the hotel. Either he didn't hear because of the wind whipping past them or he simply wasn't inclined to answer. She boiled. She seethed. He'd paid no attention to her carefully thought out speech and careened around the mountains as if all Montoya's bad guys were still after them.

Finally he zoomed off the highway onto the road that led to the restaurant he'd taken her to before. He pulled into the parking lot, turned off the motor, and after he got off offered his hand to help her.

She was windblown, frazzled and mad as a peahen. "Look at me," she said. "I'm all wrinkled."

He looked her up and down. "Hair's a mess, too." He grabbed her hand again.

Deuteronomy met them at the door. "Gentleman and pretty lady," he said. "It be so nice to see you again. You would like a table by the window, yes?"

They followed him. He held the chair out for Lisa. She loosened up enough to smile at him and say, "Thank you, Deuteronomy."

"You remember my name."

"Of course."

"And I remember you liked the planter's punch." His smile showed perfect white teeth. "One of sour, two of sweet . . ."

"Three of strong, four of weak," Lisa finished.

"Bring the damn drinks," Sam muttered.

"Of course." Deuteronomy winked at Lisa. "Anything for the pretty lady."

"You were flirting with him," Sam said when the Jamaican turned away.

"Was I?"

"Yes, dammit. And I don't like it."

"Oh?" She fluttered her lashes.

Deuteronomy returned with their drinks and a gardenia for Lisa. "It's beautiful," she said when he laid it beside her drink.

"Its beauty pales next to yours."

Sam shoved his chair back. Facing the other man he said, "Let's get one thing clear before I wipe the floor up with you, Deud. This is my woman so keep your fancy words to yourself. As for your gardenia . . ." He plucked it off the table and stuck it, none too gently, behind Deuteronomy's ear. "Now bring us a couple of steaks. Okay?"

Deuteronomy swallowed so hard his Adam's apple bounced. "Right away, boss. Yes, sir. Comin' right up."

"Let's dance," Sam said to Lisa, and without waiting for a reply took her hand and pulled her up beside him.

"Now," he said, "let's cut the crap. I meant what I said, you're my woman. Understand?"

"Oh, yeah?" Putting up a brave front.

"Yeah. You know I'm nuts about you."

She looked up at him. "Exactly what does that mean?"

"You know."

"No, I *don't* know. You made it clear back at the hotel that the way we felt about each other only happened because of the excitement and—"

"You didn't let me finish."

"Oh."

"I love you. Okay?"

She swallowed hard. "Okay."

"Is that all you've got to say?"

"At the moment."

He danced her over to an alcove almost hidden by small palms and a hanging fern. He took a small blue box out of his pocket. "This is for you," he said, and handed it to her.

Lisa held her breath. She opened the box, and a pear-shaped diamond winked up at her.

"I'm not very good at this," Sam said. "I don't have a lot of fancy words. But if you want to we could...well, you know."

"Put the ring on my finger, Sam."

His hands were clammy, but he did it.

"It's beautiful," she said. "Thank you."

"You're welcome."

"Now ask me."

He took a deep breath. "Will you marry me?"

"You bet."

He let out the breath he didn't know he'd been holding and grinned down at her. His little pint of cider. To have and to hold and to love forever.

"I was so afraid you didn't love me," she said.

"I fell in love with you the first time I kissed you. But I was scared."

"I know."

"I'm going to work for DEA. I'll be stationed in Washington. I'll find a place for us in Virginia. Is that okay?"

"Anywhere with you is okay."

He urged her closer. "Listen, if I don't kiss you pretty soon I'm going to bust a gut."

"Oh, but you're a sweet talkin' devil." She stood on her tiptoes and kissed him, kissed him till his eyes glazed, his ears burned and his breathing grew ragged. And when she stepped back, she said, "Think about that while you're having your steak."

He took a deep breath to try to steady himself. He had a good mind to sweep her up in his arms and haul her out of there. If he remembered correctly there was a stand of trees over to one side of the restaurant. He could . . .

"After dinner," she said, reading his mind.

His eyes widened. "How did you . . . ?"

"Too bad we have the Harley," she went on. "But we can probably find a secluded part of the beach. That ought to do until we get back to the hotel."

Sam put his arms around her. "Don't ever change," he said. "Don't ever stop loving me."

"Not a chance."

He took her face between his hands and kissed her. "My moonlight lady," he whispered. "From this moment on."

* * * * *

Get Ready to be Swept Away by
Silhouette's Spring Collection

Abduction & Seduction

These passion-filled stories explore both the dangerous
desires of men and the seductive powers of women.
Written by three of our most celebrated authors, they are
sure to capture your hearts.

Diana Palmer
Brings us a spin-off of her Long, Tall Texans series

Joan Johnston
Crafts a beguiling Western romance

Rebecca Brandewyne
New York Times bestselling author
makes a smashing contemporary debut

Available in March at your favorite retail outlet.

MONTANA Mavericks™

Stories that capture living and loving beneath the Big Sky, where legends live on...and mystery lingers.

This February, the plot thickens with

WAY OF THE WOLF
by Rebecca Daniels

Raeanne Martin had always been secretly drawn to the mysterious Rafe "Wolf Boy" Rawlings. Now they battled by day on opposite sides of a murder trial. But by night, Raeanne fought an even tougher battle for Rafe's love.

Don't miss a minute of the loving as the passion continues with:

THE LAW IS NO LADY
by Helen R. Myers (March)

FATHER FOUND
by Laurie Paige (April)

BABY WANTED
by Cathie Linz (May)
and many more!

Only from ▼ *Silhouette*® where passion lives.

Hot on the heels of **American Heroes** comes
Silhouette Intimate Moments' latest and greatest
lineup of men: **Heartbreakers**. They know who
they are—and *who* they want. And they're out to
steal your heart.

RITA award-winning author Emilie Richards kicks off
the series in March 1995 with *Duncan's Lady*, IM #625.
Duncan Sinclair believed in hard facts, cold reality
and his daughter's love. Then sprightly Mara MacTavish
challenged his beliefs—and hardened heart—with
her magical allure.

In April *New York Times* bestseller Nora Roberts
sends hell-raiser Rafe MacKade home in
The Return of Rafe MacKade, IM #631. Rafe had
always gotten what he wanted—until Regan Bishop
came to town. She resisted his rugged charm and
seething sensuality, but it was only a matter of time....

Don't miss these first two **Heartbreakers**, from two
stellar authors, found only in—

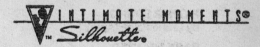

HRTBRK1

Southern
Knights

Join Marilyn Pappano in March 1995 as her **Southern Knights** series draws to a dramatic close with *A Man Like Smith*, IM #626.

Federal prosecutor Smith Kendricks was on a manhunt. His prey: crime boss Jimmy Falcone. But when his quest for justice led to ace reporter Jolie Wade, he found himself desiring both her privileged information—and the woman herself....

Don't miss the explosive conclusion to the **Southern Knights** miniseries, only in—

INTIMATE MOMENTS®
Silhouette.

KNIGHT3

EXTRA! EXTRA! READ ALL ABOUT...
MORE ROMANCE
MORE SUSPENSE
MORE INTIMATE MOMENTS

Join us in February 1995 when Silhouette Intimate Moments introduces the first title in a whole new program: INTIMATE MOMENTS EXTRA. These breakthrough, innovative novels by your favorite category writers will come out every few months, beginning with Karen Leabo's *Into Thin Air*, IM #619.

Pregnant teenagers had been disappearing without a trace, and Detectives Caroline Triece and Austin Lomax were called in for heavy-duty damage control...because now the missing girls were turning up dead.

In May, Merline Lovelace offers *Night of the Jaguar*, and other INTIMATE MOMENTS EXTRA novels will follow throughout 1995, only in—

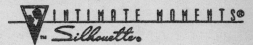

INTIMATE MOMENTS®
™ Silhouette®